A STRANGE GUEST

"He's a strange one, isn't he? Not at all like I'd thought a Russian to be. Kind of puny and . . ." Mrs. Winchell paused, her mouth twisting before she added, "He is strange . . . Something is not right with him."

Creighton wanted to agree, but he should not be speaking about his guest like this. Bidding Mrs. Winchell a good evening, he went up the stairs. He strode along the Persian runner on the floor, which shone in the candlelight from the sconces by each door.

Taking off his coat, he loosened his cravat. He stuffed it and his stiff collar into his pocket and undid the top buttons on his shirt. A good night's sleep should prepare him for another day of hosting these odd Russians.

As he passed the door to the blue guest room, he hesitated. A good host would be certain his guest was settled well for the night. With a sigh, as he hoped this would not turn into another conversation about the war, he rapped and swung the door open. "Dmitrieff, if—"

Creighton choked as he stared at the slim silhouette by the bed. The gentle curves belonged to no man or boy. He wanted to deny the truth, but it was impossible.

Count Dmitri Dmitrieff was a woman!

THE COUNTERFEIT COUNT

Jo Ann Ferguson

Zebra Books
Kensington Publishing Corp.
http://www.zebrabooks.com

ZEBRA BOOKS are published by

Kensington Publishing Corp.
850 Third Avenue
New York, NY 10022

First Printing: May, 1997
10 9 8 7 6 5 4 3 2 1

Printed in the United States of America

For Annette Blair . . . on the road again.
Thanks for being my friend over all those miles
and through all those bookstores.

One

"Why me? I have just returned from the Continent." Creighton Marshall took a glass of wine from the tray held out to him by one of the club's silent menservants. "Find another volunteer, Colonel."

Colonel Samuel Carruthers smiled while he appraised his friend who was sipping the wine with a frown. Creighton Marshall, Captain, had recovered well from his year of chasing the Frogs across the Continent. The gaunt shadows had receded from beneath his brown eyes, and his cheeks were no longer shadowed by a ruddy beard. Clean-shaven, dressed *à la modality* in a dark-brown velvet coat and pale breeches separated by a gold waistcoat, he seemed perfectly at ease in the glossy leather chair by the hearth here at White's. Only because Colonel Carruthers was so well acquainted with him did he realize what had been suffered by Captain Creighton Marshall, once again better known to the Polite World as Lord Ashcroft.

"But you have all that room in your townhouse on Berkeley Square," the colonel said, watching his young friend's face for any sign of softening.

There was none. "Damme, Colonel! I've done my duty for God, king, and country."

"This is for the Regent."

A smile tugged at Creighton's lips, and the colonel recalled his sister's reaction to the handsome viscount. Although she was older than Creighton by nearly a decade, she had complained of a delightful flutter in her stomach each time the viscount turned his glittering eyes in her direction. That charm had served Creighton well before he left for France. There were whispers of several young women who had vowed never to marry if they could not be Lady Ashcroft. Although he discounted such outrageous tales, Colonel Carruthers knew Creighton's auburn hair and the kohl eyes he had inherited from his mother would be as enticing to a young miss as the title and wealth bequeathed to him by his late father.

"Colonel, save your arguments for someone who must heed them."

"May I remind you, *Captain* Marshall, that you have not yet sold your commission to that eager young cousin of yours?"

Creighton did not answer as he took another sip of wine. Madeira. Once it had seemed too sweet for his palate, but he had come to appreciate the finer aspects of life after being denied them for so many months. France might be famed for its excellent vintages; however, he had had no chance to sample anything but wormy bread and mud during his time on its shores.

True, Gregory was anxious to buy the captaincy. True, Creighton was anxious to be rid of it. True, he wanted to spend all his time in the stylish clothes he had had made by his favorite knight of the cloth instead of the uniform that thrilled Gregory. Yet Creighton resisted making the final arrangements to sell his commission to his cousin. The idea of sending that idealistic young man into the maw of war disturbed him.

But the war with France was over! Looking down into his glass, he sighed. The ending had come without the sense of triumph he had anticipated through the torment of those months in France. Napoleon had been banished to Elba, but the rest of Europe was left to try to resurrect what remained after the fighting. Old alliances had faltered, and new ones were as uneasy as a Charley patrolling unfamiliar streets on a dark night.

"Shall we pretend, only for the sake of argument," Creighton asked, "that I am agreeable to your plan? For whom am I to play the congenial host?"

Colonel Carruthers linked his fingers over his generous expanse of belly. The garish stripes of his silk waistcoat matched the bright shade of his blue coat, but his eyes were serious beneath the silver hair brushing his thick, black brows. Signaling to a servant to refill his glass, the colonel asked, "You know the Czar of All Russia will soon disembark on our shores?"

"Of course. I do not read the *Morning Chronicle* only for the news of the élite."

He smiled at Creighton's sarcasm, which had brought common sense to many staff meetings when their fellow officers thought more of absurd honor than the needs of the men serving with them. "Then you may also realize Alexander's well-decorated General Miloradovich, who is already in town, has brought with him one of Russia's greatest heroes in the campaign against the French."

Creighton sighed. He was not sure why he had answered this invitation to join the colonel at White's today. How much more easily the time could have been spent with a ride in the park or with brandy and conversation in his book-room. His lips tightened. It would have been easier, but then he would have had to acknowledge the memories he had hoped would be forgotten by the time he returned home. Nearly every room of his home brought to mind a scene of him and Maeve. Even in his bedchamber, he could not escape the memory of her.

Damme! She had been the one who was carrying on an *affaire* with another man even while Creighton was speaking to her family of marriage.

"Which great Russian hero are you going to drop on my doorstep?" When the colonel smiled at his sour tone,

Creighton shook his head and grinned. "Listen to me. I have agreed to your request without debate."

"You know I appreciate volunteers."

"I recall your idea of a volunteer is anyone who happens to be within earshot of your bellow."

"*This* is a request only." Colonel Carruthers became suddenly serious. "I know you wish to immerse yourself in the whirl of the Season. Why not take this Russian officer with you? You will entertain him and solve my problem at the same time."

"I don't speak Russian."

"I understand the count speaks excellent English." He picked up his pipe. Taking a deep draught on his pipe, he blew smoke toward the ceiling. "From what I have heard of the count and his exploits, I think you shall find him extraordinary company. I believe you two have a great deal in common."

Creighton recognized defeat. Colonel Carruthers had the disagreeable habit of accepting no answer but the one he wanted and badgering a man until he got it. After months under his command, Creighton had learned that. He had learned as well that the colonel always had a reason for what he did.

"So what is the name of this count?"

"Count Dmitri Dmitrieff." He leaned back in his chair, but Creighton was not bamboozled by his nonchalant pose. "The count holds the rank of captain. I speculate that will change, for the czar himself arranged for the count to come to England with General Miloradovich on this visit, if the gossip-mongers are to be believed. Dmitrieff is a cavalryman. I am sure he will enjoy the hunt of the fox as well as the entertainments of Town. You two could be living in one another's pockets by the time this visit is over."

Skepticism crept into his voice. "I doubt that, Colonel."

"But you shall host Count Dmitrieff?"

"Yes," Creighton answered, hoping he would not come to regret his acquiescence more than he did at this moment.

One thing remained the same as his days before the war. Creighton Marshall hated the strictures of protocol. They were a waste of time—time that could be better spent with a hand of the devil's books and the company of good friends whose pockets were filled with gold.

Mist off the river brought the scent of rain, but he ignored it as he edged his horse through the maze of carriages clogging the street in front of the deceptively plain townhouse. Holding the leading rein of another horse, he listened to the prattle of the people filling the street and craning to see the house at its end. Everyone wanted to be the first to see the Russians, although twilight was thick along the cobbles.

Creighton considered telling them to go home. The czar would probably be busy, as soon as he arrived, plotting mischief with his sister, the Grand Duchess Catherine of Oldenburg, at the Pulteney Hotel. Rumor suggested the Regent was insulted because the czar had turned down an invitation to stay at St. James's Palace and planned to install his retinue in the hotel, save for a few who would be billeted with Colonel Carruthers's soon-to-be retired staff.

He chuckled to himself as he swung out of the saddle and handed the reins to a servant in a livery that glowed a brilliant red in the light from the streetlamp. Behind him, whispered supposition filled the air. His black coat and white breeches were fine enough for an evening at Almack's, but gave no clue to his identity. He heard the questions. Was he a Russian or an Englishman? He did nothing to satisfy the curiosity as he climbed the trio of steps. He adjusted his perfectly tied cravat and took a deep breath as he recalled the phrases he had spoken so many times in the past, the trite words of strangers who did not expect to see each other again.

The door opened, and he entered. Handing his tall beaver hat and a *carte de visite* to the footman, he glanced around the foyer. It was surprisingly empty. Straining, he could hear no sound of conversation. This was the correct evening and hour for his call, and the colonel had told him there would be a gathering of those who would be hosting the Russians.

The foyer was gaudy with gilt. Gold decorated the plaster friezes on the ceiling, the metalwork of the balusters rising along the curving staircase, and the tables set on either side of the door. Only the black marble floor offered a rest for his eyes.

When the servant returned, moments later, Creighton was escorted up the stairs and through double doors to the right. The room was choke-full, but the conversation rose barely above a whisper. What furniture remained had been pushed back against the red silk walls. No light filtered past the lace curtains set between gold brocade drapes at both of the windows.

As he entered, Creighton saw Colonel Carruthers signal to him. He crossed the parquet floor to where the colonel was involved in an intense conversation with a squat, bearded man Creighton did not know. Resplendent in his dress uniform, Colonel Carruthers emphasized every word with a broad gesture.

"And this is my aide-de-camp, Captain Creighton Marshall, Lord Ashcroft," the colonel said as he welcomed Creighton into the conversation.

"Gentlemen," Creighton said quietly. To speak louder than a murmur would shatter the smothering hush.

The colonel continued, " 'Tis my pleasure to introduce General Miloradovich."

"Miloradovich, Karl Miloradovich," the short man said, smoothing his thick beard. His arrogant tone warned that he expected Creighton to be impressed.

Creighton *was* impressed with the boorish man's girth. He struggled not to smile as he wondered if the general had a horse strong enough to support him or if he must be pulled to the vanguard of his troops in a cart. No doubt Miloradovich spent most of his time close to a laden table.

"An honor, General." He said nothing else as he scanned the room. Which one of these Russians was the count?

"You were with Colonel Carruthers in Paris?" asked Miloradovich in his thick accent. "How did you find the city?"

"In dire need of a sane leader."

"It has one now."

"At least temporarily."

"Do you expect Napoleon to escape his island prison?" The general boomed a derisive laugh that caused heads to turn throughout the room. "I can reassure you, Captain Marshall, you need not trouble yourself on that. Napoleon Bonaparte will cause us no more problems."

"I wish I could share your complacency."

Colonel Carruthers intruded to say, "Complacency is not a fault of the general's." He flashed Creighton a disapproving frown.

Creighton swallowed his irritation as he bowed his head in the general's direction and said, "Gentlemen." He had no interest in staying and listening to the rotund man's opinions. Diplomacy was just a different sort of battle, and he did not want to be embroiled in a war of words this evening.

As he turned, he nearly bumped into a man who wore the uniform of an English infantry corporal. Creighton nodded when the corporal asked if Captain Marshall would come with him. Looking wistfully at the table where wine waited, Creighton followed.

The corporal stopped suddenly and, snapping to attention, intoned, "Dmitri Dmitrieff."

Creighton's eyes widened as he looked at the man coming to his feet. This was not the hulking bear of a man he had expected. Above a red coat garishly decorated with gold trim, blond curls surrounded a slender face and accented

almond-shaped blue eyes. Dmitrieff might be a superb commander and an unparalleled master with the sword he wore
hooked to the crimson sash at his waist, but the top of his
head barely reached past Creighton's chin.

The count nodded ever so slightly toward Creighton. Only
the arch of a single eyebrow suggested the count was
amused by Creighton's reaction.

Determined not to give away any of his other thoughts,
Creighton said formally, "Welcome to London, Count
Dmitrieff. I am your host, Creighton Marshall, Captain."

"You are Lord Ashcroft as well, I believe," he replied in
nearly perfect English. His tenor voice suggested he was a
lad as lief a well-tried warrior.

"I prefer informality in my household."

"Then Marshall it shall be."

He thought he heard a hint of humor in the count's voice,
but the shorter man's face remained somber. Noting that
the man wore his riding gloves, he said, "I would be glad
to escort you to Berkeley Square at your leisure."

"Then let us take our leave. I have suffered enough of
these stilted proprieties for today. I trust my comments bring
you no insult."

"None. I learned many months ago that I would be wise
to leave politics and its intricacies to those who delight in
them. I have brandy and cigars waiting at my home. Let us
enjoy them instead."

The count turned, and a man, who was even taller than
Creighton, appeared out of the shadows. This man matched
Creighton's image of a Russian count. He wore a full brush
of beard, and he was as muscular as a bear. His uniform
was a quiet version of the count's.

"My aide, Sergeant Zass," the count said. "He, of course,
travels everywhere with me."

"Of course."

Creighton motioned for the count to lead the way to the
door but glanced at Colonel Carruthers, who flashed him

a grin. The colonel had been right. The count and he had something in common already, for they both looked upon functions such as this with distaste. Colonel Carruthers was going to be even more insufferable now as he crowed about how correct he had been.

With an ease that bespoke his reputation as a cavalryman, Count Dmitrieff mounted the extra horse Creighton had brought. "An excellent animal," he said, patting the chestnut's neck.

"He is yours to use as you wish during your stay."

"I am even more in your debt."

Creighton thought he saw a twinkle of delight in the count's eyes, but the shorter man's face remained impassive. Behind them, Sergeant Zass swung onto a black horse brought to him by a stableboy. The large man, whose face was nearly hidden in that untrimmed hedge of beard, had said nothing. Creighton wondered if he understood English.

Although he waited for Dmitrieff to speak again, the ride back to Berkeley Square passed in silence. The street was far from quiet with the rattle of wagon wheels and all the hubbub of Picadilly Street. Even when they turned onto Berkeley Street and rode around the square to the west side, the count said nothing.

The silence began to vex Creighton as he escorted his guest through the wide foyer of his townhouse and up the stairs. Zass followed like a malevolent shadow. Creighton saw the household turn to watch the two strangers with disquiet straining their polite smiles.

Creighton led the way into his book-room. The mahogany furniture was covered with heavy, dark-green fabric that was intended to invite his guests to relax and enjoy some cordial conversation. He waited for the shorter man to select a chair. Creighton kept his smile in place, but annoyance pinched him when Count Dmitrieff took Creighton's favorite chair as Zass went to sit in a corner. Shadows seemed to be his preferred milieu.

Selecting a seat opposite the count's chair, Creighton stretched out his feet on a stool. He shifted irritably. This was definitely not as cozy a chair as his own. When Mrs. Winchell bustled in with a tray holding glasses and a bottle of Creighton's best brandy, he saw the housekeeper was trying not to stare at his guests. He thanked her and waited until she backed hastily out of the room, clearly intimidated by the odd quiet.

Pouring two glasses, Creighton held out one to the count. The man turned to pass it to his sergeant. Creighton hid his surprise. He had heard tales of how cruelly Russian officers treated their men, but Dmitrieff must not fit that mold. Offering the other glass to the count, he rose to get a third glass from the sideboard by the hearth.

"So what do you think of London?" he asked, determined to put an end to the silence.

"I have seen little of it," the count replied, "but it seems a fine city. I must express my thanks to you, as a representative of England, for hosting us."

"Your czar will be a guest of my Regent." He added a bit more brandy to the glass he had poured for himself. He suspected he would need it to get himself through this conversation. Taking a deep drink, he said, "It is time to celebrate the war being over." He splashed more brandy into the goblet and raised it. "To peace."

The count lifted his glass to his lips, then lowered it. "England is fortunate to have been spared the destruction that was left after we tossed the French out of Russia."

"Winter did more to defeat Boney than the czar's army." He opened a box of cigars and offered it to the count.

Dmitrieff took one and sniffed it. With a hint of a smile, he passed it to his sergeant.

Creighton forced his smile to remain in place. Blast this Russian count to perdition! These cigars were too costly to be wasted on the palate of a Russian bear who could hardly appreciate their fine leaf. When Dmitrieff waved aside the box, Creighton wondered if the count deemed the cigars beneath his touch.

He cursed silently as he stuck a twig in the fire and used it to light a cheroot. Puffing thick smoke, he tossed the kindling back onto the hearth. His irritation crept into his voice. "If summer had been upon Russia when Boney's men arrived, the ending might have been far different. Snow makes a hero of any man."

The count motioned for Zass to light his own cigar before saying, "Odd, for there were no heroes among the French."

"Touché, if I may use that Froggish term." He smiled in spite of himself. "I withdraw my comment."

"Do not." The count hesitated, as if searching for the words he wanted in English. A hint of a smile brightened his serious face, but it was gone so swiftly Creighton wondered if he had seen it. "You are correct, Marshall. If it had not been for the blessing of Russia's fearsome winter, I fear we might, even now, be bowing our heads to a French emperor."

"The Allies would not have allowed that."

"The Allies were distant when the French marched across my homeland."

Creighton had no quick answer. It was true. For most of the campaign, the Russian army had stood alone against the French scourge. The Allies had harried Boney's army's flank, but their efforts had been no more effective than a terrier teasing a maddened bull. "The war is over now," he said, then wished he had not uttered the trite words.

"I find that unlikely."

"Do you?"

Dmitrieff did not recoil from his sharp question. "Napoleon had ambitions to meld all of Europe into his empire. Do you think he will be happy with a mere island?"

"Your general does not share your convictions on this subject. He would as lief say that Napoleon has little choice."

"There are always choices, Marshall, although we may wish to think otherwise." He put his brandy down, unfinished. "I hope General Miloradovich is correct. Let the rest of our battles be fought by diplomats."

Creighton considered asking the count if he found the brandy not to his taste, but refrained. "I think you shall find London has many entertainments planned in preparation for your czar's visit. For example, tomorrow evening there will be a gathering at Lady Eltonville's townhouse on Soho Square. Her hurricanes are always amusing, with music and conversation."

"Dancing is a skill I have never mastered."

For a moment, Creighton thought his guest was jesting, but no smile eased the stern lines of the count's face. He never had met such a controlled man. The only time the count's face became animated was when he spoke of the war. Creighton had thought he was done with zealots, but Dmitrieff was the worst he had met. The damned war was over! Let it be buried as the dead had been.

He downed his brandy, then said, "There are other choices of how to pass the evening. Cards, if you prefer a quieter entertainment."

"Then you English are unlike us Russians. Gambling is not a 'quiet' pastime for us. We roar when we win and roar when we lose."

"Mayhap I should have said a less complicated entertainment, for there is no worry if you have complimented your lady companion or the need to speak with the dowagers."

"I shall leave such obligations to my superiors." The count smiled, astounding Creighton. "General Miloradovich is a fool. He thinks himself a great favorite with the ladies, but, in truth, he cannot see his own faults. That may be the reason he was such a dreadful presence during battle. He could know no fear when he never considered he might lose. So he is a hero."

"As you are."

"And you." Dmitrieff leaned forward and asked, "What deeds did you do to win that title?"

Creighton put his glass on the sideboard. No matter what he said, the count turned the conversation back to the war. The Russian had avoided answering any direct question he had asked. Instead, Dmitrieff preferred speaking of battle and diplomacy—two topics Creighton wished to hear no more of.

His silence must have been colder than he had thought because the count set himself on his feet and said, "I believe it is time for me to retire."

At the same time, Sergeant Zass stood. Creighton had forgotten the man was sitting in the corner. "I shall have you shown to your rooms. Your sergeant is welcome to stay with my servants on the top floor."

"Thank you," the count replied.

Creighton dropped into his own chair as soon as Mrs. Winchell had led his guests out of the book-room. What a bumble-bath! This was going to be worse than intolerable. He had changed his mind. He had very little in common with that blasted count!

Silence threatened to suffocate him again. Usually he enjoyed the serenity of his house, but he could not when he should be acting a good host to his guest.

With a sigh, he pushed himself to his feet. He stubbed out what remained of his cigar, then went into the hallway. Seeing Mrs. Winchell scurrying toward him, he asked, "Are they settled?"

"Yes, my lord." When she added nothing else, he knew she was disturbed by their guests, too.

"You put the count in the blue room?"

"Yes, my lord. The other one is using James's room."

He nodded. It was appropriate for the footman to give up

his room for the servant of a guest. "Very good, Mrs. Winchell."

"My lord?" she called as he turned to climb the stairs. "He's a strange one, isn't he?"

"Sergeant Zass?"

She shook her head and brushed her hands nervously against her dark gown. "No my lord. The other one. Not at all like I'd thought a Russian to be. Kind of puny and . . ." She paused, her mouth twisting before she added, "He is strange. Something is not right with him."

"What do you mean?"

"I mean no disrespect," she said, and he knew his tone had been too sharp.

"Of course not. Just say what you wish to say, Mrs. Winchell. You know I trust your judgment."

"I don't know what I want to say." She shrugged, and a sheepish smile brightened her thin face. "Just something peculiar about him."

Creighton wanted to agree, but he should not be speaking about his guest like this. Bidding Mrs. Winchell a good evening, he went up the stairs. He strode along the Persian runner on the floor, which shone in the candlelight from sconces by each door.

Taking off his coat, he loosened his cravat. He stuffed it and his stiff collar into his pocket and undid the top buttons on his shirt. A good night's sleep should prepare him for another day of hosting these odd Russians.

As he passed the door to the blue guest room, he hesitated. A good host would be certain his guest was settled well for the night. With a sigh, as he hoped this would not turn into another conversation about the damned war, he rapped and swung the door open. "Dmitrieff, if—"

Creighton choked as he stared at the slim silhouette by the bed. The gentle curves belonged to no man or boy. He wanted to deny the truth, but it was impossible.

Count Dmitri Dmitrieff was a woman!

Two

"You are a woman?" Even as Creighton spoke the incredible words aloud, he could not believe them. Yet his eyes told him they were true.

The woman—for there was no doubt that those tempting curves beneath the linen nightshirt belonged to a woman—stared at him in horror. Her tilted blue eyes with their golden lashes were wide as all color drained from her cheeks. His gaze swept along her wine-red lips and past the firm angle of her chin to the expanse of skin visible above the deep vee of the shirt. It revealed no more than a stylish gown, but he was astonished how easily she hid the roundness of her breasts and her slim waist beneath her uniform. Her legs, which had been encased in boots and pantaloons, were displayed to entice him with their shapely length.

Mrs. Winchell's voice rang in his memory. Yes, there had been something particularly peculiar about this Russian count, and now he knew the truth.

"Is this Colonel Carruthers' idea of a hoax?" he demanded as he saw the count's uniform folded neatly on the bed.

She reached for the heavy shirt she must have been wearing under her coat, but he blocked her hand. When she tried again and he slapped her fingers aside, she glared at him.

"Answer me," he snapped. "Did Colonel Carruthers arrange this?"

"Yes."

"Why?"

"Begone! I shall not be questioned in my own private chambers."

"Your chambers? This is my home, and I wish an explanation."

When he grasped her shoulders, her fist exploded in his gut. His breath burst from him. She tried to push past him. He seized her elbow. Instincts honed during battle sped his hand to halt hers as it aimed at his chin. He gripped her around the waist and squeezed. She struggled to escape. With a grim smile, he tightened his arm. She gasped, but did not beg him to halt. Instead, she tried to shove him away. Her fingers slid from his wrist as he compressed his arm into her waist again. A soft moan oozed from her lips as she sagged against him.

He bent and slipped his arm under her knees before she could collapse. Easily, he lifted her. For all her contrariness, she weighed less than some of the equipment he had dragged across France. Dropping her, without compassion, into the pile of pillows, he stepped back and rested his hand on the upright of the tester.

He said nothing as she coughed, fighting to regain her breath, but he could not halt his gaze from tracing her splendid shape again. With her tousled, tawny curls edging her face like an aurora and her cheeks regaining their dusting of pink, she was an invitation to thoughts that had nothing to do with the present predicament. She took deep breaths to steady herself, and he followed the motion of her breasts which were covered by the undecorated linen. Her slender waist needed no corset. And her legs . . . Firmly, he told himself to keep his mind on the problems at hand. 'Twas not easy when she was half-dressed and lying in his guest bed.

She scowled at him and started to speak. Only another cough emerged. When she pulled a pillow in front of her to conceal the curves that had betrayed her, he knew she could not guess how the lace on its edges accented the femininity she fought to hide. Why had he failed to notice that her cheeks had never suffered the honed edge of a razor? Mayhap he had been beguiled, even then, by the lush wealth of gold lashes surrounding her bewitching eyes.

Damme! He must not let himself be seduced by this woman who paraded about in a man's uniform as bold as a cyprian plying her trade in Covent Garden.

Coolly, he asked, "Why?"

"Why what?"

He leaned forward until his nose was only inches from hers. In spite of himself, he noted how warmly tanned her skin was. Such a healthy hue was not the rage for ladies, but the color accented her sapphire eyes. His hand clenched on the post. More fiercely, he reminded himself again that when her lips were so close beneath his was not the time to think of how luscious she looked.

He drew back a few inches before temptation persuaded him to taste her lips. Irritation at his own reaction to this pretty sprite spiked his voice. "Answer me—" He swore, then demanded, "What is your name? Your real name!"

He expected her to demur, but she answered, without emotion, "Natalya Dmitrieff."

"Then tell me, Natalya Dmitrieff, why Colonel Carruthers arranged for you to come here."

Her eyes narrowed with bafflement, and he noted how she tensed against the pillows. Even though her hair might be as soft and silky as a kitten's, she had already proven she could fight like a lion. He would be cork-brained to trust her even for a minute.

"I had no place else to stay," she said in the warm voice that had startled him when he first heard her speak. "There was not room enough for me to stay with the Grand Duchess's party at the Pulteney Hotel."

"But why here?"

"I told you." Pressing her hand to her side where he had

held her so roughly, she swung her legs over the side of the bed. She must have sensed his gaze riveting on them, because she pulled the burgundy blanket off the bed and wrapped it around her as she stood. "My English is not perfect. Mayhap I do not make myself clear. I was told Colonel Carruthers arranged for me to stay here. But as a joke? *Ya ne ponimáyu.*" Quickly, she added, "Excuse me. I do not know what you mean."

When Lord Ashcroft stepped in front of her, Natalya glowered at him. She had faced scores of men across bared swords with the smoke of battle smothering her. This English lord would not daunt her. She had met taller men and shorter ones. She had seen their blood glisten on her sword. She had sat with her comrades while they sang and while they spoke of the women left behind . . . and while they died.

He folded his arms across his chest, but she met his brown eyes steadily. Colonel Carruthers had graciously told her that he was honored to arrange for her to stay with the captain who had been his aide-de-camp during the English campaign that ended in Paris. She tried to imagine this handsome man who wore velvet and lawn covered with the filth of battle.

She lowered her eyes when she realized she could, with ease, envision him fighting. The fervor in his ebony eyes warned he would be a ferocious opponent who would seek any flaw and exploit it to destroy her. Fighting him with no weapon other than her fists would be stupid. He had already proven he was stronger than she was, even if she could not have guessed that from his broad shoulders and strong hands. There were other ways, and she would use any form of guile to defeat him.

Edging around him, she vowed to give him no chance to best her, although he had discovered her greatest weakness. She could not trust him. She could trust no one but Petr Zass. She would not allow Lord Ashcroft to betray her when she was so close to getting what she needed to rebuild all that had been destroyed by the French.

Again he stepped in front of her. A frigid smile erased all civility from his face. The pleasant host had vanished; the savage warrior had appeared.

Squaring her shoulders, she faced him without speaking. She knew well how to deal with soldiers. Their brains usually worked in a certain, logical way she found admirable. If she could appeal to that part of him, he might be willing to forget he had seen her like this.

His finger brushed the curve of her jaw, and she flinched in spite of herself. Her breath caught, shocking her, as sweet warmth spread through her to submerge her anger. She did not want her anger smothered. This single touch should not affect her so. She leaned her face away from him, knowing this reaction, delightful though it might be, was a warning he would not be as easy to deal with as the men she had commanded. Yet, she must be as unrelentingly strong as she had been with them.

"Marshall, I—"

"I think it would be wiser if you called me Lord Ashcroft. Under the circumstances, informality might not be the wisest course."

"As you wish."

"I doubt you are always so compliant." His smile broadened.

"You are my host."

"And you are no *Count* Dmitrieff!"

Natalya took a step toward her left and her small knife which she had placed on a table on the far side of the room. He countered and put his hand on the tester pole at the foot of the bed. The only way she could get past him was to sneak beneath his arm. She would—if she must—but she wished to hold onto whatever dignity she had remaining.

"You are wrong, my lord. I *am* Count Dmitrieff."

"A captain in the czar's army?"

"As Kapitán Dmitrieff, I led one of his most decorated troops. We Cossacks do not like to lose." She hoped he would take that as a portent of the trouble he could bring upon himself if he continued this conversation.

He did not, for he asked, "Was the czar so desperate for soldiers that he forced women into his army?"

"I volunteered!"

"As a carpet-knight, no doubt."

Baffled, she said, *"Ya ne ponimáyu."*

"You said that before. You don't understand?"

She smiled slightly. "You apparently understand better than I, for that is what I said. What is a carpet-knight?"

"Allow me the honor of explaining." His sarcasm lashed her, stealing her smile. "A carpet-knight is any soldier whose battles are fought in a parlor."

She tapped a ribbon pinned beneath the fur collar of her uniform. "The czar does not award decorations to the best dancer. I earned the title of hero, my lord."

"And you were made an officer just like that?"

Her voice was as hard as the steel in her ceremonial sword on the carved blanket chest at the foot of the ornate bed. "I was no *portupej-junker.*"

"What?"

"A cadet who is waiting to better his skills to become an officer." She could not help smiling when she saw his astonishment as she added, "I was breveted immediately to my rank."

He laughed as he sat on a chair covered in red velvet and set his feet on a tufted stool. Folding his arms on his chest, he gave her a superior smile. "So, you simply walked up to a Russian officer and offered your services?"

Natalya knew her cheeks were afire, turning them the shade of the wool of her coat. His insult was clear. She had been no camp-follower, but a respected officer who had won decorations and the czar's attention for her valor.

"Yes, my lord, but you must understand that my services

consisted only of a strong arm and the ability to maintain my seat during a battle as well as being able to inspire my men to deeds of greatness."

"Then the Russians are bigger blocks than I had thought." Not giving her a chance to respond to his double insult, he went on, "I cannot conceive of what would make a young woman search out the war, so she could play a part in it."

"I did not need to search for it. The war found me." A deep sigh punctuated her words as she slowly sat on the chest. Twisting the fringe on her sword about her fingers, she said softly, "My father and my older brother joined the czar's men to battle in Prussia against the French. Dmitri came back. Father did not. Then the French came to Russia."

"And your brother went again to fight?"

"Yes." For the first time, she looked at him directly. No sympathy eased the hard lines of his face, but the derision was gone. "When he did not come back, we tried to manage as well as we could until the French overran our home. My mother, my younger brothers, and my sisters died. I did not. It was my duty to avenge their deaths." She touched the scabbard. *"This* was my way of doing it."

"Where is your older brother?"

"Who knows?" She shrugged, although she was sure the weight of a cannon sat on her shoulders. "I have to assume he is dead."

"So you took over his life?"

"Yes."

"And Zass?"

"He served in my father's household. He and I are the sole survivors of the attack on our lands by the French. I can assure you that he shared my determination to let our swords taste the blood of those who killed our families." Her smile returned. "I would warn you, my lord, not to underestimate Petr Zass. He may be a peasant by birth, but he has proven his worth more times than you can count."

Lord Ashcroft pyramided his fingers in front of his face, concealing it in shadow. "Does he know you are a woman?"

"Yes, of course. He served my father for many years. He taught me to shoot when I was a child."

"He is the only one who knows the truth?"

"Until now, yes."

When Lord Ashcroft did not reply, Natalya stood. She was careful to keep the coverlet around her shoulders. The comparative informality of civilian life had betrayed her, because she had been accustomed to the ways of the army. No one would have entered her tent without knocking first, which always gave her a chance to hide the truth. As she crossed the rug, which was roughly pliable beneath her bare feet, she realized she had become soft on the journey from Russia. During the campaign against the French, she had slept in her uncomfortable uniform so she was ready at all times to answer the call to arms.

A shadow climbed up the wall in front of her, and she slowly turned to face Lord Ashcroft. With his shirt open at the throat, the robust muscles of his chest moved smoothly as he walked toward her. Her fingers closed into fists at her sides. To defend herself . . . or to keep from touching him?

"You are lying," he said in a low rumble. "I have no idea what you have planned, but I shall not be a part of it."

"I can assure you, my lord, I am speaking the truth."

"Count—" He swore under his breath, then said, "Miss Dmitrieff—"

"You may address me as *Kapitán* Dmitrieff. That is, unquestionably, the truth."

With a sharp laugh, he said, "I shall call you what I please. You said your name is Natalya, right?"

"I would prefer—"

"Natalya, I want to know the truth." He put out his hand, but she backed away, shocking herself.

She had never been frightened like this. So many times, she had looked death in the face, and never had she shied away as she did now. She did not know how to fight this kind of battle. The wisest thing would be retreat until she could gather her wits, like a shield, about her.

"I wish to retire, if you would give me leave," she said, as she walked to the door. Opening it, she went on, "Good evening, my lord."

He started to speak, then seemed to think better of it. When he walked toward the door, his steps pounding out his frustration, she stepped back to give him room to depart. A terrifying thought struck her, and she grasped his sleeve as he would have walked past her.

"Lord Ashcroft, you must tell no one what you have discovered." She hated the pleading sound of her voice, but she had to win this promise from him.

"Lying is abhorrent to me."

"It is necessary to me."

"That is where we differ." He caught her by the elbows and tugged her away from the door, closing it. He pulled her against him.

Natalya could not halt the shriek that burst from her throat. As Lord Ashcroft released her, astonishment on his face, the door crashed open. She whirled to see Petr Zass's face alter into fury. He leapt toward Lord Ashcroft.

"Nyet!" Natalya's order stopped him with his hands on Lord Ashcroft's throat. She motioned for him to release the astonished Englishman. Stepping between the two men, she said in Russian, "Petr, let me deal with this in my own way."

Petr looked from Lord Ashcroft, who was rubbing his neck, to her, and she saw his bafflement. She understood, for she had asked Petr to help her conceal the truth that, until tonight, only the two of them had known. It was an oath he had taken at the same time he vowed to kill the French who had murdered his family.

"Yes, Kapitán," he replied in the same language, but disappointment was jagged in his voice. He ground his fist into his palm and stared at Lord Ashcroft, then asked, "Do you want me to stay?"

"Go to bed." Rage was altering to exasperation and curiosity on Lord Ashcroft's face, but she continued in Russian, "This man will not betray us."

"He knows."

"He will tell no one."

Petr spat, "If he does, I shall break his neck with my bare hands."

"Go to bed," she repeated.

With a ruthless scowl at Lord Ashcroft, he bid her a good night. She knew Petr would not sleep until he heard Lord Ashcroft seek his own bed. For that, she was grateful. What English hospitality might demand under these circumstances was something she did not know, but she would find a way to convince Lord Ashcroft of the wisdom of keeping her secret.

"You have him well trained."

Natalya spun to face Lord Ashcroft, expecting to see a contemptuous smile on his lips. Instead, he was sitting on the thick sill of the window by the bed, a puzzled expression on his face.

Quietly, she said, "Sergeant Zass is a good soldier."

"Does he speak English?"

"He understands some of what is said, but I do not think he speaks any himself."

"So he cannot corroborate your tale to me?"

"I am unaccustomed to having to prove the truth, my lord."

With a smile, he stood. "You have both the arrogance of a Russian count and General Miloradovich's narrow-mindedness. I could almost believe you are a Russian soldier."

"You should believe it, because 'tis the truth."

"I am beginning to believe that, although I suspect I am

dicked in the nob to entertain the idea that you could be a decorated hero."

Natalya did not trust his charming smile. Her gaze met his dark eyes, and she knew she had been wise. They remained as cold as before.

When she said nothing, Lord Ashcroft asked in a purely conversational tone, "Will Zass kill at your command?"

"He has." She drew the coverlet more tightly to her chin because his gaze continued to sweep along her, constantly reminding her how vulnerable she was without her uniform. "My lord, once more I would ask your leave to retire. It has been an uncommonly long day."

"And an uncommonly long night?"

"I do not understand," she said as she had before.

"Then let me show you." When he seized her again by the shoulders, he pulled her closer. She tried to raise her fists, but they were caught in the bulky blanket. His finger beneath her chin thrust her face up so she could not look away. A satisfied smile was hard on his face.

"Lord Ashcroft—" The coarse caress of his fingertip against her cheek stole every thought from her head. An odd tingle burst outward from his touch. It flowed through her, settling over her rapidly beating heart.

His fingers combed upward through her hair, tilting her mouth beneath his. Each touch threatened to weaken her more. When his face lowered toward hers, she freed one hand and put her hand up to halt him. She touched the bare skin of his chest and jerked her hand back, for it burned as if a flame had arched from him to her. This was absurd. She did not so much as like this man. He could destroy everything that mattered to her. Yet his touch enticed her into thoughts of forbidden pleasure.

"You are, without question, the most beautiful cavalry captain I have ever seen," he murmured, his breath flavored by the brandy he had served her. "Is every man in Russia blind that he cannot see the truth?"

"I have learned that illusion is self-fulfilling." She wanted to shout the words at him, but her voice rose no louder than a whisper. "I presented myself as Count Dmitrieff. You accepted me as the count. No one in Russia questioned my identity either, especially once I proved my aim was true."

"And your wit sharp." His hand curved along her cheek, the tip of his finger grazing her ear.

Fear coursed through her along with the undeniable delight. She was an idiot to allow him to touch her like this. Lowering her eyes, she turned away. Running from any battle was odious, but letting him lure her into insanity with nothing more than this caress was worse.

"My lord," she said, her back to him, "you must tell no one what you know."

"You cannot intend to continue this masquerade in England."

"I must." She took a deep breath, then, sitting on the red velvet chair, realized the complete truth might be the only way to convince him of how precious her deception was. "As Count Dmitrieff, I can, upon my return to Russia, claim the lands that belonged to my father. In addition, to thank me for my loyalty and my heroism, the czar will give me a rich reward. That will be enough to resurrect my father's home which the French left in ruins. I have done all I have done for that moment, Lord Ashcroft, and now I need your word you will acknowledge me publicly as Count Dmitrieff."

"Ridiculous!"

"Would you allow your birthright to be taken from you by an accident of birth?"

He sat on the windowsill again and laughed. "You call your feminine sex 'an accident of birth'?"

"I am the only one left. I must be allowed to claim my father's lands."

"Very well."

"Very well?" she repeated, baffled.

"I, too, would do what I could to hold what is mine. I shall acknowledge you publicly as Count Dmitrieff."

"And tell no one the truth?"

"Who would believe me?" he fired back.

"Good, for I shall continue to be Dmitri Dmitrieff. You must do nothing to halt me." She tilted her chin and smiled. With a lightning-quick motion she had learned from Petr, she leapt to her feet and grabbed the knife. She pulled it from its sheath. The steel caught the light in a blinding glint as she held it before Lord Ashcroft's astonished eyes. "I can assure you that you will be sorry if you reveal the truth."

Three

Natalya closed the last button on the front of her uniform jacket and settled the gold braid in place around her shoulder. She brushed her hair back from her face. A quick glance into the cheval glass told her that she once again looked like the courageous Kapitán Dmitrieff. How she wished she could turn back time! If she could go back to last night, she would not have readied herself for bed until she had been sure Lord Ashcroft had found his.

She snarled a curse at her reflection and the pink warmth dusting on her cheeks. If solely his name in her thoughts brought about this feminine color, everything she had fought to hold on to could be swept away. The czar might be more progressive than his predecessors in his determination to make Russia like the western nations of Europe, but she doubted if he would be pleased to learn that one of his decorated soldiers was living a deception that could embarrass her homeland.

With a sigh, she turned away from the glass. She should have stayed in Russia, but had wanted to do nothing that might bring any less of the czar's favor on her. When Alexander had decided to display some of his heroes to the British, the invitation offered to her was one she could not refuse.

Fool that she was, she had dared to believe she could come here and go back to Russia without anyone being the wiser to the truth. Now Lord Ashcroft knew.

Her eyes squeezed shut, but she could not close out the memory of the handsome viscount standing so near, his hands setting her skin aflame with sensations she had vowed never to feel. His fingers had been amazingly gentle, but the passions they roused were more dangerous than a French assault. When she had touched his naked chest, she had sensed the galloping pace of his heartbeat, but hers had been pounding more swiftly. If she had let him kiss her . . .

She dared not savor such thoughts, delightful though they might be. She had no time for a dalliance, especially with an English lord whose smile was as cold as a Siberian winter. Yet, if that were so, why did fire sear her each time he looked in her direction? Coming to this house had been wrong. Staying would be the most foolhardy thing she could do. She had to leave before she did more to destroy all she, as Count Dmitrieff, had struggled to win.

Even though Lord Ashcroft had vowed to keep her secret and not expose her deception, she could not keep from wondering if his word had any value. So little she knew of the English. They had proven worthy allies in the war, but their ways were alien. With a sigh, she knew she had no choice but to trust Lord Ashcroft.

"For as long as he proves trustworthy," she whispered as she adjusted the wide sash at her waist. Her hand grazed the haft of the knife tucked into it. She had hoped the war was over, but Lord Ashcroft's knowledge of the truth jeopardized everything.

Her fingers clenched as she stared at the door from her bedchamber. If he spoke the truth to a single person, she would have no choice save to slay both of them. She shuddered as she imagined driving her knife into the chest that had pressed against her last night. A scowl strained her lips. She had killed other men to obtain the glory she needed to regain her family's home.

But they were faceless enemies.

"Enough!" she murmured as she took a deep breath. "You must do what you must do."

Natalya was not surprised when she opened the door to find Petr asleep against it. Knowing better than to touch him—for she had seen him, while still half-asleep, drive his knife into a Frenchman who had managed to sneak up on their camp in the middle of the night—she whispered his name.

"Kapitán, are we leaving?" he asked, jumping to his feet.

"General Miloradovich ordered us here. Until I have his approval, we cannot remove ourselves." She smiled and patted his arm when he scowled through his thick beard.

"We must leave." He cracked the knuckles of one hand against the other.

"I intend to speak to the general on that very topic before midday."

"The *anglíski* lord—"

"Will say nothing for now."

"You cannot trust him."

His words echoed the small voice inside her. Lord Ashcroft might not be trustworthy, but the fact remained that she must comply with the general's orders. To disobey was incomprehensible.

"I do not trust him, Petr," she said quietly.

He smiled as she knew he would when she used his given name as she had when they spent summers together at her family's dacha along the Dnieper. Wrinkles, left by the sun and the icy breath of winter winds, smoothed as he said, "You are wise." His dark eyes twinkled. "If you change your mind, I would be honored to slit his throat."

"That is not the way to treat our host."

"But if he is no longer our host, how can you be certain he will not reveal the truth?"

Natalya shook her head. "I have tried to find an answer to that, but it eludes me."

"He must die."

"No, for that would draw attention to us that we cannot afford."

Petr's long face drooped. "You are wise."

"I am not so sure about that." She forced a smile. "Let us hope the general is wise enough to allow us to go to other quarters."

"Do you wish me to pack your things, Kapitán?"

She almost said yes, then answered, "Wait until I return."

He nodded, and she knew he understood what she did not wish to say. General Miloradovich was as unpredictable off the battlefield as on it. Trying to guess what he might decide was as useless as attempting to catch the sunshine in her hands.

"Petr, find yourself something in the kitchen to eat. If fortune smiles on us, we shall sup somewhere else this evening."

Natalya hurried down the stairs, knowing he would obey her orders. She always could depend on Petr Zass. Ties to the land where they had been born bound them together. No matter what happened here in England, he would be her ally.

She slowed as she admired the paintings on the wall along the gently curving stairwell. Several were landscapes with softly rolling hills that were nothing like the flat land she had called home. An elegant house could be seen in each of them, and she guessed it belonged to Lord Ashcroft's family. When she returned to Russia, she would build a house as fine on the blackened ruins of the estate the French had razed on their way to Moscow.

As she reached the ground floor, the thin housekeeper bustled over to her. "Good morning, my lord—I mean, Captain D—Dm—" Then she halted, an apprehensive expression stealing her smile.

"Dmitrieff," Natalya supplied. "If it is easier for you, you may call me Demi. My mother often used the name."

"Oh, no!" the gray-haired woman gasped, pressing her

hand to her nearly flat bosom. "I could not do that, my lord. I'll just be calling you my lord, if that is agreeable with you."

"Yes, that's agreeable," she answered, wondering if the woman would have suffered an apoplectic fit if she had given any other answer. "And your name is?"

"Mrs. Winchell." She dipped in a curtsy. "If you will come with me, my lord, I shall be right glad to show you where the breakfast-parlor is." With a fearful look up the stairs, she asked, "Where is your man?"

"Sergeant Zass is on his way to the kitchen. I assume you can provide food for him there."

For a moment, Natalya thought the gaunt woman would swoon, but Mrs. Winchell gathered herself together and nodded. "He's right welcome. This household prides itself on our hospitality to Lord Ashcroft's guests."

"Is Lord Ashcroft in the breakfast-parlor?"

"He has already eaten." The housekeeper started along the hall. Once begun, her prattle did not slow. "The viscount keeps no regular hours, you should know. Says he had to live with too much regimentation in the army, so he comes and goes as he pleases. Not that there's anyone to worry about him if he is late for dinner. I thought he would settle down with a fine lady when he returned from the Continent, but he was too hurt by—" With a gulp, she glanced guiltily at Natalya and added only, "This way, my lord."

Her curiosity piqued, Natalya asked, "Hurt by what? A ball? A knife? Cannon?"

"This way, my lord," the housekeeper repeated, staring at the floor.

Natalya's eyes widened. Mrs. Winchell's reticence spoke more than any answer. 'Twas not a wound of the flesh the viscount suffered, but one of the heart. She wanted to find out more about the enigmatic man who was her host, but she recognized the dismay on the housekeeper's face. She would get nothing from Mrs. Winchell now. It would be better to wait and ask a probing question later.

Not later! She must not stay in this house a second longer than it took to get General Miloradovich's permission to leave. What did she care about Lord Ashcroft and his apparently broken heart? Any woman would be prudent to turn down his offer of marriage, for he was as wily as a snake and might be less trustworthy.

The breakfast-parlor would be welcoming on a sunny day, but the sky was little lighter than Natalya's dank spirits. The wallcovering of a rich violet silk vanished into shadows near the friezes edging the ceiling. A brass lantern hung over the cherry table, but its light could not sweep aside the lackluster aura of the room.

Mrs. Winchell fluttered about like an emaciated songbird, twittering and never alighting anywhere for long, as she made sure Natalya had a seat with a view of the rain-soaked garden. The housekeeper had chocolate and eggs and muffins and fresh butter brought. Only Natalya's insistence that she did not want fish or jam or sugar kept the housekeeper from sending servants for them.

When the housekeeper apologized that Lord Ashcroft had taken the newspaper, she added in a small voice, "You do read, don't you, my lord?"

"Russian and English, Mrs. Winchell," she answered as quietly.

"Oh, my! Isn't that wondrous?"

Natalya was spared from having to answer the curious question when the housekeeper was called away. Grateful for the silence, she ate quickly. She would have liked to have read the morning's newspaper, but that could wait. For now, her only duty was speaking to General Miloradovich.

Going back through the passage to the foyer, Natalya was aware of curious gazes cutting in her back. She saw no one, but she guessed Lord Ashcroft's servants were peering from the doorways. She could not fault them for being interested in the strangers in their midst. Wanting to tell them they need not worry about her and Petr intruding on their quiet existence much longer, she pulled her riding gloves from her sash.

A footman waited in the foyer. He bowed toward her, but his eyes were large in his face as he stared at her. "Good morning, Lord Dem—"

Hoping she would not have to repeat the same conversation with everyone in the house, she said, "I would like the horse Lord Ashcroft has made available brought about."

"Yes—"

"My lord," she supplied quietly.

"Yes, my lord." Relief lit his face as he hurried to convey her orders to the stable.

Natalya went to look out the window by the door. The rain had faded to dreary drops diving into the puddles in the street. A few carts were on the far side of the square, but no one stood near this door. As her fingers lingered near her knife, she scanned the shadows beneath the trees in the heart of the square.

"I doubt you shall be ambushed in the foyer of my house."

She whirled. Lord Ashcroft's laugh came down the stairs before him. Stiffening, she slowly released her grip on her knife. "I know that."

"Then why are you acting as if you are reconnoitering the enemy's position?"

"I was merely looking at the square."

"Is that so?"

As he stepped off the bottom riser, she fought not to throw back a sharp retort. She should have as little to do with Lord Ashcroft as possible. Last night, she had let him seduce sense from her head with his thrilling touch. Today, she must be resilient to him. Still, she could not help admiring how his light-brown pantaloons accented the lithe strength of his body. He moved with the grace of a dancer, each step measured until she was sure her very breath matched the pace. The coat he wore over a blue silk waist-coat matched the dark color of his mysterious eyes, which pierced her as his lips tightened into a straight line.

"I see nothing has changed," he continued when she did not answer.

Let him be discomforted by her appearance! This was her life. *And,* whispered the small voice in her head, *if he is angry, he will not touch you.*

"Did you expect it to?" she replied. "I bid you a good morning, Lord Ashcroft."

His brows lowered in a scowl worthy of Petr. "Why? You cannot be planning to go out alone."

"No?" She rested her hands on the hips of her gray pan-taloons and tapped the toe of her boot against a bench by the door. "As you can see, my lord, I am dressed appropri-ately for a ride."

"For a man. But you are——"

"Say no more!" She cursed under her breath in Russian, then demanded, "Is your pledge of such slight value to you that you break it without thought?"

His face hardened into a mask of stone, and his voice contained no emotion. "I recall what I promised, Captain Dmitrieff, but my orders are to see to your comfort while you are a guest of my nation. I suspect you would find it most uncomfortable to be set upon by conveyancers."

"Conveyancers?"

"Thieves." His smile became ironic. "Surely you have their like in your homeland."

"Do not fear for me, my lord. A thief would be foolish to risk my ire." Pulling on her riding gloves, she forced a smile. No other man discountenanced her as Lord Ashcroft did. She must put a swift end to this conversation before he discovered the truth. Even more vehemently than she was fighting him, she had to fight her own yearning to touch him.

"But think of the fair prize they could steal from you."

"My lord, say nothing—"

"Of the gold braid on your shoulder?" He ran a single finger along it and chuckled coldly when she stepped back before he could follow it along the front of her breast. Grasping the sash at her waist, he said, "This is, I believe, silk, which would bring a fair prize in the lowest shops."

She did not move as he tugged on the fabric. She gripped the sash and said, "Release me, my lord."

"Or?"

She faltered. With another laugh, he wound the sash around his hand as he edged closer to her. She reached up to push him away, then drew back her hands before she could touch him.

"Or what, Natalya?" he whispered. "What will you do?"

"Do not ask of what you do not wish to know."

"Such as why I still breathe this morning?" He smiled icily. "Imagine my shock at waking this morning when I had half expected you to set your man upon me while I slept."

"You were able to sleep while that was in your mind?" She frowned, unable to imagine letting slumber overcome her while she awaited an attack.

His eyes glittered a warning, but she could not look away before he murmured, "You should heed your own advice and not ask of what you do not wish to know. Or do you truly wish to know of what was in my mind while I slept, Natalya?" He grinned. "Or who?"

"No!"

"But, if I wish to tell you—" He cursed as she pulled her knife.

Sharply, she cut through the sash, then slid the knife back in its sheath. "But, my lord, I do not wish to hear of it." Without a pause, she added, "I trust I did not overstep myself by having a horse brought about to the front. You said it was available to me at all times during my visit."

"I do not renege on offers of hospitality." He threw the piece of sash onto the banister.

"I am pleased to hear that you hold that pledge dear, my lord."

"I hold all my pledges dear, my dear count." His frigid words failed to cover the fury sparking his eyes to dusky fire. With his hands clasped behind his back and his chin jutted in her direction, she guessed he was about ready to explode. She girded herself for the detonation.

When he added only, "Good morning, Captain," she was left to stare after him as he strode down the hall toward the breakfast-parlor. He did not look back, dismissing her as completely as she had him the night before.

Baffled by his bizarre ways, but glad to have the encounter at an end, Natalya hurried out to where the horse was waiting. She swung easily into the saddle. Mounted, she was ready for any battle, but the feel of the leather against her legs offered sparse comfort. She had defeated stronger enemies than Lord Ashcroft, although, she had to own, none stranger. He should be her ally, but she could not trust him. Even though he had tried to hide the fact from the outset, she knew he wanted nothing to do with a Russian houseguest. To him, that she was a woman was just another bothersome detail. He wanted her gone as much as she wished to be elsewhere.

She set the horse to a gallop around the square. The odd sound of cobbles beneath its hoofs made her yearn for the noise of frozen earth or fresh mud. The scents of the chimney pots were stifling on the morning breeze, and she longed to smell the aromas of campfires and the fats the men used to clean their weapons. She had hated London from the moment she saw it. She liked no city, not even beautiful St. Petersburg or Kiev. All of her life, save for the past months, had been spent in the country.

Wishing she now could ride across the fields of her father's estate was futile. Soon she would be back there. Then she would not have to think about Lord Ashcroft and the dangerous power his touch had over her. She must be gone from his house before his bewitchment claimed every ounce of sense in her head.

General Miloradovich put down a crumpled newspaper as Natalya was ushered into his grand bedchamber, which appeared twice the size of her generous room at Lord Ashcroft's house. He dismissed the servant with a flick of his hand and motioned for Natalya to come closer. Ignoring the buxom woman who was brushing her hair at the dressing table beside the bed, which was as rumpled as the newspaper, Natalya obeyed. She wondered when the general had managed to find this woman, for he had left his collection of mistresses in Russia.

She almost smiled, but kept her face emotionless. No doubt Kapitán Radishchev had found this woman for the general. That seemed the insipid coward's primary job.

"Who is this?" asked the woman, whose red hair was several shades lighter than Lord Ashcroft's. Her gaze swept Natalya up and down, and she giggled. "Is *this* one of your heroes, Karl?"

"Be silent," Miloradovich answered, flashing Natalya a wry smile. "Go, my dear, and ring for more hot chocolate. I think you emptied this pot."

She rose and gave him a kiss on his left jowl. Her smile vanished as she gave Natalya a sneer. When Natalya did not react, the woman left, slamming the door behind her.

Natalya arched a single brow at the general, and he chuckled.

"Pay her no mind, Dmitrieff. Her head is as empty as the chocolate pot." Scratching his bewhiskered chin, he lit his pipe and asked, "Why are you bothering me at this hour?"

"General Miloradovich, I am sorry to intrude, but I wish to request a change of residence."

He shook his head, rearranging the heavy smoke around it. "Impossible."

"But, General—"

"Do not pester me with worthless requests, Dmitrieff." He regarded her intently. "It is not like you to whine like a vexing woman. What is amiss?"

Wanting to tell him the truth, but knowing that she could not explain without revealing the whole, she sighed. "I had thought to be closer to the Russian delegation in order to serve our czar better."

He puffed on his pipe as he rose and paced. His dressing gown of a most outrageous emerald green rippled across his full body. "You serve me best where you are right now." Miloradovich rounded to face her. "Begone, Kapitán Dmitrieff, and do what you were brought here to do."

"Which is?"

A feral smile pulled his thin lips back over his teeth. "Get to know *Angliya* and its people and their ways, of course. The czar wishes us to be more like these western Europeans. Now, begone."

Natalya obeyed, knowing she had no other choice, but, as she walked along the long corridor and down the stairs to the street, she could not shake off the feeling that General Miloradovich's words had a meaning she was not privy to.

But what could that be? She hoped her disquiet was nothing more than knowing she must go back and tell Petr she had failed to do as she had promised. It was going to be a most troublesome day.

Four

Creighton climbed the steps to the front door of the club, not stopping to answer any of the questions fired at him. He had not come to White's for the company of his tie-mates, especially when all they wanted to speak of was his blasted guest. With that hulking Zass popping up at odd places throughout his house, Creighton needed to find a place where no Russian would be welcomed. Here, he could think clearly.

What a to-do! All he had wanted, in the aftermath of the war, was to enjoy the whirl of the Season with his friends and the rest of the Polite World. Now he was afflicted with this Russian woman and her ridiculous secret.

His hand clenched on the railing. How dare Natalya Dmitrieff wander about London in such a guise! If she had been honest—and he had no doubts that she had been—not even her superior officers knew of her sex. Was the male half of the world suddenly want-witted? Every motion she made betrayed she was a woman, from her slender hands emphasizing her words to the enticing sway of her hips as she had stormed out of his house.

The small parlor was empty when he opened the door. That was good. He did not want even the hushed rumble of gambling to intrude on his thoughts. Going to a wing chair, he dropped into it and glowered at the unlit fire in the hearth.

He had been a cabbage-head to agree to do nothing to expose Natalya Dmitrieff as the liar she was. His jaw clenched as he wondered if he could believe her, even now. Her story seemed a bit too pat. After she had spent years in service to Czar Alexander, it was unlikely no one knew the truth of her identity, save for Zass. Could everyone be blind?

He had thought something was wrong from the moment he met Count Dmitrieff. Were all the Russians stupid that they had failed to take note of her unshaven cheeks and feminine features? No man had ever had such soft hair and inviting lips and her eyes . . . Those exotic eyes had burned into his brain last night and refused to be dislodged.

Damme! Why had the chit been foisted off on him? Colonel Carruthers! Creighton's brow furrowed with fury, then he warned himself that jumping to conclusions would prove he wanted for sense. Until he had a chance to question his colonel—obliquely, of course—he must assume that no one knew Natalya's secret except for him and Zass.

The sound of the latch lifting brought another curse to his lips, but it went unspoken as he recognized the man in the doorway. Barclay Lawson was as thin as an anatomy and had no more hair than a streetlamp. Wisely, in Creighton's estimation, Barclay never had heard the summons to duty to protect England. Mayhap because he never had suffered the pain that had stalked Creighton during those last months before he sailed for the Continent. Barclay, the younger son of a baron who sat on a penniless bench, enjoyed the benevolence of his friends who were more plump in the pocket. His repartee and ability to drink all night and still play an intimidating game of cards endeared him to the *ton*.

"Creighton! Enright told me he had seen you racing up the stairs as if all the dogs of hell were nipping at your heels." He handed Creighton a glass of wine and sat in the chair across from him. "What is bothering you? I have seen a man on his way to die of a hempen fever with a more cheerful countenance."

Tapping the side of his glass, he took a reflective drink. "It is nothing of import."

"Nothing?" Barclay perched on the edge of his chair and clenched his fists on his knees. "Can this be the same man who announced to all who would listen that he was done with dreary thoughts of faithless Maeve Wilton and wished only to enjoy the pleasures of the Season?"

"I did say that, but—"

"No buts. How can you be so glum when we have been invited to Lady Eltonville's hurricane tonight?" Putting his glass on the table next to his chair, he rubbed his hands together and laughed. "I have vowed to lighten John Hotz's pocket of a few centuries before dawn. If you are to be my partner, Creighton, I need you to be in the proper state of mind."

Rising, Creighton walked to the window that overlooked St. James's Street. Cheerless rain splattered at the window, but that did nothing to curtail the traffic below. Carriages rolled up to the door of the clubs, and men scurried through the downpour to pass the day with their comrades.

With his hands locked behind him, he continued to stare out the window as he said, "I am obligated to play host to Count Dmitrieff."

"Who in the devil is that?"

Creighton did not pretend to smile as he faced his friend. "Count Dmitrieff is my guest."

"Dmitrieff?" He nearly choked as he gasped, "But that name is—"

"Russian." He laughed without humor. "Colonel Carruthers took it into his idea-box to foist one of the officers in the Russian delegation into my house, so Dmitri Dmitrieff is my guest."

"You need to rid yourself of that commission with all due haste."

"True, but even if I were rid of the blasted thing today, I am obligated to play host to the count for the duration of his stay."

"You have too strong a sense of honor, Creighton. I thought I had broken you of such bad habits." Barclay set himself on his feet. "I have heard the Russians can outdrink anyone. Mayhap we should get a few good bottles of brandy and see how long it takes to get this one altogethery."

"I think not." He could not imagine Natalya allowing herself to become intoxicated.

"So why is this Russian a problem?"

Creighton foiled the urge to laugh. It was tempting to answer with the truth. What would Barclay think of a Russian war hero who was, in truth, a beautiful woman with beguiling eyes? His hands recalled the smoothness of her skin against them even as the memory of the scent of her skin raced through his mind.

Fiercely, he clenched his fingers to squeeze out the sensation he could not keep from wanting to feel again. Was he queer in his attic? Her style of dress made it clear she wished nothing from any man but camaraderie. That was all to the best. He should have learned his lesson with Maeve. A teasing smile, an intoxicating touch, lips that promised him everything—as they had promised too many others.

"Forget I mentioned it," Creighton said as he picked up his glass and drained it. The warmth of the wine could not melt the icy lump of disquiet within him.

Barclay laughed. "I think that is unlikely. I know you, too well, old man. Having this Russian about unsettles you greatly."

"Then I would have guts in my brain to put my guest right out of my head."

Barclay Lawson stepped from his carriage onto Berkeley Square and settled his hat on his head. Taking his gold-topped walking stick from the footman, he looked both ways along the street. It was a shame no lovely lady was about to see him when he was dressed in his finest. Beau Brummel himself would be envious of the cut of this new scarlet coat and cream breeches.

He strode out into the street, then leapt back as a horse sped past. Mud struck him, spotting from head to foot. Shaking his hands, he looked down at his ruined clothes. Mire dripped from him.

Shoving aside his footman, who was trying, in vain, to clean the filth from him, Barclay strode to where the horse had stopped. The rider was swinging down from the saddle, an expression of consternation on the young pup's face. Barclay swore under his breath when he saw the gaudy uniform the rider wore.

Russian!

The damned Russians had infected Town with a fever of excitement and anticipation of the celebrations now that the war on the Continent was over, but they ran about as if London were their private playground. This one would learn that he could not ride down an Englishman with impunity.

"Look at what you have done!" he snapped. "I am fortunate I have suffered no more damage than this. You could have killed me! How could you be so stupid?"

Natalya held the reins easily as she listened to this bald man's ranting. The idiot had stepped almost beneath her horse's hoofs. If she had not pulled the beast aside, the man would be suffering more than a splattered coat. She had not been certain if Lord Ashcroft's horse would respond with the speed of her own mount, but fortunately the steed had been well-trained.

"You should be more cautious where you walk, sir," she said.

"Me?" He muttered something she could not understand. He gave her no chance to reply as he wagged a finger in front of her nose. "You were riding neck-or-nothing. I demand satisfaction for this indignity."

"Satisfaction? Of what sort?"

"Look at me!"

She eyed him up and down. As far as she could see, the mud was an improvement, for it muted the garish crimson of his coat, which would have better suited a parade ground than a city street. She frowned as she realized it was not designed to be worn by a soldier. Swallowing her snicker of derision, she said, "You are lucky I did look at you, sir, or you would be lying wounded on the cobbles now."

"I am wounded!"

"Are you?" She had been certain she had missed him by yanking wildly on the reins.

"My coat is ruined."

"It is muddy, sir."

"Mud will ruin good wool, even good English wool." He looked down his long nose at her. "Which is finer than anything you might have in Russia."

Natalya sighed. Arguing about the durability of English wool in comparison to what had been raised on her father's land was futile. Not a single sheep remained. Nothing remained there, only scorched stones and stumps. Wondering what an English tailor would charge to make another coat in that hideous shade, she said, "You were clearly at fault on this matter. You cannot expect me to replace your coat under these circumstances."

" 'Tis not just my coat." He slapped at his breeches, making the mess worse. "I am soaked to the skin. Everything I am wearing is ruined."

"I shall be glad to assume the cost of your coat, sir," she said, wanting to be done with this and be on her way, although she did not look forward to telling Petr about the general's decision that they were to remain as Lord Ashcroft's guests. "But you must be as willing to take your share of the blame for this accident."

The man snarled an insult, and she clenched her hand more tightly around the reins. Becoming embroiled in an argument with this plaguily foolish man would only complicate an already complicated situation.

"Sir," she began. "I said—"

"I would ask you to name your friends for grass before breakfast."

"What did you say?" His words made no sense to her. *Grass before breakfast.* She could not guess what the bizarre phrase meant. If only these Englishmen would speak their own language!

"I challenge you—"

"To find a finer day for a ride," interrupted a deeper voice.

Natalya watched the man in the scarlet coat whirl to confront the intruder, but she moved more cautiously. She was unsure what this half-cocked Englishman might do if she made a sudden motion. When she saw Lord Ashcroft standing with his hand on the wrought-iron fence by the walkway in front of his house, she did not know whether to feel relieved or more distressed. A smile curved along his lips, and she suspected her day was going to go from troublesome to disaster.

Five

As he listened to Barclay's fury, Creighton kept all his thoughts from his face, but he had to fight harder to keep his gaze from following the alluring curves that Natalya's uniform could not hide from him any longer. How much easier this would have been if she were as bracket-faced as Zass! Instead, she possessed, even in that concealing uniform, a faerie beauty that had crept into his head and refused to be dislodged. Through the night, every attempt to sleep had been haunted by the icy blue passions he had seen in her exotic eyes.

He had been a complete block to touch her last night and again today. Now his hands itched to caress her surprisingly silken skin again, to become lost in the soft jumble of her golden curls, to bring her beguiling lips to his so he could determine if they were as sweet as the strawberries they resembled or as bitter as the dregs at the bottom of a bottle of burgundy.

He resisted the yearning to seize her and discover the truth. She would fight him now as she had before. He almost smiled as he recalled her slim body against him, each motion an invitation he knew she did not mean.

"Barclay, you are late," he said, but paused as he heard the huskiness in his voice. Damme! He would not be an air-dreamer, repining for a woman whose style of dress made it clear she had no interest in anything from a man.

"What? Speak what you have to say loud enough so I can hear past the mud cloaking me," demanded Barclay, bristling like a rooster whose yard had been invaded.

"Mayhap I should say your timing is perfect." Creighton walked toward the street and smiled. "Allow me to introduce a visitor to England. Captain Dmitri Dmitrieff. Captain, this is Barclay Lawson, a friend of mine."

Creighton was not surprised Natalya was the first to react, for he had seen that her wits were as sharp as her tongue. *"Zdrástvuyte,* Mr. Lawson." She smiled. "Good day."

"This is *your* Russian?" Barclay choked.

Natalya's eyes widened as she glanced at Creighton, but he had no chance to do more than smile before she said in a cool voice, "I advise you again, Mr. Lawson, to accept my generous offer of replacing your coat. I would not wish to have a friend of my host Lord Ashcroft assume the complete damages for his foolishness of stepping in front of my horse."

"Listen to him!" Barclay's cheeks were becoming a choleric shade which approached the color of his coat. "He has done this to me." He shook more mud from the tail of his coat. "Now he thinks he can allay my anger with that preposterous offer while he shunts the blame off on me. Creighton, tell me that you will be my second when—"

Creighton saw comprehension brighten Natalya's eyes. If he did not do something quickly, he feared Barclay would become a victim of his own stubbornness. He was certain of one thing. Natalya would not back down from the challenge to a duel, for to accept would be the only way to protect her identity.

Taking his friend's arm, he said, "Come in. Mrs. Winchell will get the worst of the mud out of your coat."

"Not until I have had my satisfaction from this damned Russian." He jerked his arm away and faced Natalya. "You need to learn you cannot ride hell-for-leather through London streets."

"I have made my offer for reparation, Mr. Lawson. It is up to you to decide if you wish to accept it. I will not stand here and argue with a—" She glanced at Creighton and smiled. "I believe the term, if I heard it correctly, is carpet-knight."

Creighton snatched his friend's arm as it rose and pulled him toward the front door. Mrs. Winchell was peeking around it, shock on her thin face. Barclay sputtered like a man who had been dunked in the village pond, but he climbed the steps to the door.

When Creighton looked back, he did not see a triumphant smile on Natalya's face. Uneasiness stole the light from her eyes. Something—something much more important than Barclay's blusterings—had upset her. A pinch of sympathy startled him. He did not want to feel sorry for her. He did not want to feel anything for her. Maybe that way he could stifle the longing that rose through him like a heated wellspring each time her blue eyes turned toward him.

His curse at his own caper-witted musings was muted by Barclay's complaints. Peeling Barclay's coat from his shoulders, Creighton said, "Mrs. Winchell, please do what you can with this."

"Yes, my lord." She lowered her voice as Barclay stamped up the stairs. "I never saw its like."

"In what way?" Mayhap Mrs. Winchell's eyes were clearer than the others in the household.

"The count, my lord." She leaned toward him as she continued in a conspiratorial whisper, "I saw the whole. Mr. Lawson stepped right in front of the count's horse. I could not believe the count was able to pull his horse away from trampling Mr. Lawson. 'Twas right fine riding, Lord Ashcroft."

"The count did ride with the cavalry into battle."

Mrs. Winchell nodded. "True, but 'twas fine riding nonetheless. Never saw its like." She straightened and said, "Good afternoon, my lord."

Creighton turned to see Natalya behind him. Damme! She was as light on her feet as a will-o'-the-wisp. Clasping his hands behind his back, he said, "You continue to disrupt this household in ways I could not have imagined, Captain Dmitrieff."

"Nor I." She glanced up the stairs and sighed. "Please convey to Mr. Lawson that my offer still stands. I will replace his coat if he feels it is ruined beyond repair."

Mrs. Winchell clucked her tongue. " 'Twill be fine once it dries and I brush it." Quickly, she lowered her eyes. "Excuse me, Lord Ashcroft." She scurried away.

Natalya said, "If I misspoke—"

"You apparently have done nothing wrong through all of this, save for riding well enough to prevent Barclay's absentmindedness from causing him to be injured."

"Mr. Lawson does not seem the type to be absent his mind," she replied, her forehead ruffled with bafflement.

"You do not know him well." Creighton again fought with temptation—this time not to laugh. At the shout of his name down the stairs, he called, "I shall be with you directly, Barclay. Natalya—"

She put her gloved hand on his arm. "Please do not call me that."

"It *is* your name. I do not wish to call you 'count' or 'captain' for the duration of your stay."

"Yes," she murmured, "the duration of my stay . . ."

He caught her hand before she could draw it off his sleeve and turn away. "What is it— Damme! I must have something I can call you."

"My fellow officers called me Demi as a familiar version of Dmitri."

"Then, Demi, what is it that upset you about what I just said?" He laughed, halting her answer when he saw the truth on her bleak face. "You went to General Miloradovich today, didn't you?"

"He insists we serve the czar best by remaining here." Again, charming confusion threaded her forehead, giving him a hint of the gentle young woman she might have been, save for Napoleon's greed for power. "I fail to understand why."

"Nor do I. What is it you told me? *Ya pon*—"

She laughed. *"Ya ne ponimáyu.* I do not understand."

He stroked her fingers and folded them beneath his against his chest. "On that, if nothing else, we are in agreement, Demi." Smiling, he said, "That name suits you even less well than the others you claim."

"Demi? It is a good name."

"But in French, demi means half, and I cannot envision you ever doing anything by half." He watched how the soft glow in her eyes deepened as he drew her closer as he whispered, "You give all of yourself to your goals. You—"

"Creighton!" Barclay leaned over the banister on the upper floor. "Where in blazes are you?"

When Natalya snatched her hands away, Creighton did not speak the curse battering his lips. He should be grateful to his friend for interrupting. In fact, if he had half an ounce of wit about him, he would not delay in inviting Barclay to move into the townhouse as well. He had never understood the need for a watch-dog . . . until now when he was constantly bombarded by his curiosity to taste Natalya's lips.

"I shall be right there," he called back. As Barclay's furious footfalls resounded from upstairs to the ground floor, he added, "I think it would be wise, Natalya, if you do not join us."

"I agree."

He was unsure if he detected a tremor of amusement in her voice, and she was striding away before he could ask her another question. When he saw something move in the shadows beyond the staircase, he frowned. He should have guessed Zass would not stray far from Natalya once she returned to the house.

Creighton took the steps, two at a time, up to his bookroom. The Russian sergeant was enough to give any man second thoughts about Natalya. Wryly, he smiled. Second thoughts about her did not seem to be a problem for him. He thought about her every second.

Closing the door behind him, he hoped nothing would intrude before he convinced Barclay to forget that he had challenged her to a duel. It would not be simple. Barclay prowled about the room, his virtually bald head catching the glint of the sunshine each time he passed a window. On every step, he muttered a condemnation of the Russian who, he was certain, had humiliated him.

Creighton sat in his favorite chair and watched. When brandy was brought, he poured a glass for himself and one for his friend. He sipped his and listened to Barclay's rumbles.

Finally, when it seemed his tie-mate could go on indefinitely, he interrupted to say, "Barclay, I can listen to no more of this. Count Dmitrieff is my guest."

"That changes nothing."

"The count reiterated the offer to replace your coat, although Mrs. Winchell has assured both of us that it can be cleaned without looking the worse for wear."

"That changes nothing," he repeated grimly. "I shall have my satisfaction for his outrageous taunts. Carpet-knight, indeed!"

"You cannot duel Count Dmitrieff."

"Why not?"

Creighton lifted his glass of brandy. "You have no second."

"Why not you?" He gripped the back of the chair facing Creighton and scowled.

"Tonight I plan to attend Lady Eltonville's soirée and I

have no desire to rise before the sun to stride across wet grass to allow you to vent your spleen. Even if I did, you cannot duel Count Dmitrieff."

"If you will not stand as my second, Creighton, I shall find someone who will."

"You cannot duel Count Dmitrieff," he repeated, prepared to say the words over and over until his friend would listen.

Barclay slammed his fist into the chair. "Tell me one reason why not."

"Because the count will air your skull for you with a single shot."

"I can best any half-pint Russian in any affair of honor."

"The count is a war hero. You have faced nothing more fierce than a fox seeking earth."

Barclay's lips worked, but no sound came out. Seizing his glass, he downed a hefty drink of brandy. "Are *you* now questioning my abilities, Creighton? I thought you were my friend."

"I am your friend. That is why I am urging you to rethink this." He set his glass on the table by his chair. "Barclay, you cannot duel Count Dmitrieff."

With a curse, Barclay threw his glass onto the hearth. The flames leapt wildly. He strode toward the door and flung it open. "I shall not let my honor go unavenged. Those words were spoken publicly."

Creighton jumped to his feet. Taking his friend by the lapel, he shook him as he kicked the door closed. "Listen, you stubborn dull-swift! You have more hair than wit, and you have no hair! Listen to me! You cannot duel Count Dmitrieff."

"You cannot halt me."

"I shall!"

Barclay jerked away. "If you are afraid I shall wound your guest and embarrass you—"

"I doubt you shall get a shot off before the count lets fly the pop."

He laughed coldly. "I invite you to join us for the duel, Creighton, and you shall see how mistaken you are. My shot shall strike that damned Russian and put an end to the insults to decent Englishmen!"

"No."

"No?"

Creighton sighed. Walking away from the door, he shook his head. The simplest way to halt Barclay from embarking on this nick-ninny's quest was with the truth, and he was forsworn to say nothing of it. Yet, if he remained silent, he knew what the results of the duel would be as surely as if he were a soothsayer who could discern the future. Natalya would finish Barclay's life for him with a single shot. She could not risk being struck, for, as soon as anyone examined her wound, the truth would reveal itself along with her feminine curves.

Staring down at the fire, he sighed again. "The count is my guest. I will not allow you to duel him."

"Not allow?" Something else followed the question, but Creighton could not understand the words spat through Barclay's clenched teeth.

"I am saying, Barclay, that you cannot duel Count Dmitrieff. You are fooling yourself if you think you will get off the first shot. The count will see you dead."

"Let me show you how well I shoot!"

"It does not matter. I shall not allow it."

Barclay jabbed a finger at Creighton's waistcoat. "This is between me and that witless Russian. Do not interfere."

Creighton arched a single brow, then stepped away from Barclay's bony finger. Obviously good sense was not going to prevail when his friend was in such a pelter. Clasping his hands behind his back, he said, "Very well."

"Very well?"

"Are you going to parrot back everything I say?"

"I am astonished."

"I suspect so, but I hope you are not so astonished that

you see the wisdom of what I am about to say." Creighton held up his hands to forestall Barclay's next comment. "Listen to me. The count is nearly arrived from the Continent. I do not know how they handle these challenges in Russia, so allow me to discern what procedures the count is familiar with before you set the time and place of your death."

Barclay started to nod, then snapped, "Don't assume the count will be the better man."

Creighton smiled. "That is one thing, my friend, you can be certain I shall never assume."

Six

Natalya jumped to her feet when someone rapped on the door of her bedchamber. Throwing it open, she said, "Petr, *mózhno!*"

Mrs. Winchell regarded her, wide-eyed. "Is that Russian, my lord?"

"Yes." She buttoned the front of her jacket quickly. "Excuse me. I thought you were Sergeant Zass."

"No, my lord." An extraordinary flush splashed across her thin cheeks. "Lord Ashcroft asks that you join him and Mr. Lawson in the book-room."

Noting a motion at the other end of the passage, she nodded. "Please let Lord Ashcroft know I shall be there directly."

Mrs. Winchell glanced along the hall, shuddered, and whispered, "Of course, my lord." She scurried away as if a hungry wolf were at her heels.

Natalya switched effortlessly to Russian as Petr came toward her. "What have you done to frighten that poor woman away from her wits?"

"I vow to you, Kapitán, I have said nothing to her." His eyes twinkled. "She will be pleased when we are gone."

"Which shall not be soon, Petr." Walking along the soft rug that swallowed the sound of her boot heels, she explained the general's insistence that they remain here. "It is most odd."

"How?"

"It was as if General Miloradovich were laughing at a joke I could not be privy to."

He combed his fingers through his beard as he did whenever he was deep in thought. "The general often has done odd things."

"Like ordering us to the flank of the other hussars outside Vitebsk?"

"Fortunately for him, we were there in time to halt that band of French and Hessian mercenaries from sneaking away."

"Fortunately for him," she agreed. Only because she had been serving as a liaison between the field and the general's headquarters, which were comfortably out of the range of French artillery, had she—and Petr—known the truth. General Miloradovich had panicked and given the wrong orders, turning too many of the men away from the main thrust of the French vanguard.

If only they had been so lucky when Moscow came under siege . . .

"How long will we be billeted here?" Petr asked, freeing her from her dreary memories.

"Until the state visit is over, if I know the general. He is preoccupied with other matters."

"A blonde or a brunette?"

"A redhead."

"That is something new for him to sample." Petr's chuckle rumbled along the silent hallway. "All the general's appetites are well-renowned."

Natalya's answer went unspoken when a door opened to spill light across the dark carpet. "Say nothing, Petr."

"They will understand nothing I say, even if I do." His dark brows lowered in a fierce scowl. "Kapitán, what trouble are we in now?"

"We are in no trouble." That much was the truth, although she had few doubts how Petr would react when he discovered she had been challenged to a duel. During their campaigns, he had been insistent that she should fight only when necessary—and only against the enemy. The expediences of war had demanded that *Grazhdánka* Natalya change to become *Kapitán* Dmitrieff, but she knew, even though he had not spoken of it, how Petr longed to return to their home and the life they once had known.

Natalya swept all emotion from her face as Lord Ashcroft motioned for her to enter. He was not as successful in concealing his thoughts, for she saw his eyes narrow when Petr followed her into the cozy room. Did he think Petr was accompanying her as her second so she could face his loud-mouthed friend over bare swords right here in his house?

"Gentlemen," she said cautiously.

Mr. Lawson stared at her, glanced at Lord Ashcroft, and then swallowed roughly. "Creighton has persuaded me to wait before issuing my challenge to you." His tone was as strained as hers.

"Wait? Why?" She looked at Lord Ashcroft who was smiling coldly.

"That is something," the viscount said, "we shall discuss at length later."

She nodded, although she was not sure what outlandish English custom this might be. In Russia, an insult was dealt with swiftly. "Very well. However, my offer to replace your coat remains, Mr. Lawson."

"Mrs. Winchell has been known to work miracles," Lord Ashcroft said as he held out a glass of wine to her. "I think both you and Barclay shall discover she can clean the coat until it looks as good as new."

"If even a hint of *grjaz'* remains—"

"What?" Mr. Lawson asked, frowning.

"Mud." She smiled as she heard Petr's chuckle. "Forgive me, for my tongue yearns for the words of my birth. If even a hint of mud remains, I shall gladly replace your coat."

Mr. Lawson tilted his head as he stared at her. "Mayhap

that is not such a bad idea. Then I can introduce you to
Mr. Hardy, who is my knight of the thimble."

"Tailor," Lord Ashcroft supplied before Natalya could
ask. "Barclay, you shall discover the count is unfamiliar
with the cant we use daily."

"A tailor is not necessary," she said quietly.

"You cannot plan to wear that heavy uniform during the
rest of your stay in London. Mayhap it is comfortable
enough for a Russian winter, but you will swelter in such
thick wool here." Mr. Lawson came around the chair and
flicked a disdainful finger at the fur on her stiff collar. He
jumped back as Petr growled under his breath.

"Petr, please do not make things more tense," she said
in Russian.

"Kapitán . . ."

"Serve yourself some of the lord's wine and sit. If I need
you, you shall be nearby."

He smiled, his expression growing frigid as he stared at
the two Englishmen.

Natalya was unsure what Lord Ashcroft might do when
Petr poured a generous serving of the red wine and raised
it to his lips. Although Mr. Lawson grumbled something,
Lord Ashcroft leaned one shoulder against the mantel and
continued to regard them with a smile.

When Petr had chosen a stool in the back corner, Natalya
said, "I thank you for your concern, Mr. Lawson." She took
a sip of her wine, then went to stand by the window overlooking the street. Putting her shiny boot on the stool not
far from Petr's feet, she smiled. "A soldier is not accustomed to comfort. However, you may be correct. If I am
granted such liberties by General Miloradovich, I shall
thank you for such an introduction, Mr. Lawson."

"Soldiers!"

She held up her hand to halt Petr from surging to his
feet. He did not need to know much English to recognize
the aspersion. Mr. Lawson's insult included Lord Ashcroft

as well. They must take a hint of how to respond from their host.

Lord Ashcroft laughed. "Do not make it sound as if we are as vile as the slimiest grub beneath an overturned rock." Sitting, he added, "Barclay, you must restrain your opinions. The good captain and I have agreed to disagree."

"On what?" Mr. Lawson asked.

"Many things." He flashed a smile at Natalya. That now familiar, unwanted pulse of delight throbbed through her. She fought to keep any expression from her face as he added, "For example, the count does not share my estimation of the usefulness of our superiors now that the war has been won."

"Yes, I do." Natalya wished she could take the words back, but they had slipped from her lips.

"Do you now?"

When the viscount motioned for her to sit across from him, she silenced her sigh and lowered herself into the chair. The general had ordered her to learn more of the ways of the English. How else could she do it other than to spend time with them? She could not go back to the general with the complaint that she was uneasy in Lord Ashcroft's company because she could not keep from thinking of the exciting danger of his touch which urged her to be as bold.

She watched Mr. Lawson as he prowled from the hearth to the door, keeping a wide expanse of floor between him and Petr. His rage punctuated every motion. She must watch him closely. She would not be ambushed if he sought satisfaction now.

Lord Ashcroft rested his chin on his fist as he smiled. She was not fooled. His eyes were as stern as the uncompromising line of his jaw. Aware of Mr. Lawson coming to stand behind her, she longed to jump to her feet and rush away. She was surrounded, and Petr, who would watch closely, could not guess how facilely Lord Ashcroft used words as a weapon to skewer her.

"My colonel," Lord Ashcroft said in a purely conversational voice, "left no doubts in my mind that you were the most competent among General Miloradovich's men."

She whirled when Mr. Lawson choked. He took a hasty drink and muttered, "Swallowed the wrong way."

"Be more careful," chided Lord Ashcroft.

"Some things are hard to swallow." Mr. Lawson's grin returned as he leaned over the back of her chair.

Natalya stiffened. Were his words an insult?

"Then take more care!" Without giving his friend a chance to answer, Lord Ashcroft said, "It is good to know, Captain Dmitrieff, that the Russians think much as we do. Our leaders have built their careers more on luck than skill."

"And more on the skill of those who serve them than their own," she said, resting her arm on the chair. "It is said you are a hero, Lord Ashcroft."

"I am sure my so-called exploits pale before yours."

With a grumble, Mr. Lawson downed his wine and set the glass on the table. "I shall leave you soldiers to your stories of war. I have other matters to concern myself with before this evening." He scowled at Natalya. "We shall meet with all due speed, Count, to resolve this matter between us."

"Barclay . . ."

He included Lord Ashcroft in his frown. "The challenge remains—"

"And shall be dealt with at the proper time. There will be opportunities to discuss it. I think you shall be seeing quite a bit of the count."

"I wish only to see the count's blood mixed with the mud that splattered my coat." He pulled a glove from beneath his waistcoat.

Creighton stood. "No!"

Natalya tensed, then gasped as Mr. Lawson struck her cheek with the glove.

Petr leapt forward, pulling his knife.

"Nyet!" cried Natalya.

Mr. Lawson's face bleached with fear. "Tell your beast there I meant that as a token of challenge."

Natalya turned and said, "Petr, it is nothing. He clearly sees me as a gentleman who has affronted him."

"Then he sees no more than anyone else, Kapitán, save for the other."

She nodded. "Our host has pledged to keep my secret from anyone else."

"He will, or he will die."

Again she nodded, knowing this was not the time to remind Petr they must cause no trouble while in England.

"Will you share what Sergeant Zass has to say?" Lord Ashcroft asked quietly. "He looks unconvinced."

She clasped her hands behind her back. She must not give free rein to their yearning to touch the shimmering warmth of the satin waistcoat accenting his broad chest. Other men had touched her, but none with an invitation to such sweet madness. She could counter the greatest thrust of a lance, yet she could not force aside the memory of Lord Ashcroft's fingers grazing her cheek.

"He understands," she began, then heard her voice tremble. She looked hastily away as a smile curved along Lord Ashcroft's lips. Taking a deep breath, she focused her eyes on Mr. Lawson's face. If she did not look at the viscount, she could not be caught by the promise of pleasure in his eyes. "Mr. Lawson, Petr understands your *angliski* ways are different from ours."

"I can see that."

"Good," she said.

"And I can see," he continued, "that there is little reason to continue this conversation."

Lord Ashcroft said in the same quiet tone, "I shall speak with Count Dmitrieff without delay, Barclay. Then the three of us shall complete the arrangements this evening at Lady Eltonville's gathering."

"A dandy of an idea." He smiled broadly.

Natalya looked from one to the other. Was she missing something in their words? Something that they found amusing? A pinch of dismay struck her. If Lord Ashcroft had divulged the truth to his friend . . . No, he had given her his word. *As an Englishman,* she reminded herself, not sure what that was worth. "A gathering? What sort of gathering?"

"An evening with music and dancing and cards." Mr. Lawson shrugged. "You may not have its counterpart in that uncivilized land of yours."

"Yes, we do," she said slowly. If he wished to enrage her into doing something foolish, he would soon learn how mistaken he was. She would not have survived five minutes on the battlefield if she were prone to surrendering to impulse.

"Then join us." Lord Ashcroft chuckled. "We shall have a roaring good time at the card table, if I recall your description of Russian habits correctly, Count Dmitrieff."

Mr. Lawson gave her no chance to demur as he strode to the door. "It is settled then. I look forward to seeing the two of you—" He glanced at Petr. "Yes, I look forward to seeing the two of you this evening."

"But Petr would serve as my second for the challenge," she said.

Mr. Lawson's lips tightened. "It seems Russian ways are quite similar to ours in these matters. Why are we delaying? Tonight, once the moon has risen, we can—"

"We will discuss this at the gathering," Lord Ashcroft said, the ice returning to his voice. "Agreed?"

Natalya said, "If there is no reason to delay—"

Again he interrupted, "Agreed?"

"Yes," she said quietly.

Mr. Lawson muttered, "Yes." The door slammed, resounding through the room, in his wake.

She looked at Petr who wore a strained frown. This was

Seven

Lord Ashcroft shook his head as the door closed behind his friend. "It seems Barclay is set on dueling you, Natalya."

"My lord, you should not—"

"Barclay cannot hear me from here when the door is closed. And who knows? You may wish to tell him the truth."

"Me? I doubt that."

"You and Barclay may become the best of friends."

"And so may you and Petr."

Creighton looked across the room as the huge Russian stood at the mention of his name. He wondered how many French soldiers had quailed before the very sight of this man.

"Possible," he said.

When she laughed, he watched Zass relax. He noticed that from the corner of his eye because his gaze riveted on Natalya. Her somber expression had vanished, sweeping aside the façade she hid behind so successfully. With her incredible eyes crinkled and her soft lips tilted in a smile, she again possessed the vulnerability he had discovered when he drew her close.

"At least we shall get that matter settled," she said, as she sat again. "I honestly do not want to meet your friend across sabers."

"Pistols would have been Barclay's choice, if he were choosing."

"Pistols?" She sat straighter. "Is honor served here only with death?"

He smiled. "Ofttimes. That fact, however, was somewhat useful when I persuaded Barclay to wait. Mayhap once the haze of his ire vanishes, he will know better than to demand satisfaction from a decorated war hero."

"I am glad you convinced him to listen to reason."

"So am I." With a low chuckle, he asked, "Can you imagine the complications it would cause if he shot you and it was revealed to everyone that Creighton Marshall could not even recognize a woman when she was living under his roof?"

"Your concern for Mr. Lawson and me is extraordinary." She stood and set her glass next to the other one on the table. When Sergeant Zass came to his feet, she said, "Thank you for your help in handling this, my lord, scanty though it might be. I assume you have preparations to make for this evening."

"Actually, I have none." Crossing his arms in front of him, he said, "I thought you might enjoy a ride."

Her eyes grew wide again, offering him a chance to enjoy their blue glow. "A ride?"

"You seemed eager to get out earlier." He smiled coolly. "I thought you might like a guide to show you around London while we discuss this blasted duel. Don't you wish to learn more about the city and those of us who live here?"

She flinched.

"What is wrong?" he asked.

"If I did not know it was impossible, I would be certain you have been eavesdropping on General Miloradovich's orders to me."

"For you to see the city?" His laugh was less rigid. "Mayhap because Colonel Carruthers' orders to me as your host were much the same."

"These are most unusual orders."

He stepped closer to her. "These are most unusual times, Natalya." He raised his hand to cup her cheek, but pulled it back as he heard the low rumble of disapproval from Zass. Blast it! The giant was too good a duenna. Putting his hand on the back of the chair as if that had been his intention from the first, he asked, "Do your general's orders and my colonel's make you uncomfortable?"

Again she laughed, and Creighton silently vowed to give her ample cause to laugh as often as possible. That enticing glitter in her eyes sent a pulse of pleasurable heat through him.

"Lord Ashcroft," she said, folding her arms on the back of the other chair, "I have followed many uncomfortable orders, but I have made my enemies rue them even more." Her smile scintillated like the sunlight on the rain-jeweled leaves in the tree beyond the window. "I do recall a time during the French withdrawal from Moscow that—"

He put his hand over hers. "Let us enjoy this fine spring day as lief think of the hellish cold we suffered during that winter."

"You were on the Continent then?"

Natalya was not surprised when, instead of answering, he asked, "Would you enjoy a ride about the city?"

As she nodded, she tried to puzzle out her host. He acted as if he had not been a participant in the struggle to free Europe from Napoleon. Yet all the general had told her of Captain Creighton Marshall led her to believe he was a man of rare bravery.

"Petr and I—"

"The invitation was for you, Natalya."

She recognized the challenge in his eyes. Unlike his friend, he did not need to parade his prowess about the room with a shouted demand for a duel. As lief, he possessed a quiet dignity that warned her there was more to him than his fascinating good looks and quick wit. He was dangerous to anyone—man or woman—who did not acknowledge that.

"Then I would be glad to accept your invitation. One moment." She faced Petr and switched to Russian. "Tonight I will be attending a gathering with Lord Ashcroft and Mr. Lawson. I must learn how the challenge from Mr. Lawson will unfold."

"You could simply shoot him," he said rather wistfully.

Natalya smiled. "There would be nothing simple about doing something that would complicate this visit to England in ways I don't want to imagine."

"True." He sighed with regret. "I will make certain your other uniform is ready, Kapitán." A frown creased his face and lowered his brows toward his bushy beard. "Your pistol will be ready as well."

"I doubt that will be necessary. There will be ladies at this party." She smiled. "If you need anything, I am sure you can find a way to explain to Mrs. Winchell. Otherwise, it shall have to wait until I return."

"From where?"

Natalya faltered as she had been about to turn back to Lord Ashcroft. Petr had never questioned where she might be going. Even in the midst of battle or while delivering a message to headquarters, he had trusted her to take care of herself.

"What is wrong?" she asked.

"I do not trust the *anglíski* lord."

"Why?" She had learned to heed Petr's intuition.

"He has accepted what he knows too easily."

"No, he hasn't."

Petr surged from his corner to scowl at Lord Ashcroft, but the viscount did not step back. Lord Ashcroft continued to regard them with the concentration of a man who was trying to puzzle out their words. Not to discover what they said, she guessed, but as lief to learn more about the language she spoke to Petr.

"What has he done to you, Kapitán?"

"Nothing." She put her hand on Petr's burly arm. "You are worrying too much."

He did not meet her eyes as he said, "I hope you are right, but the truth is, you are not a man."

She could not help laughing. "That we all know."

"But I am." He pointed at his chest, then glared at Lord Ashcroft. "I know how a man thinks, Kapitán, and this *angliski* milord has many thoughts about you."

"Of course, he is curious, but—"

"Natalya," intruded Lord Ashcroft, "if you do not want to go for a ride, all you need is to say so. Then you and Sergeant Zass can continue your conversation in private."

"Our conversation is over," she said in English, adding in Russian, "Do not worry, Petr."

He grumbled something beneath his breath that even she could not understand and left.

"Friendly chap." Lord Ashcroft motioned to the open door. "Shall we, Captain Dmitrieff?" His eyes twinkled with merriment. "See? I am learning to be cautious."

"I suspect you learned that long ago if you survived the war."

Natalya was becoming accustomed to his sudden silences when she mentioned the war, but she could not swallow her sigh as she went with him down the stairs. Setting her black hat with its gold trim on her head, she waited for Lord Ashcroft to lead the way out the door.

"I thought," he said, breaking the silence as they emerged into the faint sunshine, "we might take a leisurely ride around Hyde Park."

"Leisurely?"

"There are rules within the park all of us must follow. Many ride there, so it is expected we will ride at a decorous pace."

She smiled and set aside her retort when she saw the fine horse she had ridden earlier waiting by the walkway. As she walked to the horse, she heard Lord Ashcroft ask, "Do you want help?"

She faced him, amazement widening her eyes. "Help? With what?"

"I thought you might wish to be thrown up in the saddle."

"Why would you think that?"

Irritation struck Creighton as sharply as a blow. "Forgive me for being gracious."

Easily, she swung onto her horse. "If you would recall I have requested that you treat me exactly as you would any other gentleman, there would be nothing to forgive."

"Easier said than done." He mounted and leaned toward her. He dropped his voice to a whisper. "No other gentleman of my acquaintance has such intriguing curves hidden beneath his waistcoat."

Her curse needed no translation as she sent her horse along the street at a speed still quite suitable for the city. That proved Barclay had put all his blame for the near accident on Natalya. Even when she was exasperated, she recalled the need to watch out for others along this busy road.

Creighton laughed as he set his horse to follow. Barclay would be more furious when he discovered he had shown Creighton that hosting this wild-hearted woman could provide just the diversion Creighton needed. What better way to erode away the rough edges of his memories than by rubbing this woman the wrong way—and mayhap the right? One would provide pleasure for his soul, the other for his body and mind that were plagued with the yearning to draw her into his arms again.

He bent closer to his horse as Natalya lengthened the distance between them. If she wished to prove herself the better rider, she had a lesson to learn. Weaving around carriages, he ignored the shouts of coachees who waved whips at him in frustration. He kept his eyes focused on her back. She did ride well.

He smiled. But did she ride well enough?

Natalya recognized pursuit with a sense that had no name. It had been honed by nights on watch when not-so-distant French campfires pierced the darkness like earthbound stars. Glancing over her shoulder, she smiled when she saw Lord Ashcroft riding after her. She turned the horse around a tight corner and shouted. The beast would not understand the Russian command, but her excitement should reach it.

She raced from dappled sunlight to shadow through the street that was edged with houses and trees. As she turned another corner, she saw open space ahead of her. She urged the horse forward. Lord Ashcroft could not catch her now!

Shouts merged in her ears. Her scream and the horse's shriek merged with the bellow of a teamster as he drove directly in her path. She pulled back on the reins. The horse rose on two feet, pawing the air over the wagon that was filled with refuse. Holding tightly to the reins, she calmed the horse and fired a ferocious scowl at the driver.

A blur fled past her. Lord Ashcroft! She slapped her hand against the horse's haunch. They could not be beaten now.

Cobbles became hard dirt, but Natalya gained little on Lord Ashcroft. When he drew in his horse and raised his hand, he was nearly a dozen lengths in front of her. She slowed her horse. With a reluctant laugh, she leaned forward and patted her horse on the neck. She sat back in the saddle and took a deep breath of the fresh air. She had not guessed she could find the countryside within the environs of London.

When he rode back toward her, he was frowning. "I told you to ride with more care! Can't you follow orders?"

"Not yours, my lord." She shook her head and threw out her hands. "I am tired of following orders. Like you, I am eager to set aside the war for a few glorious moments and delight in just being alive."

"Which you shan't be if you ride *ventre-à-terre* through the city."

"As you did."

"Chasing you."

"And surpassing me. The victory is yours, my lord," she said, as he drew even with her.

"Something I suspect you have said seldom."

She smiled. "Recently, that is true, although, as a child, I was often the loser in races with my brothers."

Turning from her, Creighton gazed at the city. Smoke poured from chimney pots, and sunlight glistened on the tiles of the roofs that ran together like a variegated river pouring into the Thames. "And your sisters? Did they lead a life as wild as yours?"

"No."

He shifted in his saddle. Her face was as sorrowful as her voice. Although she stared back at the City, he doubted if she saw anything but scenes drawn from the precious cache of her memories.

She slowly met his eyes, and the grief vanished. "You may be startled to discover I am as competent with a needle as I am with a saber."

"Both are valuable skills in the army."

"That I found out when many of the uniforms started to suffer from wear. In the depths of winter, few washerwomen were willing to follow the army, even with the promise of food in exchange for their work. My men were shocked to learn their captain could teach them to repair their own clothes." She laughed, and he was astonished anew at his reaction to that unbridled gaiety.

Unlike the ladies who gathered here in London for the Season, Natalya was honest with her feelings. She might hide the truth behind a hussar's uniform, but he never had to guess if she were distressed or happy or angry. Every emotion played across her face.

Such honesty might be a liability among the *ton*, who concealed their thoughts behind flowery compliments which could be, in truth, an insult. Mayhap it was time for him to be as honest.

"Natalya," he said quietly, "you know I shall not allow Barclay to face you in a duel."

"You are a better friend than he deserves." She frowned. "I find it odd that you are friends. He is nothing like you, and I have seen how he irritates you."

"You irritate me, too."

Her frown became a bright smile. "I had noticed that." Shifting on her horse, she said, "All right. As a boon to my host, I will refrain from accepting the challenge to a duel, but how do you propose to keep Mr. Lawson from insisting?"

"A first-class lie."

"I do not like lying."

"No?"

She did not lower her eyes as he regarded her with amusement. "No matter what you think, I am Kapitán Dmitrieff. That is no lie."

"But are you *Count* Dmitrieff?"

"I shall be." She took a deep breath and released it slowly, and he could not keep his gaze from following the motion of her breasts against her coat.

Blast! It would be so much simpler if he could ignore the fact—for even a moment—that she was a most desirable woman.

"What lie?" she asked, forcing his gaze back to her face.

"If you will devise some cock-and-bull tale of how Russians duel—"

"But I believe it is much as it is done in England."

"Don't tell Barclay that. Tell him a tale of preparations that must be made. Preparations that will take some time, so I can come up with an inspired solution that will soothe his bruised pride."

She wrinkled her nose. "His pride is not all that will be bruised if he continues to step out onto the street without watching for riders and carriages."

"Will you help me on this, Natalya?"

Creighton watched as she glanced again at the buildings of Town. She did not answer for so long that he began to wonder if she had failed to hear the question or could not understand it. Both excuses he knew were false.

"My lord," she said quietly, "I will help you on this matter. I owe you that much for keeping the truth secret when you could have halted this duel by simply telling Mr. Lawson I am a woman."

"That is true."

"It is honorable to help a man of honor, my lord."

"It would be better, I believe," he said, "if you call me Creighton, and I shall remember to call you Demi when we are with others."

"I would prefer—"

His hand settled over hers on the reins. "Heed the counsel of one who knows the Polite World far better than you do. If your intention is to keep from gathering notice, you would be wise to treat me as a tie-mate."

She slowly drew her fingers from beneath his. When she swallowed harshly, he fought to keep his smile from his face. Did she think he could not sense that gentle quiver as he touched her?

"I acquiesce to your superior knowledge on that detail," she said stiffly.

"Is that the only thing you will acquiesce on?" he murmured, taking her hand in his again. Edging his horse closer to hers, he pressed his lips to her fingers. They were not as soft as other fingers he had kissed, for even leather gloves could not protect her hands from the rigors of her long months of riding with the Russian army, but the luscious flavor of her skin sent craving resonating through him. He wanted more than this chaste sample.

She jerked her hand back and twisted her horse away from his. "Yes!" With a shout, she rode toward the cobbled streets.

Creighton smiled as he watched her leave. Chuckling, he

said, "Do not be so certain of that, my dear count. I convinced Barclay to wait and think things through this afternoon, something I had been sure was impossible. I suspect I may just be able to persuade you to change your mind as well."

Eight

Wiggling her toes in her boots, Natalya listened to the conversation around the card table. She longed to shout that if they were going to play cards, then they should play them as lief spend all this time in worthless prattle. With an envious glance toward the table where a group of her countrymen were laughing and tilting back a jug which she knew held something much stronger than the wine served by their hosts, she resisted tapping her fingers impatiently on the table.

"Mr. Vosley is, I have heard said, a gentleman of three inns," Mr. Hotz said as he shuffled the cards. The man, who must be able to claim as many years as Petr, chuckled.

"He is following a whereas? I thought his pockets were quite plump." The hook-nosed man sitting beside Natalya rested his elbows on the table and whispered, "It must be that woman."

"Lady Elizabeth?" Mr. Hotz shook his head. "You cannot blame the lady. He has been gathering a preserve of long bills for several years now."

"She certainly has not helped the situation. She wears more baubles than the Regent." The hook-nosed man laughed at his own sally.

Natalya glanced across the table to where Creighton was listening without comment. He smiled when his gaze caught hers.

"Gentlemen," he said without releasing her from his cool

stare, "I believe we have baffled Count Dmitrieff with our words. He wears the expression of a man who has no idea of what we speak."

"I came to play cards, not to talk," she returned quietly.

"That we can see." Creighton pointed to the pile of coins in front of her. "And we can see how competent you have proven to be at the board of green cloth. Much practice, I suspect."

"Cards travel easily when an army is on the move." She motioned for Mr. Hotz to deal the next hand. "Also, they fill the long hours of a midnight watch."

"You were with the army the whole time the Russians chased the French from Moscow back to Paris?" asked a man who had not spoken before. Lord Pleasonton had merely grunted a greeting when Natalya was introduced to him.

"Yes."

"Many of your countrymen did not survive."

"Fewer of the French did."

Laughter rounded the table, but Creighton pushed back his chair and rose. When Natalya regarded him with surprise, wondering what she had said mistakenly now, he murmured, "Excuse me, gentlemen. I think I would show uncommon good sense to let my commanding officer know I am in attendance this evening."

"That's right," Lord Pleasonton grumbled. "You still are shackled with that silly commission, aren't you? I swore you had taken a maggot in your head when you rushed off on some want-witted hero's quest."

Natalya clenched her hands on the table as she stood. "You insult my host, my lord. Lord Ashcroft is truly a distinguished hero who—"

"Demi, there is no need to leap to my defense."

She scowled at him. How senseless and complacent could these English be? "No, I need not come to your defense, Creighton, but I regret your friends do not share your clear-sightedness of the danger that threatened all of us. If not for the combined strength of all the Allies against Napoleon, even now the treacherous French might be bringing their dreams of empire to your soil, gentlemen."

"Nonsense!" Mr. Hotz announced. "We would never allow that."

"Once we believed the same. We did not have your good fortune of never having to prove that." She pushed herself away from the table. "Good evening, gentlemen."

She clenched her hands at her side as she walked out of the card room. When she heard her name called, she paused. She turned to face Creighton, her fingers resting on the knife in the sash at her waist.

He held out his hand. "Don't you want this?" He poured the money she had won onto her palm.

"Spasíbo."

"Thank you?" With a low chuckle, he said, "You're welcome. Do I owe *you* thanks for leaping to my defense with such fervor?"

"They have no idea what they are prattling about. The fools!"

Putting his hand on her arm, he steered her along the corridor that was decorated with paintings in gilt frames and statues set on little shelves that were guaranteed to draw the eye. "Of course they don't," Creighton said calmly. "Are the civilians in Russia so different?"

"Every person along the path of the French destruction knew the war firsthand." She tugged away and faced him. "Those blocks should realize how lucky they are to have men like you who were willing to risk their lives to protect England."

"I am glad they do not." Lifting one hand, he said, "We have spoken enough of this. I came here to enjoy myself this evening, not to keep you out of trouble."

"I can take care of myself."

"I have no doubts on that. I just don't want to have to

stop all my friends from challenging you for your incendiary words."

"Those?" She pointed back toward the card room. "Save for Mr. Hotz, there is not enough spirit within the lot to confront more than a kitten. Even their gambling is boring, nothing like we have in Russia. I cannot imagine any of my men chattering like a group of *babas*."

"Let me guess. *Babas* means babies?"

She laughed. "Not even close. It means old women."

With a grimace, he motioned for her to continue walking with him along the corridor. "Watch what you say, for I may not be able to cajole the next man who challenges you to delay the duel."

"You really don't want to play cards any longer?"

"I did not like the turn the conversation took."

"You would as lief hear a man's misfortune aired about among those more fortunate?"

He shook his head. "No, I did not like that either, but I find it preferable to rehashing the war."

"People are curious about what happened."

"That is no reason to satisfy it with such babble."

"It does no harm to ease someone's curiosity."

"Never?"

She frowned. "Never."

When he took her arm and tugged her out onto a balcony overlooking the back garden, she tried to pull away. He smiled as he pressed her shoulders against the stone wall of the house. "Then," he whispered, "ease my curiosity."

She stared up at him. The sharp angles of his face were not muted by the darkness, for the faint light from within the house highlighted his jaw and cheekbones. Even though his eyes were hidden in pools of shadow, she could guess they were bright with amusement.

"About what?" she asked as quietly.

"About you."

"Creighton, please . . ." She closed her eyes as his fingertip traced the curve of her ear. Shaking her head, she said more fiercely, "Enough!"

"I shall desist if you think I should, although I do not believe you are speaking the truth." His hand cupped her chin, and he brought her face to his. The soft brush of his words caressed her as he asked, "How is it that a woman with a woman's desires can think solely of something as hideous as war?" His laugh had a ragged edge. "Mayhap not solely, for your reaction when I touch you so chastely suggests you can think of more feminine pursuits."

With a curse, she pushed herself away from the wall. "Pursuits of feminine prey are *your* thoughts. I prefer the strategy of planning and winning a battle to courting and wooing. If you have no interest in what interests me, I shall ask you to excuse me."

Creighton smiled as Natalya went back into the house. Every inch of her glowed with fury. A feminine fury, which was as charming as the splendid motion of her hips. A fury which would escalate if she guessed the course of his thoughts.

Mayhap this would have been a simpler thing if Barclay had not flown up to the boughs this afternoon. During the card game, he had avoided looking for Barclay. Barclay would like nothing better than to announce his challenge to Natalya at the moment when it would cause the most commotion. It was Creighton's duty now, in addition to playing host to Natalya when he could easily have played something more pleasurable with her, to keep Barclay from finding out what must stay hidden.

This was certainly not going to be the lighthearted Season he had planned in the wake of the war. The battle continued on, but now his most fierce foe was his own desire to draw Natalya back into his arms. It was a battle he must not lose.

Nine

"Do tell us, Count Dmitrieff, what you think of London."

"Yes, do tell us."

"Is it anything like your cities in Russia?"

"Can you say something for us in Russian? I do hear it is a most unusual language."

"What colors do the ladies prefer in Russia?"

Natalya struggled to keep her smile from vanishing as she tried to ease away from the circle of women which had formed around her within seconds of her arrival in the bright gold ballroom. It was impossible. She was defeated more soundly than she had ever believed possible. Elbowing aside one of the women, all of whom were dressed in white silk as foamy as the plaster friezes edging the ceiling, was unthinkable. How easily she had forgotten the skills women employed when they wished to flirt with an unknown gentleman! Now she knew why she had so readily assumed the plain-speaking ways of the men in her command.

"You would be better served by asking the Grand Duchess what colors the ladies prefer," she said to a slender blonde who was nearly as tall as Creighton.

"But you, Count Dmitrieff, are a man, and we wish to know what the Russian men have noticed about the gowns that are worn by the ladies of Russia—" The blond Englishwoman took a step closer and flashed a coquettish smile. "—and England."

"Miss—"

"Wilton, my lord." The elegant design of her gown, which gained her envious stares from the other women, shimmered in the candlelight. Holding out her hand, she offered Natalya a warm smile.

Too warm for Natalya's comfort, but she took the woman's hand and bowed over it as she had bowed over what seemed like countless hands since her arrival in England.

"Count Dmitrieff, meeting you is a pleasure I have been anticipating with the greatest pleasure." Her low voice was husky and inviting.

"I am pleased to meet you, Miss Wilton," she mumbled.

Natalya noted Miss Wilton's superior smile. If these ladies thought to compete for her favor, they were sadly wasting their time. Although a flirtation with one of the women would serve her disguise well, she did not want to risk hurting anyone.

"Miss Wilton," she asked, hoping this excuse would allow her to make her escape, "may I get a glass of something cool for you?"

She held up a goblet of champagne. "No need, my lord." Linking her arm through Natalya's, she glanced around the circle of women and said, "Allow me to steal you from these admirers so I might introduce you to some of the other ladies who are eager to make the acquaintance of one of Russia's greatest heroes."

"You flatter me." Natalya tried to think of some other reason to free herself from this predicament. If she had had half an ounce of foresight, she would have remained in the card room where she could have avoided this discomfort. "However, I have to speak with General Miloradovich about a matter he expressed interest in earlier this afternoon. If you will excuse me . . ."

"Do stay and speak with us a moment longer." Miss Wilton squeezed her arm.

Again the volley of voices bounced over Natalya.

"Yes, do. Do stay and speak with us."

"Tell us about what you saw in Paris."

"Yes, what are they wearing?"

"Did you see Napoleon before he was exiled?"

"When is the czar arriving in England?"

Natalya longed to roll her eyes, spit a curse that was sure to offend all of them, and leave. In near desperation, she glanced around the room. She wished she had brought Petr with her. He always could be depended on to know when she needed his assistance. Somewhere there must be help to escape this silliness.

Her breath caught as her gaze locked with Creighton's. He stood in one of the trio of doorways opening into the corridor. With him were the gentlemen who had joined them at the card table, but she took no more than casual note of them. Every thought was focused on Creighton. Her feet yearned to run across the ballroom to bring her against the firm warmth of his chest.

Impossible! Had she lost every bit of sense she possessed? Tonight she was Count Dmitrieff, not a woman determined to capture a man's attention.

"Count Dmitrieff," said Miss Wilton, "do tell us how you won that medal." She put her finger out to the ribbon set above the braid on Natalya's uniform.

Natalya drew back before Miss Wilton could touch her breast. Forcing a smile, she said, "That was for a battle whose retelling may not be fit for the ears of ladies."

"Oh, do tell us," Miss Wilton urged. Her blue eyes were tinted with specks as gold as her lashes. "We would so like to know."

"Yes, yes," said another of the ladies, and they all echoed the words like well-trained acolytes.

"If you wish . . ." Natalya glanced again at Creighton. He had not moved, so she would have to devise her own escape.

Creighton surrendered to his urge to smile as Natalya turned back to speak to the group of ladies who had clumped around her. One had her arm through Natalya's. This late in the Season, some women were willing to chance even exile in distant Russia in order to win a titled husband. He chuckled to himself. What a surprise would await that bride on their wedding night!

"Count Dmitrieff is quite the ladies' man, I would say," murmured Lord Pleasonton."

"I think I shall play the good host and rescue my guest from Lady Eltonville's guests," Creighton replied.

"I doubt the man wants rescuing. Even icy Russian blood needs heating once in a while, I suspect." Lord Pleasonton sighed. "As for me, I profess an interest in what our hostess has provided for us to drink this evening. I know my black coat is no match in the ladies' eyes for Count Dmitrieff's gold piping and buttons."

"Count Dmitrieff?" intruded a voice laced with rum. "Where in perdition is that blackguard?"

Creighton caught Barclay's arm as his friend was about to stride across the ballroom in pursuit of Natalya, although Creighton doubted Barclay could see anything clearly past the tip of his nose. "Slow down," Creighton ordered.

"Want to talk to him. Now!"

Lord Pleasonton cleared his throat, gave Creighton a pitying smile, and then turned to talk to someone else.

Creighton steered his friend in the other direction. "We shall talk, Barclay, but later."

"I want to talk to him now!" He raised his hand and fired an invisible pistol. At least it was invisible to Creighton. He was unsure what Barclay was seeing right now.

"Barclay?" Creighton did not want to leave his friend, who was top-heavy with wine, among ears which would be delighted to listen to his challenge to Count Dmitrieff. They did not need an audience for this blasted duel.

Barclay pulled away and dropped into a chair. "Go and get your count. I shall wait right here like a good lad and speak only when spoken to."

"I doubt that."

Creighton got a grin in response. With a deep sigh, he tried to guess what he had done to deserve this muddle being dumped in his lap. It was enough to persuade him to volunteer for service at the farthest edge of England's holdings. He frowned. Mayhap that had been Colonel Carruthers' intention from the beginning with this assignment. If so, Creighton would endure being Natalya's host until he could get that damned commission transferred.

He offered a smile to a pair of dowagers as he crossed the smooth marble floor. Lady Eltonville's assemblies were without par, but tonight he wished he had stayed home. There was something unsettling about catching only the attention of two women old enough to be his mother while half the ladies in the room were clustered around Natalya. He never thought he would have to consider a woman as a rival for the eyes of the ladies.

"Good evening," he said, as he came to stand behind Natalya. "I hope I am not interrupting something that cannot be continued. I . . ." He took a step back as the woman holding on to Natalya's arm faced him. He swallowed his curse as he met familiar eyes. "This is an unexpected pleasure to find *you* keeping Count Dmitrieff busy this evening."

Natalya stiffened at the frozen edge on Creighton's voice. Even though she had known him but a short time, she recognized the tension straining his tight smile. Something was amiss here. She knew it as well as she knew the best moment to send her men into battle.

"It *is* an unexpected pleasure," Miss Wilton said as she fluttered her fan in front of her face. "I had not thought to see you here tonight either, Creighton."

Natalya wondered what Miss Wilton was trying to hide.

Or was the fan a shield to protect her from the flurry of emotions racing through Creighton's eyes?

"Count Dmitrieff is my guest," Creighton said, shrugging his shoulders in a nonchalant pose she knew was false. His hands were too tightly clenched behind him. "It is my duty and my honor to show the count every facet of the Season, both the glorious and the ghastly."

A quick glance at the other women warned Natalya something was happening here that she was not privy to. Her fingers went instinctively to her knife, but she forced them to relax as Miss Wilton murmured, "Am I the glorious or the ghastly?"

"That," Creighton said without faltering, "is something I shall leave you to decide, for I must ask you to excuse the count and me. Duty calls, you know."

"Must you go?" Miss Wilton asked, turning back to Natalya.

"It appears I must." She bowed toward the women. "Thank you for your pleasant conversation, ladies."

"Do consider calling on Mama and me, Count Dmitrieff," Miss Wilton cooed, her long lashes fluttering as rapidly as her fan. "I know Mama would be so pleased to meet a brave hero from such a distant land." She held out her hand. "We are at home on Tuesdays."

Natalya frowned. "Where are you the rest of the time?"

Miss Wilton gave a laugh as light as the music for the quadrille rolling through the room. Tapping Creighton lightly on the arm with her fan, she chided, "You need to give your guest much more tuition in the ways of a London Season."

"A difficult task," he said, drawing his arm away, "when I have not proven to be the master of such myself." Motioning toward the far wall, he added, "Count Dmitrieff?"

Gladly, Natalya followed him across the dance floor where couples twirled to the cheery music. When she sighed deeply, he glanced at her with a hint of a smile.

"Is that sigh happy or sad?" he asked.

"Glorious or ghastly, don't you mean?"

"Mayhap."

When the whisper of his smile vanished, she locked her hands behind her as she surveyed the room. "Do English ladies speak of nothing but fashion and gossip?"

"Farradiddles consume much of the conversation among the élite."

"They twitter like birds."

He dropped his arm companionably over her shoulders. "So you have suffered ennui among the men and are over-mastered by indifference at the conversation the women share. You are clearly neither fish nor fowl, Demi."

"Fish? Fowl?"

"An English saying. It means you are neither one thing nor another." He chuckled. "Why did you come to London when you should have known you would never fit in here?"

"Orders."

"An easy answer, but I suspect you could have given your superiors good reasons for you to remain behind in Paris or go directly to Vienna."

She shuddered. "Another experience I am not anticipating with pleasure."

"More parties, but there shall be many exotic heroes among the diplomatic corps. You need not be the center of attention."

"I'm glad." She rubbed her hands together. "How much longer will this gathering last?"

"A few hours."

"Hours?"

He laughed at her astonishment. "If you could find something to interest you, the time would go quickly. However, it seems as if this gathering has nothing to appeal to you."

Natalya stepped away. Something here appealed to her, something appealed to her very much. Nearly every word Creighton spoke to her was an invitation to throw off her guise and urge him to pull her back into his arms while she discovered if his kisses were as mind-sapping as his suggestion of such intimacy.

"Nor does much appeal to you," she said quietly. "You walked away from the card table."

"To catch you."

"And you were beneath reproach in speaking with Miss Wilton."

"You looked as if you wished to flee."

She smiled. "True, but being rude was not the way I planned to do that."

"Trust me." He put his hand on her shoulder and turned her to face him. The motion, which should have been a sign of friendship, sent a flurry of delight swirling through her with the strength of a blizzard across the steppes. His fingers stroked her shoulder surreptitiously as he said, "I know these people, and you do not. Some of them do not understand subtlety. They see hesitation as weakness."

"We are speaking of the guests at this party, not enemies."

"For you, when you are as you are," he said, lowering his voice to the whisper which resonated through her, "each one of these people is an enemy who could uncover the truth."

She laughed and moved away again. "Trust *me*, Creighton. Nobody has seen the truth before tonight."

"Save me."

"But only because I was careless. I shan't be again. If you judge by the women who expressed interest in my male opinion on ladies' clothing, no one here will guess at my deception."

"Mayhap I am being overcautious."

"Or jealous of the attention I am garnering?"

His chuckle was terse. "Of all you have said to me, that is the most ludicrous. If I did not know the truth, my good count, I would challenge you to see which of us could first win the good favors of one of these fine ladies. I assure you that you would again grant me the victory."

"Easy for you to boast when you know it is impossible."

"Exactly."

"As for challenges, is Mr. Lawson here?"

"Yes."

"And?"

"And I'm still waiting for inspiration." He gestured toward the back of the room. "I see General Miloradovich has arrived."

She sighed. "I should greet him."

"Good. Let's go. Mayhap talking with the general will give me time to let some inspiration blossom in my head."

Although she had hoped Creighton would take her words as an excuse to go elsewhere, Natalya led the way to where the general was enjoying a crowd of admirers of his own, including, she noted with astonishment, Colonel Carruthers. The general waved for her to join them.

"And bring Marshall with you, Kapitán," General Miloradovich ordered in a roar. Putting his broad hand on Natalya's arm, he unceremoniously shoved her aside as he said, "Marshall, allow me to introduce my niece Tatiana Suvorov."

Natalya swore under her breath and counted backward from ten. She had thought Tatiana Suvorov would not arrive in London until the czar's party did. As she watched, the black-haired woman, whose skin was as smooth as a porcelain doll's, held out her hand to Creighton and offered him a smile as warm as Miss Wilton had given her. She wanted to shout *"Osteregáytes!,"* but she doubted if Creighton would heed her call for caution. She knew General Miloradovich would be furious, for he did not see his niece was a harlot as surely as the mistresses he collected.

With a frown, she scanned the room. No, she saw no sign of Kapitán Radishchev. Could General Miloradovich have found his ginger-hackled mistress by himself? Having

Radishchev far from London might be the only good part of this muddle.

Clasping her hands behind her back, Natalya bit her lip as Creighton said, "Miss Suvorov, a true honor." He raised Tatiana's gloved hand to his lips and bowed over it.

Her fingers curved around his, not letting him release them. In a heavier accent than Natalya's, she said, "No, my lord. I am the one honored. So much I have heard about the brave Kapitán Marshall."

Her uncle bent and whispered something in her ear. Creighton saw Natalya's lips tighten, but his gaze went back to the lustrously beautiful brunette as Tatiana laughed. She was dressed *à la modality,* and every motion gave off the scent of an enticing perfume that urged a man to give his fantasies free rein.

"Forgive me," Tatiana said. "I should have said 'the brave Lord Ashcroft.' My uncle tells me you already have plans under way to leave the British army."

"That is true."

Thick lashes danced on her cheek as she moved closer and gazed up at him. "However can they bear to let you leave? Colonel, can your army endure the loss of such a dashing hero?"

As Carruthers chuckled, Creighton said, "I have few doubts they will give my departure more than passing notice." Putting his hand on Natalya's stiff shoulder, he asked, "Miss Suvorov, if you wish to meet a true hero, allow me to introduce someone from your own homeland, Captain Dmitrieff."

"You are Kapitán Dmitrieff?" Tatiana gasped, then recovered to hold out her hand.

Natalya bowed over it so smoothly that Creighton began to understand how she had managed to conceal she was a woman. Her manners were as polished as a courtier's. "And you are Tatiana Suvorov," she answered pleasantly. "Although we have not had the opportunity to meet before this, I can tell you that your uncle has spoken of you often."

"And with honesty," General Miloradovich prompted.

"Without question."

Creighton watched Miss Suvorov preen at her uncle's compliment and Natalya's quick confirmation. Then his gaze went back to Natalya. She was chatting with Colonel Carruthers with an ease he had never attained. Mayhap tragedy had thrown her into the life of a soldier, but she had assumed the guise of her brother as if she had been born to it.

"Oh, listen to the music! 'Tis a waltz," cried Tatiana as she whirled, the ruffles on her hem brushing Creighton's legs. She put her hand on his arm. "Is it considered too bold for a lady who knows so few people here to ask if a kind gentleman might find her a partner so she can dance?"

General Miloradovich chuckled. "You will help my niece, won't you, Dmitrieff?"

"I would be delighted to find her an escort." Natalya almost laughed aloud when she saw the exasperation on Tatiana's face. The young woman had hoped her uncle would ask Creighton. She turned to the older man beside her. "As senior officer here, Colonel Carruthers, you should have the honor."

"I regret I am too senior. That dance was not one I learned in my youth."

"Then, Creighton, may I be so presumptuous as to ask you for a favor on behalf of General Miloradovich and his niece? She seems to find you in good favor already." To Tatiana, she added, "I suppose you would not be averse to dancing with Lord Ashcroft."

"Not if he wishes to dance with me," she said, putting her hand on his arm again.

Before Creighton could answer, Colonel Carruthers ordered with an indifferent wave, "Go and dance, Captain. It's an excellent idea. You need not worry about being the good host at this moment. Captain Dmitrieff and I can exchange stories for hours, I believe."

Natalya tried to wipe her face clear of any emotion as Creighton looked at her. Letting him see her sympathy was a guarantee of trouble, for the general and his empty-headed niece would be watching her, too. She could not hold back her smile as Creighton said, "Very true, Colonel. Miss Suvorov, would you stand up with me for this dance?"

When Creighton fired a glance at her again as he walked with the brunette to the dancing area, Natalya struggled not to laugh. She was not daunted by his annoyed expression, and, if she were wise, she would recall the first lesson Petr had taught her when they rode to join the Russian army. Use whatever tools were at hand as a weapon to protect herself. Mayhap Tatiana Suvorov was the very tool she needed to strengthen her resolve not to surrender to Creighton Marshall's seductive touch.

But if that were so, why did some despairing emotion she did not recognize whirl through her as she watched Tatiana laugh and spin in Creighton's arms?

Ten

"This is all that is left for old soldiers, I fear," General Miloradovich grumbled beneath the blithe music. When Natalya plucked a glass of champagne from a tray and handed it to him, he added, "Nothing but to stand by the side of a ballroom and watch the young fools flirt with the women."

"A respite from the war is welcome," Natalya answered in the Russian he spoke, although Colonel Carruthers still stood beside him. "You have said so yourself, sir."

He focused his frown on her. "But for the rest of our days? I forget. You are as eager to put your military days behind you as your host Marshall. You are determined to return to that patch of ground the French destroyed."

"It is my duty."

"As mine is to protect our country, and I may never have another chance." Folding his arms atop his broad belly, he stamped away.

Colonel Carruthers gasped, "Is something amiss with General Miloradovich? If there is something he wishes which has not been provided, he needs only to request it."

Natalya smiled and switched to English. " 'Tis nothing. The general always growls like a leashed dog when he grows tired of his latest mistress. It appears his newest conquest has already begun to bore him, even though he must have met her less than two days ago."

"Women!" the colonel muttered with a sigh.

"Now there is an uncommonly interesting topic."

At Creighton's wry tone, Natalya glanced over her shoulder. She was surprised he had returned without Miss Suvorov in tow. "It seems, Creighton, your fortune has turned as sour as the general's."

"He did seem distressed when he halted me from asking Miss Suvorov for a second dance."

"Did he?" She turned to look across the room, although she cared less about finding the general than avoiding Creighton's gaze. A second dance! She had thought Creighton would be eager to rid himself of Miss Suvorov's company with all due speed. Brushing her hands against her gray pantaloons, she kept her voice light as she said, "I believe he might have matters other than this evening's entertainment on his mind."

"She *is* his niece, isn't she?" asked Colonel Carruthers.

Natalya smiled at the colonel, who wore a most discomfited frown. "Yes, she is, and I doubt if she often gets a second thought from him."

"Mayhap he thinks of the czar's impending arrival," the colonel offered.

"That should be soon," Creighton said, drawing Natalya's eyes back to him. "Then all of London will be agog with excitement." He smiled and gestured toward the opposite wall. "Colonel, if you will excuse us, I have a friend who needs rescuing from his own folly. Demi?"

Natalya walked with him across the ballroom. She affixed a smile on her lips as she paused again and again as she was greeted by the many young women filling the room. A quick glance at Creighton warned her he was amused by the attention paid to her.

His hand on her shoulder steered her away from one miss who was more persistent than the others. "You have an odd effect on the ladies, Demi."

"I doubt if any of them have met a Russian cavalry officer before tonight. They think of me as unique."

"Or, mayhap, they think of you as a kindred spirit."

"Creighton, be careful what—"

He chuckled. "I am most careful. 'Tis you who reads more into my words than they contain. I spoke only of these ladies who are looking for exotic adventure and think they have found it in you who epitomize the daring rake who has set his nation's welfare above his own."

"A description that fits you as well."

"Does it?" He did not give her a chance to answer as he stopped in front of Mr. Lawson. The balding man was sitting, his arms folded in front of his chest, his toe tapping impatiently against the floor. "I thought to find you gone and looking for trouble by now, Barclay."

Mr. Lawson scowled at her, then squinted at Creighton. "And miss the entertaining tableau of you dancing with a fair Russian bauble? You have garnered quite the eye for Russian ladies, Creighton."

"Have you met many others?" Natalya asked, keeping her voice even.

"No." Creighton's mouth worked, and she hoped he would not betray her with a laugh.

She sighed with relief when Mr. Lawson came to his feet and swayed. He slapped Creighton soundly on the arm. "What do you say to us gentlemen retiring somewhere to where we might enjoy the cloud of a funker?"

"A what?" She was beginning to think these Englishmen never spoke the language she had struggled to learn.

"A cigar." Creighton smiled. "Lead on, Barclay. Coming, Demi?"

She was about to say no when Lawson clamped his arm around her shoulders. The odor of rum billowed from him, and she wondered where he had obtained a bottle. Lady Eltonville was serving only champagne.

"Of course the count is going to come with us," he announced. "No man in his right mind would stay here when he could enjoy raising a cloud while we arrange our duel. Correct?"

Natalya nodded, although she had hoped the night would come to an end now. She was too tired to play out another charade. Sleep had been elusive last night, and today had been long and tense as she struggled to deal with these English who were nothing as she had expected and sensations she had never guessed existed. Sensations that rushed through her whenever she was close to Creighton.

Following Creighton, who was half-supporting Mr. Lawson, into a small room across the hall, she was surprised to discover it was empty. A trio of lamps burned brightly, glowing on the white satin covering the pair of settees and the chairs flanking them. Paintings of horses and dogs filled the walls, which were sheathed in light-blue silk. A window might hide behind the massive navy drapes, but not even a hint of starlight could get through the thick fabric.

Mr. Lawson reeled to a table behind a settee. He opened a box and withdrew a cigar. Fumbling, he lit it and held it out to Natalya. When she shook her head, he took a puff himself before saying, "Creighton, it is time to talk about the duel."

"Yes, it is." He motioned surreptitiously to Natalya.

She squared her shoulders. Just the thought of lying was bitter on her tongue, but she had to admire Creighton's loyalty to a friend who was so obnoxious. "Mr. Lawson, I have accepted your challenge to a duel, but I request we follow the procedures that we follow in Russia."

" 'When in Rome . . .' " Mr. Lawson slapped his leg, laughing uproariously.

"Barclay, heed the count."

Swaying, he dropped into a chair. "Speak on, my good man."

Natalya nodded. "Very well. In Russia, it is customary to allow a week—"

"Or two," interjected Creighton.

"Yes," she said, as his compelling gaze held hers. "A week or two, usually a fortnight, is traditional."

"Why?" asked Barclay.

"Why?" she repeated. Mayhap the fool was not as intoxicated as she had believed. She did not dare to falter at this point. "To be honest, Mr. Lawson, I do not know. You know how traditions are. They get started, and people follow them, even if they don't know why."

"Absurd!"

"Mayhap so, but that is the way things are done in my homeland." She regarded him coolly. "Do you agree to these terms?"

"Only if your traditions allow the challenger to have the choice of weapons."

Creighton scowled. "Now see here, Barclay. You are asking too much of her—" He gulped as Natalya gasped. Flashing her an apologetic smile, he hurried to add, "Sorry. *Herr* is Prussian, not Russian. You are asking too much of the count."

Natalya bit her lip, fearing Mr. Lawson might take too much notice of Creighton's near slip. She realized she had no need for worry when he came to his feet and grinned.

"Very well. I withdraw my request," the bald man said. "However, I will accede to your request for a delay of two weeks. It will give me time to enjoy imagining how I shall make you rue the day you nearly ran me down."

"I regret that already," she said, but quietly. She did not want to infuriate him more. It might bring unwanted attention to her.

Again she discovered she did not need to fret, for Mr. Lawson continued, "Creighton, you always have the good fortune to find the most beautiful and willing woman among a crowd. Who was that dark-haired Russian angel I saw you dancing with?"

"Tatiana Suvorov, and I would say she found me."

Natalya sat on a wing chair and clasped her hands around her knee as she balanced one polished boot on the other knee. Glad at the turn of the conversation, she chuckled. "More accurately, she has *selected* you to entertain her while she is in London."

Lawson laughed. "What better?"

"As she selected a duke in Prussia and a *comte* in France, I should add."

"I thought she did not know you." Creighton opened a bottle and poured three glasses of brandy.

"The general's niece and her activities have long entertained the men under his command." She took the glass he held out to her, being careful his fingers did not brush hers. Raising it, she said, *"Za váshe zdoróv'ye!"*

"Leave off with those blasted Russian words! Who do you think can understand such sounds?" grumbled Lawson. "Why can't you just speak English?"

"To your health!" she said with a smile. It was shockingly easy to unsettle Barclay Lawson.

Creighton chuckled as he asked, "Do you offer me a warning about Miss Suvorov, my friend? Or simply do you wish to inform me that her tastes usually are for peers of higher rank than I?"

Natalya managed to mumble some answer. Not sure if Creighton heard it as Lawson continued to jest with him, she stared down into the brandy in her glass. He had not called her "my friend" before, and the term bothered her more than it should. She was not sure why, for as long as she was required to remain beneath his roof, it would be better to have an amicable relationship.

Looking at him, she could not keep from admiring the breadth of his shoulders and the cool confidence of his voice, which came from those lips she must not imagine on hers. Yes, she knew exactly why the term bothered her. When he had touched her, the sensations, sweet and irrefutably seductive, had been nothing she should feel for a man who called her friend. That she understood, but what she could not understand was why she was drowning in misery when he was offering her exactly what she wanted.

She did not understand at all.

"How can you maintain this pace?" Natalya yawned widely as she reached for the morning paper in the middle of the table in the breakfast-parlor. "For the past week, we have spent every night at some soirée until long past midnight. I am more exhausted than I was during the march on Paris. I have heard your Season here in London goes on for months. What do you do to keep from falling asleep in the middle of a hand of cards?"

Taking a sip of his coffee, Creighton said, "Few in the *ton* rise with the dawn as you choose to do, Natalya. They wisely prefer to view the sun only when it is reaching its zenith."

"After so many years, rising early is a habit I cannot disabuse myself of."

"My problem as well." He smiled. "The solution to your other problem seems to be unfolding perfectly. Barclay is totally bamboozled by all the customs you keep inventing for a Russian duel." He chuckled. "What is this I hear about the so-called Russian custom of having to dance a waltz the night before the duel?"

She smiled. "He was insistent for an explanation."

"And that was the best you could do?"

"I fear I am running out of ideas. I spoke of the need to have the weapons sit in the light of a full moon and how the duelists must not sleep for two nights before the duel and . . ." She shook her head. "I don't remember what else. If he were not drunk every evening, he would soon see through my silly stories."

"Be thankful he is foxed. Otherwise, you would have been obligated to meet him on the field of honor."

"Honor?" She smiled her disagreement. "Only a carpet-knight's honor."

"By Jove! Watch your tongue. 'Twas such talk that started all of this." Standing, he said, "Bring that muffin and your coffee. It is too fine a morn to sit in this stuffy room."

"Where are we going?"

"Come, and you shall see."

Natalya smiled as she tucked the paper under her arm and picked up her plate and cup. He plucked the paper away and tossed it back on the table. "Creighton—"

"Let the Polite World go for a moment."

"Gladly."

"Come with me."

Motioning with his head, he led the way from the breakfast-parlor to a closed door on the other side of the hall.

"Be careful," she said, as he balanced his plate on top of his cup.

"Don't worry. I have done this hundreds of times." He opened the door, then shouldered it aside. The muffin teetered.

With a laugh, she caught his muffin on her plate. "I would say you need a bit more practice."

"I must be rusty after so many months away." He laughed as she dropped his muffin back on his plate. "Follow me."

Natalya did, then wondered why he hurried through the elegant room as if he could not wait to put it behind him. With the drapes drawn against the morning sun, the walls were in shadow. Still, she could see hints of portraits above the furniture that was covered with sheets. At the back, a case held finely carved guns. Although she wanted to go and admire them, she followed Creighton. She hoped he would explain why this room had been left closed like this while he was living in London.

The prick of despair was so strong her steps faltered. If someone had died within these walls, the room might be left like this as a memorial. There was no memorial for her family, save for a pile of scorched and decaying timbers. Tears filled her eyes, but she blinked them away.

"This is a pretty room," she whispered. She was not certain she could manage anything louder.

"Yes."

"The front windows must overlook the square."

"Yes."

"Why—?"

"Blast it!" He dabbed at his coat with his napkin. He thrust his plate toward her. "Hold this, Natalya, while I open the doors."

She bit back her questions as he threw aside the French doors. Beyond she saw a balcony that overlooked the tiny garden between the house and the stables. The fragrance of roses blended with hay and oats and other aromas that had become familiar during her years with the cavalry. Walking to the ironwork railing that twisted and contorted in a copy of the rose vines on the arbor below, she took a deep breath and smiled.

"What a perfect place!" she said.

He chuckled, his good spirits returning as he gestured for her to sit on the bench by the small glass-topped table set to the left of the door. Putting the cup and plates on the table, she went back and folded her arms on the railing.

"Not hungry?" he asked.

"Not any longer. Nor am I tired either." She closed her eyes and breathed in deeply again. "I love that scent."

"Which one?" He came to stand beside her, leaving a hand's breadth between them as he rested his arms on the railing, too. "The roses?"

She shook her head. "That aroma is charming, but what I love is the aroma of freshly turned earth and hay and the polish used to keep saddles from cracking. It smells like home. I didn't realize home had a smell until the first time Papa took me to St. Petersburg. Then I realized the wonder

of all I had taken for granted. Even the stench of the pigs'
sty was welcome when I came back home."

His voice dropped to a sibilant whisper, no stronger than
the indolent breeze curling through the space between the
buildings. "And soon you'll be home again."

"Not soon, for I am obligated to travel with General
Miloradovich to Vienna." She faced him and smiled when
she saw honesty on his face. It was an expression she saw
too seldom, for he did not wear it among the Polite World
where a practiced smile always tilted his lips, save when
he frowned at her in the wake of some badly chosen question.

"How long will you stay there?"

"As long as I am required to stay. Who knows how long
it will take for the diplomats to carve up Europe to every
government's satisfaction?"

"Forever."

"So I fear." Looking at the low building on the other
side of the garden, she said, "I appreciate you letting Petr
run tame through your stables."

He chuckled. "You are gaining a competency in our cant
with rare skill."

"My language master lauded me for my quick ear."

"You had a language teacher?"

Going to the table, she sat on the low bench and locked
her fingers around her knee. "He was hired to instruct my
brothers, but, save for Demi, they were more interested in
things beyond the walls of the classroom than the study of
words of other lands. So, while our brothers frolicked
among the hills, Demi and I studied."

"And your sisters?"

"Anna pretended to be interested, but I think she was
more absorbed by our teacher's strong chin and smile than
in his lessons. Sof'ja was the youngest and wished to do
whatever Demi did, for she worshipped him."

"As you did." He sat beside her.

"Yes."

Around them, silence dropped, broken only by the rustle of leaves and the trill of the birds in the trees. The tears again were heavy in Natalya's eyes. It must be the lack of sleep, for she had not fallen victim to such feminine frailty since she had assumed Demi's place in the cavalry.

When Creighton's finger brushed her cheek, she pulled back. He said nothing as he held up the finger which was jeweled with a single teardrop. With a curse he could not understand, she wiped it away.

"It is nothing to be ashamed of," he murmured.

"It?"

"Grieving for those who are lost."

"Weeping does nothing to avenge their deaths or rebuild my father's estate."

"Is that all you think of? Vengeance and power?"

She scowled. "I owe my family—"

"And you have done your duty to them. It is time to think of your future, Natalya, not what has happened before." Again his finger grazed her cheek before his hand curved along it, tilting it toward him. "No matter what you pretend, the truth is that you are a beautiful young woman who cannot live the rest of her life as her brother's ghost."

His hand kept her from glancing toward the door to be certain no one was near enough to overhear. Warmth spread outward from his palm that was as coarse as horse hair. She wanted to close her eyes to savor what was so sweet, but his gaze held hers.

"What is so funny?" she demanded when he grinned.

"Imagining you as a gnarled old man still telling tales of your exploits against the French." He released her and sighed. "Truthfully, 'tis not amusing. 'Tis tragic that you are throwing away your life when I cannot believe that is what your family would wish for you."

"Demi would have—"

"Blast it, Natalya!" He lowered his voice when she

tensed. "I cannot believe your brother would have ridden off to war if he had not wanted to defend what he had at home, including his sister who should have a chance to grow up into the woman she was meant to become."

"Mayhap that is what he wished." She reached for her cup and took a hasty sip. When Creighton's eyes burned into her, she raised her gaze to meet his. "Mayhap that is what he wished," she whispered, "but not all dreams come true, do they?"

She was startled when he looked away as he said, "No, they don't."

Although he turned the conversation to talk of other sights he wished to show her in London, Natalya knew his thoughts were elsewhere. The twinkle had disappeared from his eyes, and he was ignoring the muffin in front of him.

Which dream of Creighton's had been destroyed? She resisted reopening the French doors and asking if his dream had died within that shrouded chamber. For the first time, she wondered how many secrets, other than her identity, Creighton Marshall hid behind his easy smile.

Eleven

Natalya tried to curb her impatience. How long could it take Creighton to do something as simple as selecting a waistcoat and tying his cravat? She glanced at her reflection as she passed a tall glass. Vanity had been set aside when she donned a man's uniform, and today she was grateful she had no choice but to wear it. They were wasting the pretty sunshine which might soon disappear beneath one of the showers that seemed to plague London.

She swallowed a yawn as she heard the street door open below. If she had even an ounce of sense, she would send her regrets to Lady Webley, who had invited them to this evening's musicale. She needed to sleep tonight.

When she heard footfalls on the stairs, she turned and nearly struck Barclay Lawson. The bald man hastily retreated a step, then scowled.

"Why are you lurking here?" he asked, the irritation in his voice matching the high color in his face. The odor of wine billowed from around him, and she guessed he was intoxicated . . . again.

"I was not lurking. I'm waiting for Creighton to finish dressing so we might ride about London." She folded her arms over her chest. "He seems unduly concerned about his clothing whenever we go out."

"Can you blame him?"

"I do not blame Creighton for anything." She frowned. "Please explain your question."

He circled her slowly. She turned to keep her eyes locked with his that were shadowed with fatigue. Why was he calling at this hour? She had no time to ask as his lips tightened into a sneer. "Why should I waste my breath explaining anything when you are such a gawney?"

She was not sure what the word meant, but she recognized his insulting tone. Trading demure hits with him would be worthless. Walking toward the stairs, she said, "Creighton should be down in a few minutes. I will leave you two to—"

Mr. Lawson seized her arm and twisted her to face him. She reached for her belt. "Don't!" he growled. "You may be a great war hero, but you know nothing about anything off the battlefield."

"Take your hand off me."

"You brag about deeds done," he continued as if she had not spoken. Stepping closer to her, he laughed tersely. "So will you take the knife in your belt and free my blood here on my friend's rugs? Go ahead. You have hurt him enough already. Why not more?"

She lifted her fingers away from her belt and stared at Mr. Lawson. "Speak more clearly. I don't understand your riddles."

He laughed again. "Didn't you see how everyone watched you and Maeve Wilton last night while you spoke for nearly an hour?"

"No." She drew her arm out of his grip. "No, I did not, although I do not understand why you think that is surprising. Everyone is curious—"

"If Count Dmitrieff will succeed where Lord Ashcroft failed."

"What are you speaking of?"

"Persuading Maeve Wilton to join you at the altar."

Natalya stared at him in shock. "She— He—"

His laugh remained honed. "Does your English fail you, Count?" He did not give her a chance to answer. "Now you understand why Creighton is concerned about his appearance while amid the Polite World."

"I still don't understand. Does he wish to win Miss Wilton back? If—"

Instead of answering her, he turned to look at the stairs leading to the second floor. Heat slapped Natalya's cheeks when she saw Creighton coming down them. She had to own he had chosen his clothing well. Not only was its cut in prime kick, but the sand color of his coat deepened the brown of his eyes and his green waistcoat was the perfect foil for his auburn hair.

Creighton reached out and clasped his friend's arm. "What stirs you out of your bed before noon, Barclay?"

Mr. Lawson glanced at Natalya as he replied, "The count's winnings were left behind at Lord Marr's last night, so I thought to retrieve them and bring them here." He tossed a small pouch to Natalya.

"Good of you." Creighton adjusted his waistcoat. "Will you join us on a few errands?"

He shook his head. "No, for I find I am quite exhausted. I shall seek some sleep while you do what you must. Good day, Count Dmitrieff. I am counting the few days left in our fortnight with the greatest glee."

Natalya struggled to keep her face from betraying her thoughts. 'Twas nothing she had done that had caused Miss Wilton to end her betrothal to Creighton, for that must have happened before she came to this house. She met Mr. Lawson's icy gaze evenly and nodded as he went down the stairs to the door.

Clasping her hands behind her back, she watched Creighton as he went to bid his friend a good day. He did not appear to be suffering from the demise of Miss Wilton's affection. His smile bore no shadows of strain, and his eyes were cheerful.

Unlike when they had walked through the closed room.
The thought came unbidden. She glanced over her shoulder
at the door which was once again shut as tightly as a tomb's.
Was it closed because of a silly woman's change of heart?
This was all too absurd.

Natalya had no chance to ask because Creighton kept up
a steady prattle as they went down the steps and out to the
phaeton he had waiting. Even as he drove them along the
busy streets, he seemed resolved to allow no silence to settle
between them. She tried to get caught up in his excitement
as he pointed out the homes of his friends and of titled
lords she had met during the week.

When they turned onto a narrow street and halted, she
broke into his monologue to ask, "Do you have an errand
here?"

He jumped down. As he reached up to her, he hastily
pulled back his hands. Instead, he waited until she stood
by him on the walkway. "I thought it would be wise to
replenish the box of cigars that Barclay has raided on every
look-in."

Natalya stared at the collection of shop signs that hung
off the buildings. They were jumbled together as if they
had been blown here by a harsh winter wind. One was hung
atop another, so she guessed some of the shops must be on
the upper floors.

Without hesitation, Creighton opened a door and ushered
her into a shop. Her nose wrinkled. It was scented with
roses, not tobacco. When she saw stacks of books opened
to reveal drawings of ladies' gowns and a drape of white
silk and lace across a bench, she winced. Her heart cramped
as she recalled giggling with Mama and her sisters when
the seamstresses brought fine fabrics for them to choose.
Mama had wanted them to dress as befit the daughters and
wife of a respected count. A barrage of emotions she had
thought long forgotten surged forth to attack her like a row
of French infantry. Mama . . . her sisters . . . Papa . . .

Demi . . . Always Demi, who had treated her with kindness and never made her feel insignificant because she was a girl, even when he had teased her about her skirts getting in the way as she waded a stream or rode.

She forced the memories back within the chamber of her heart, which she hoped would remain locked forever. This was her life now, and she would choose no other. Yet . . . her fingers itched to caress the silks hanging over a table.

"I hope you do not mind this stop before we go upstairs to the tobacco shop," Creighton said.

"No." She winced at the pitiful sound of her voice. Squaring her shoulders, she forced a smile. "Do you come to a seamstress's shop often?"

His smile was as cold as hers. "If you are suggesting, Demi, that I opt to wear unexpected clothing as you do, you are sadly mistaken."

"I meant no such thing." She drew off her gloves and fingered the silk, unable to resist. A soft gasp bubbled in her throat. She had forgotten how luscious such fabric was against her skin. When it caught on her rough fingertip, she drew back her hand. She was no longer the daughter of a count. She *was* Count Dmitrieff. "I am simply curious why we are here now." She faced him. "I have no need for such a shop as this."

"But I do." He turned away as a plump woman pushed through the curtained doorway.

"Lord Ashcroft, *soyez le bienvenue!*"

At the Frenchwoman's greeting, Natalya's fingers curled so tightly her nails cut into her palm. How could Creighton bring her here? The French had destroyed all of her family. She did not want to patronize the shop of one of those heartless vermin.

Creighton put his hand on her arm and drew her forward as he said, "Madame Barbeau, allow me to introduce a guest in our country. This is Count Dmitrieff. Demi, Madame has been a fixture in this shop since she fled Napoleon's excesses almost fifteen years ago."

"Count Dmitrieff," the round woman said with a smile, "you are welcome here, too. How may I help you gentlemen?"

Natalya forced the tension from her shoulders. Creighton's introduction warned that her reaction to the seamstress's French had been obvious. Dash it! She was too tired to think clearly. Her emotions were so close to her skin, the slightest slice of dismay burst them out into the open.

Wandering away, she admired the exquisite silks as she listened to the low rumble of Creighton's voice. She turned when he called her name. Her eyes widened as she saw the glorious fan he held. Golden lace edged the top and dripped off into two long strips that would brush a lady's gown. Painted silk unfolded to reveal the design of some nameless Chinese pagoda surrounded by flowers she also could not name. It was the most beautiful thing she had ever seen.

"What do you think?" Creighton asked. "Will Miss Suvorov like this?"

Natalya locked her fingers behind her back to keep from caressing the lace falling from the fan. She turned away, not wanting him to read what her face might reveal. "I know nothing of her taste."

"She likes me."

"Then she probably will enjoy something as ostentatious as that fan." Walking toward the window, she gazed out at the street. Carriages passed, rattling the glass in front of her. She had not thought Creighton so foolish as to ignore the warning she had given him. Tatiana Suvorov would forget him as soon as she left London.

As Natalya Dmitrieff must.

She bit her lip as she wondered if that were possible. Even the brush of his fingers against her arm as he had greeted the *modiste* had sent delight rushing through her like a tempest. She never had met a man of Creighton Marshall's like, and she feared she never would again. No, she should be happy she never would meet his match. He was dangerous to her and her plans. She should be thrilled he was enthralled by Tatiana Suvorov's blatant flirtations.

But she was not.

Creighton laughed lowly as he motioned for her to follow him out of the shop. When they stood on the street again, he said, "You were oddly quiet in there. Could it be you are jealous that I am buying a gift for Miss Suvorov?"

"Jealous? Of you and Tatiana Suvorov?" She smiled and shook her head. "No, for how can I be jealous of nothing?"

"Nothing?"

"I believe you truly have as little honest interest in her as she does in you."

He paused on the street and pressed his hand to his chest. "You cannot believe I have a true *tendre* for the young lady?"

"No." She laughed, still astonished how he drew emotions from her that she had not expected she would feel. "Do not try to bamblusterate me with such silliness. I have seen as much of this world as you."

"Most likely you have seen more, for I have not strayed so far from my homeland as you have."

"I would not need to journey far to know you cannot use Miss Suvorov to find your way back into Miss Wilton's heart."

All amusement vanished from his eyes, which grew as hard as cannon balls. "I don't know who has been filling your head with bangers, but—"

"Bangers?"

"Falsehoods!" he snapped. "Be certain of one thing, my dear Count Dmitrieff. I would as lief be in some water-filled trench facing the French again than be within Miss Wilton's fickle heart. I leave you to enjoy her cloying company."

He strode away before she could reply. As he climbed into the phaeton, she sighed. Yes, someone had told her lies,

Twelve

"You are doing so well!"

Creighton grimaced at Colonel Carruthers. This call too closely echoed the one when he had been invited here and had left with orders to take Natalya into his house. He had hoped the afternoon would provide an escape from the dreary thoughts that had plagued him since the disastrous errand to the *modiste*'s shop.

Barclay! It must have been Barclay who had, in some misguided, half-foxed attempt at being a good friend, told Natalya about the failed betrothal. Creighton should have expected this after seeing the tension between his friend and Natalya this morning. Barclay clearly had come to the house on the flimsy excuse of bringing her winnings so he could share the truth with her.

Why would Creighton care if Maeve practiced her fascinating arts on Natalya? Even if Natalya truly were a man, why should it bother him? He had no answer for either question, which unsettled him more than he wished to own. War and death should have seared the wounds of his heart long ago, yet he could not honestly say he was not distressed.

He fingered the cards in his hand, then threw them onto the table. By Jove! 'Twas not Maeve who consumed his thoughts, but Natalya. He disliked the idea of Natalya getting caught up in that web of half-truths and broken promises as he had been. That was it. As her host, he should be protecting her from what she clearly did not understand. She might be the finest rider he had ever raced, and she might possess a keen eye and a quick wit, but she was a babe in comparison with Maeve's well-practiced wiles.

No, she was no babe. She was a lovely woman whom he could not keep from his thoughts. Since he had discovered her, so soft and enticing, in her *déshabillé,* he had longed to pull her back into his arms and give freedom to his fantasies of tasting her soft mouth. His fingers curled into a frustrated fist as the image of her in her uniform filled his mind. Its lines accented her lithe curves until he was grateful to find an excuse, such as this invitation to call upon his colonel, to keep from being alone with her.

"Yes, you are doing well." Colonel Carruthers's laugh brought Creighton's attention back to his commander. "Just as I had anticipated."

"I am glad someone thinks so." He leaned back in his chair.

"At least two of us do." The colonel chuckled again. "General Miloradovich has developed an intense interest in your background."

"Military or financial?"

Resting his elbows on the table, Colonel Carruthers smiled. "The good general seems very anxious to follow his czar's orders to blend western Europe and Russia. What better way than the announcement of a match between his niece and an English war hero?"

"I trust *this* is not an order, Colonel."

"I think you can safely say that goes beyond duty to country and king."

"And Regent," Creighton added dryly.

"And most certainly Regent." He gathered up the cards and began to shuffle them. "I understand the czar and his party shall be arriving within a few days."

"That is good news."

"Because you shall bid your guest farewell shortly after that?"

"The count and I have become more tolerant of each other, and no more of my friends has challenged Demi to a duel since that first day."

"How did that resolve itself? I have seen no outward wounds on Lawson."

Creighton chuckled. "The duel has not been held yet."

"Not yet? How—?"

He quickly explained the traditions Natalya had invented. "Barclay swallowed every out-and-outer whole."

"His good fortune, for Captain Dmitrieff is a renowned marksman."

"Even that argument failed with Barclay when he flew off his hooks."

The colonel crowed with laughter, then slanted forward. "What do you say to the idea we give your guest and his fellow Russians something to do with the pistols they wear to every function much to the distress of the ladies?"

"I have yet to see a lady who is distressed by Count Dmitrieff."

"True."

Creighton was stunned when Colonel Carruthers bowed his head and made a business of shuffling the cards some more. His lips tightened as he realized why his colonel was averting his eyes. No one could be indifferent to the pretty blonde who hung on to every word Count Dmitrieff uttered from the moment they arrived at any gathering to the second they left. Blast her! Her? Natalya or Maeve? Both!

"So I thought," the colonel said as if there had been no pause, "we might invite General Miloradovich and his party to join us for a ride out to grassville to engage in a bit of hunting. It should be a diverting day before we all are sucked into our dress uniforms for the events that will begin unfolding with the arrival of Alexander and King Frederick." Looking up, he grimaced. "Those pompous Prussians are going to make the whole of this a bore."

"You speak of our Regent's distant cousins."

"I would say the same of my own cousins, who have as little life in them." With another chuckle, he regained his smile. "So what do you think, Creighton? Do you think Count Dmitrieff would enjoy a visit to the country?"

Creighton arched a single brow as he thought of the wistful sound of Natalya's words when they had enjoyed their breakfast on the garden balcony. "I believe the count would."

"Then it is set. We leave at dawn on the morrow." He began to deal the cards. "It should prove to be interesting."

That was what Creighton dreaded. Interesting might prove too pale a word to describe anything Natalya Dmitrieff was involved in, and he knew it would be his duty to make sure the sojourn remained simply interesting. He wondered if that were possible.

Natalya rubbed harder on the stubborn spot on the right toe of her best boots. Petr had offered to have them ready for the czar's arrival, but she needed to do this task herself. Every stroke against the leather worked out a bit of her irritation at Creighton's high-handed ways. He should not be angry with her simply because she had been gracious to his one-time fiancée. If he were always this unreasonable, Natalya could understand why Miss Wilton had given him his *congé*. Mayhap the next time Natalya had the opportunity to speak to Miss Wilton, she would say exactly that.

With a sigh, she sat back in the chair and stared at the book-room hearth. How much longer must they endure this visit to London? Once she returned to Russia, she could rebuild the life she had known, the life she understood. There she could trust people to say what they meant as lief hiding their true feelings behind pretty words and deceitful compliments.

The door opened. Her fingers clenched on the cloth as her gaze locked with Creighton's. Some emotion raced through his eyes so swiftly she could not guess what it was before his smile became coolly polite. He closed the door behind him, then reopened it. She frowned at his curious action, but he did not explain as he peered over her shoulder.

"Polishing your boots, Demi?" he asked. "My bookroom is an odd choice of site for such a chore."

"The sunlight is better here than in my bedchamber, so I thought to take advantage of it."

He sat in a chair facing hers. Pyramiding his fingers in front of his face, he prevented her from seeing his expression. What was he hiding, she wondered, and, more importantly, why?

She dampened her lips. The words would be distasteful in her mouth, but they must be said. "Creighton?"

"Yes?" He did not move his fingers.

"Óchen'zhal'."

"In English, please."

"I am sorry." Reaching out, she grasped his hands and pulled them away from his face. "The very least you could do when I am apologizing is not hide."

"Hide?" With a quick move, he pulled his hands out of hers and caught her fingers beneath his. He pinned her hands to his knees. "I find it most strange that you would accuse me of that when I do not conceal the truth of who I am."

She jerked her hands away and picked up her boot, rubbing it fiercely. "Must you repeat that whenever we speak? I have no wish to continue this discussion."

"Now that sounds just like a woman!"

"Creighton!"

He waved her protest aside. He started to speak, but

turned as the sound of rapid footfalls came up the stairs and toward the room.

Barclay Lawson burst in. "Great news!" His smile wavered as he glanced at Natalya. "Dmitrieff," he added with a terse nod.

"Mr. Lawson," she said as coldly, although she had to be grateful for his intrusion. It would give her the excuse she needed to leave.

Creighton grasped the arms of his chair and shoved himself to his feet. "I think it's time the two of you stopped acting like strangers. As frequently as you call here, Barclay, the very least you can do is be pleasant to my guest."

"You expect me to be pleasant to this cur?"

"Yes." Creighton gestured to Natalya to remain silent. "This is my home, and I wish for harmony within its walls. I care little what you two do at the end of this blasted fortnight, but, for now, be pleasant to the count."

"Leather-headed notion!"

"Will you be pleasant, or will you leave?"

Mr. Lawson breathed in through his clenched teeth, then hissed, "I shall be pleasant if I must."

Natalya lowered her eyes when she saw how Creighton was struggling not to laugh. "I shall endeavor," she said, "to be more gracious to Mr. Lawson."

"Gracious? That is for strangers." Creighton raised his hands in defeat. "If you two wish to be foes while we ride out to grassville tomorrow—"

"Grassville?" she asked.

"Excuse me, Demi." His bow in her direction was as mocking as Mr. Lawson's words. "Since you have begun to sprinkle your conversation with our slang, I fear I forget which phrases slip easily from your lips."

"Russian ones are the simplest for me, but I fear you would be saying little more than *Ya ne ponimáyu* if you were in Russia."

"That phrase I know means I do not understand." He

bent toward her, and she was as startled as he was when she drew back. Seeing his astonishment in his eyes, she squared her shoulders. She should not act like a frightened deer being set upon by the hounds. "Grassville, my dear count," he continued, "simply means the country."

"Which country?"

Mr. Lawson mumbled something, then said, "The countryside, Dmitrieff. What is beyond the city."

Natalya sat straighter and smiled when Creighton moved aside so her head did not strike his chin. "The countryside? We are leaving the city?"

"For only a day or two, I fear. My colonel has invited your general and his staff to enjoy some hunting at his country estate not far from London. There will be a gathering with the ladies in the evening as well, I am sure, so while we are there, Barclay, you shall call the count Demi, and the count shall call you Barclay."

"Cannot go," muttered Mr. Lawson.

"Why not?" Creighton asked.

"I am allergic to grassville. It makes me sneeze."

"What part of it?"

"All of it. The good Lord granted us the skills to make enough blunt to raise roofs over our head. It behooves us to enjoy them."

Creighton dropped back into his chair and smiled. "As you are not joining us, it would seem logical for you two to start calling each other by your given names here and now. Is that settled?"

"I would say so," Natalya answered.

Barclay grumbled, but sat by the hearth.

"What is wrong?" Creighton asked.

"You have become too accustomed to giving orders, Creighton," Barclay muttered.

He laughed. "Why should that worry you? I do not recall you obeying a single order in your life."

"Which is why I had the good sense to stay away from

the army. I did not want to become an unthinking puppet
of officers who were superior in rank only. I still have no
idea why either of you jumped into that fury. You appear
to be otherwise in full control of your faculties."

Natalya stood and crossed her arms over the front of her
uniform. "Did you consider it might be for the challenge?"

"What challenge?" asked Creighton, surprising her, for
she had thought he would understand.

"The challenge of testing yourself to see if you can do
all you have vowed."

Barclay sniffed. "I have vowed never to be at the wrong
end of a gun. That is a vow I feel no challenge to keep."

Creighton glanced at him. "Is that so? Even now?"

When Barclay sputtered and sat quickly, Natalya resisted
smiling. It would make the situation more explosive. What
a bizarre man Barclay Lawson was. All air and no sub-
stance, so unlike Creighton.

"You must know which challenge I speak of, Creighton,"
she said into the silence. "The challenge of daring to trust
those who trust you, the challenge of testing the strength
of your arm and the speed of your mount, the challenge—"

"Enough of the war!" Creighton set himself on his feet.
"I see there is little brandy here. Why don't I ring for some
to be brought?"

As he turned, rage tightening his face, she thought he
would push past her without another word, but he paused
and put his hand on her arm. She took a half-step toward
him, wanting to be even closer to the gentle madness that
suffused her whenever he touched her. His fingers stroked
her arm out of Barclay's view. As she gazed up into his
eyes, she saw the pain he tried so desperately to hide.

"Stay and have some brandy with us, Demi," he murmured. "Mayhap speaking of what I wish had never happened might help me forget."

"I should go and—"

"Stay."

"Yes," she answered as quietly, for she might argue with him, but she could not with her own longings. She wanted to be with Creighton as much as she could, for she knew the time was coming when she must bid him farewell. If she had a bit of sense, she would look forward to that time with eagerness. Instead, she wanted to linger here as she rested her cheek against his and let his breath warm her skin. She longed for more than that. As her gaze rested on his lips, she thought of them on hers. Would his kiss be tender or demanding?

Her hand rose toward his jaw, but she pulled it back. Barclay! Dash it!

When Creighton smiled with regret, she knew his thoughts dangerously matched hers. His fingers drew reluctantly away, and she watched him walk out of the bookroom. A sigh drifted from her lips. Wanting what was impossible was a certain path to heartache, but she could not resist savoring a single moment she might spend with him.

"Mayhap 'tis not a bad idea," Barclay said.

She faced him, hoping these were the first words he had spoken, for she had heard no others. "What?"

"Using given names, for I fear my tongue will be sprained if I try to use your full name too many more times, Demi, as I announce my victory over you."

She smiled. "Do not be premature with your celebrations."

"I know you are the war hero, but things are different here. Look at how Creighton acts. He doesn't parade around himself like a cheap cyprian."

Her smile vanished. "I know, and I don't understand why Creighton joined the army. He hates even to speak of it."

"You chucklehead!" He gave her a superior grin. "Isn't it obvious? Maeve Wilton is the reason Creighton bought that blasted commission."

"He wanted to prove his bravery to her?" She could

a gasp as he put his other hand on her head and shoved her down, too.

"Shh!" he said, holding his finger to his lips.

Before she could ask what madness had possessed him now, she heard what he had. Two men were coming toward them. And they were arguing. She smiled. General Miloradovich was one of them. She did not recognize the other voice, but they were speaking in Russian.

The men passed right behind their blind in the cattails at the edge of the pond. Natalya bit her lip to keep from laughing when she heard the general deride the mud and the steep hill and the birds which flew too fast.

"England is too proud of itself," mumbled the general.

"They act as if they won the war alone." She strained to match a name to the voice as it added, "Think how they will act when everything explodes during the czar's visit with the Regent."

"It will serve them right to underestimate what the Russians have done."

When Natalya chuckled lowly, Creighton whispered, "What is so funny?"

"The general is not happy with this outing or anything else about this visit to England. I think he hopes the czar will share his feelings." She explained what General Miloradovich had said.

"You would be wise to hide from the good general trophies you have shot today."

"He would not appreciate being reminded how long it has been since he aimed at anything moving." She sat cross-legged and balanced her gun on her knees. "Too much fresh country air unnerves him. He prefers the soot of the city, but this is what I prefer." She leaned her elbow on her knee and rested her chin on her hand. "This is nearly as lovely as Russia."

Creighton could not help chuckling. When she sat there looking like a golden-topped elf and spoke of home in such

Thirteen

"Bravo!" Creighton called above the dogs splashing into the pond. "An excellent shot, Demi!"

As Natalya reloaded her gun with easy efficiency, she smiled. "It is much simpler, you must admit, when the beasts do not fire back at us."

"Now there is a horrendous thought."

She sat on the knoll and gazed across the pond. Beyond the trees, she could see the chimneys of Colonel Carruthers' country home. No rustic dacha, the elegant stone house was grand enough to have at least forty rooms. Even as she watched, another carriage came up the curved drive and paused to deposit more guests.

"I thought this was to be a quiet gathering," she said, as Creighton took the dead bird from one of the dogs. She patted another of the brown-and-white spaniels on the head and was rewarded with a lick across her cheek. Laughing as she wiped her face on her sleeve, she motioned for the dog to take its place with the rest of the pack.

"Anything less than one hundred people is a small gathering for the colonel. Remember that he commanded a battalion. He is accustomed to having many folks around." He pointed skyward. "Here comes more."

Natalya sighted her gun on the first bird flushed out by the dogs. When Creighton grasped the barrel and pushed it toward the ground, she started to protest. Her words became imagine no better way for a man to show a woman his love than by protecting the very earth she walked upon.

"Prove his bravery?" Barclay snorted his disagreement. "All he wanted to do was forget her, even if it took getting his head blown off his shoulders to do it. I don't know who was more surprised—Creighton to discover she was still unwed when he returned or Maeve when she found out he did not do the heroic thing and die."

"What a horrible thing to say!"

"But it is the truth." He glanced toward the door again. "Where is Creighton with that brandy? I still haven't boasted to him how much I won last night."

When he left the room, Natalya bent to retrieve her half-polished boot. This was becoming too complicated, and she feared the tangles would only tighten during the days to come. She wondered if she would be able to free herself from the snarls when the time came to leave London, or, she had to confess as she looked at the chair where Creighton had sat, if she would wish to.

"Yes," she answered as quietly, for she might argue with him, but she could not with her own longings. She wanted to be with Creighton as much as she could, for she knew the time was coming when she must bid him farewell. If she had a bit of sense, she would look forward to that time with eagerness. Instead, she wanted to linger here as she rested her cheek against his and let his breath warm her skin. She longed for more than that. As her gaze rested on his lips, she thought of them on hers. Would his kiss be tender or demanding?

Her hand rose toward his jaw, but she pulled it back. Barclay! Dash it!

When Creighton smiled with regret, she knew his thoughts dangerously matched hers. His fingers drew reluctantly away, and she watched him walk out of the book-room. A sigh drifted from her lips. Wanting what was impossible was a certain path to heartache, but she could not resist savoring a single moment she might spend with him.

"Mayhap 'tis not a bad idea," Barclay said.

She faced him, hoping these were the first words he had spoken, for she had heard no others. "What?"

"Using given names, for I fear my tongue will be sprained if I try to use your full name too many more times, Demi, as I announce my victory over you."

She smiled. "Do not be premature with your celebrations."

"I know you are the war hero, but things are different here. Look at how Creighton acts. He doesn't parade around himself like a cheap cyprian."

Her smile vanished. "I know, and I don't understand why Creighton joined the army. He hates even to speak of it."

"You chucklehead!" He gave her a superior grin. "Isn't it obvious? Maeve Wilton is the reason Creighton bought that blasted commission."

"He wanted to prove his bravery to her?" She could

"Of course." With a shuddering sigh, she turned away.

"Did you mourn for them?"

"What kind of question is that?"

"Did you cry, Natalya?"

"A Russian kapitán does not weep for fallen comrades. I must exult in their bravery and retell it to anyone who will listen until they are known as *bogatyrs.*"

"What is that?"

"*Bogatyrs* are the heroes of the poems we call *byliny.* Their brave exploits become legend."

He shook his head. "Do you use such tales to seduce another generation into believing war is glorious when it is nothing but degrading and filthy and hideous?"

"We use them to teach that Russia has had many brave sons who were willing to defend her borders."

"And brave daughters?"

She glanced around. "Be careful what you say."

"I merely ask a question about your history. Are all your heroes men?"

"Most of them."

"Now there shall be a heroine among them." He reached beneath his coat and said, "Here. I want you to have this."

She took the leather sheath he held out to her. Her mouth became as round as her eyes when she drew the hunting blade out and tilted it so the honed edge caught the light. When she saw the design engraved into the fancily carved handle, she gasped, "Isn't this your family crest?"

"Yes."

She slipped the knife back into its sheath. "Is it yours?"

"It belonged to my brother." He sighed and looked past her. "I think he would have liked a brave war hero using it."

"Your brother? I didn't know you have a brother."

"I *had* a brother. Like your brother, Napoleon's imperial dreams stole him from his family."

"He died in battle?"

"He was wounded in battle. He died in my arms."

She pressed her hand to her lips as she stared at him, not sure what to say. So many men she had seen die. A few she had been able to offer comfort by telling them she would share tales of their valiant sacrifice with their families. But to imagine watching Demi or any of her siblings die as she prayed for them to live . . . Tears filled her eyes.

"I did not know," she whispered.

"How could you?" He took in a deep breath and released it slowly as if it could cleanse his soul of pain. "It is not a memory I have shared with anyone else."

"Now I understand why you hate the war."

"No, you don't!" He gripped her chin in his hand, twisting her to face him. "You have no idea, Natalya! You think I hate the war simply because it stole my brother from me."

"But don't you?"

"I hate it more for all those people who lauded Kenneth as a hero and then will forget him until they need to parade his name out to find volunteers for the next war." He shook his head. "Of all I do not understand about you, Natalya, I understand least how you can love war."

"I do not love it."

He laughed tersely. "You speak of it endlessly, and you proudly wear that uniform every day."

"I wear this as a reminder of what has been lost and what must be recovered." She blinked back tears. "And I would gladly trade it all to bring my family back to life. It is easy to be a hero when you have nothing to lose but grief."

She rose as far as her knees, then halted as he grasped her arms. Slowly, his hand slid along her right shoulder. She could not mute the heated shiver as his cool fingers glided up her neck. As he cupped her nape, teasing her curls with a gentle caress, her hands settled on his arms. Her anguish melted in the sweet fires burning in his eyes.

"Creighton—"

"Don't speak," he murmured. "I know all the perils of touching you. I know you could lose everything you have fought to hold on to, but I still profess to being curious."

"Curious? About what?"

His lips brushed her ear when he murmured, "How does a mouth that is more familiar with vodka than madeira taste against my mouth?"

"I do not drink vodka, but Petr does." She put her hands up against his chest and pushed him away. Jumping to her feet, she said, "Mayhap he would be willing to help you satisfy your curiosity."

He laughed as he set himself on his feet. Closing the distance between them again, he herded her back against the tree. "Yet it is not his lips I am curious about." Twisting his finger in some of the gold braid dripping from her shoulder, he said, " 'Tis your lips."

"I am afraid my lips would not help you satisfy your curiosity."

"My curiosity is not the only thing I wish to satisfy."

She tried to slide away from him, but the rough bark caught at the braid on the back of her coat. From the moment he had come into her bedchamber and learned the truth, she would have had to be dull-witted not to see the desire in his eyes. She knew the ways of men, for she had lived with them for the past two years. She had heard their tales and seen the women who waited upon their favor. It would seem Creighton Marshall, whether he claimed the title captain or lord, was much the same. A woman was a challenge to be conquered. *She* would not be forced into surrender.

"That you shall not satisfy with me either," she said, but her voice grew soft as his fingers moved aimlessly across her cheek.

"That? Of what do you speak?"

"You know as well as I."

"There would be no need to ask if I did."

"I shall not be seduced by you, Creighton Marshall."

He smiled. "Such words, my dear count, when I speak only of a friendly kiss."

"Really?"

"No." He put his hands on the tree. "You are so wondrously naïve in so many ways. I would gladly teach you of maneuvers you never learned on the battlefield."

"I need not learn them."

"So you are as expert in the ways of love as in the ways of war?" When she faltered, he demanded, "What do you know of passions shared by a man and a woman?"

"Much."

He leaned toward her, and she wished she had had the good sense to insist Petr ride with them. "Is that so? What vast experiences do you have, Natalya?"

"One cannot spend more than a few minutes around a campfire before one is regaled with all sorts of stories, most of them false, about men's conquests of women." She brushed the hem of her coat in an effort to hide her trembling fingers. This topic was too uncomfortable, and she had been successful in avoiding such battle as the Russian army chased Napoleon across Eu

"What of a woman's conquest of a man?" he asked softly. "Did they speak of lustrous blue eyes which promise more than a woman could guess?"

She ducked beneath his arms and scooped up her gun. Holding it across her chest, she backed away as she said, "I think we have done enough hunting today."

Creighton laughed lowly as he watched her rush down the hillside as if half the French army were at her heels. Clasping his hands behind his back, he said, "My dear count, the hunt has only begun."

Fourteen

Natalya wandered about the grand ballroom of Carruthers' house. She did not pause anywhere, for she did not wish to be caught up in another conversation with a young miss who was intent on making a match with a foreign officer.

She smiled when she saw Creighton surrounded by Tatiana and several of the Englishwomen who had decided they must have the Russian woman as their bosom bow. Creighton wore the expression of a man who had been told he would have the dawn watch on a freezing night.

"My dear count," purred a too familiar voice as a slender arm slipped through Natalya's.

Her smile threatened to abandon her as she turned to face Maeve Wilton. What was *she* doing here? No doubt Colonel Carruthers thought he was doing Count Dmitrieff a great favor by inviting Miss Wilton to this gathering.

"Good evening," Natalya said with a stiff bow.

"I heard you were the best hunter of all who went out today." She fluttered her gold fan, which matched her elegant gown. "Not that I am surprised by such tidings. I am sure you could capture anything you wished—whether it be the fox or a duck or . . ." Her voice softened to a husky whisper. "Or a woman's heart."

"Well, well, who is this, Dmitrieff?" rumbled a deep voice.

Natalya was certain she would be forever grateful to General Miloradovich for giving her an excuse not to have to answer Miss Wilton. Smiling, she said, "General Miloradovich, allow me to present Miss Maeve Wilton."

The general smirked at Maeve and said, "I have seen you often in the company of my aide-de-camp. My greatest regret when I leave England will be that the count caught your eye first."

"How kind of you, General!" cooed Maeve.

"I only speak the truth."

"And so beautifully. Your English is excellent, sir."

Natalya locked her hands behind her back as Miss Wilton continued spewing compliments on the general. She watched as General Miloradovich ogled Miss Wilton openly. This might be the solution to her problem. The general was not accustomed to being alone, and he might be willing to invite Miss Wilton to Vienna with them. What a peculiar turn of events that would be!

Her hopes were dashed when Miss Wilton possessively slipped her arm through Natalya's again. "Pardon me for being bold, Count Dmitrieff," she said with the same coo she had used to flatter the general. "I hear the music beginning. Do stand up with me."

She shook her head. "I do not waltz, Miss Wilton."

"A war injury?"

Lies were bitter on her tongue. She decided to speak the truth. "As lief you should say, the war kept me more involved with the need to have a fencing master than a dancing master."

"I would gladly teach you."

"I doubt if your lovely slippers could endure the number of times my boots would stamp them."

Miss Wilton said, "We are in luck. It is not a waltz but a quadrille."

"Go, go, Dmitrieff," ordered the general. "Go and keep a watchful eye on my niece." He gestured toward where

Miss Suvorov was facing Creighton as the line of the dance formed. "Go and then come back with Miss Wilton. I would get to know her better."

"Why, General, how charming you are," murmured Miss Wilton. "I await that moment with delight."

Natalya was sure every eye in the room was centered on her as she walked with Miss Wilton onto the dance floor. Barclay's words echoed in her ears. Everyone was eager to see if Count Dmitrieff stole the heart of the woman who had broken his host's heart.

Or had Miss Wilton hurt him so badly? Natalya was not so sure when Creighton raised a single brow as Natalya came to stand beside him. "I thought you did not dance," he said.

Before she could answer, Miss Wilton intruded to say, "You should listen to poker-talk more carefully, Creighton. Count Dmitrieff does not waltz."

"I stand corrected." He bowed his head to her, then to his own partner. So lowly only Natalya could hear him, he said, "This should be most interesting."

Natalya doubted that, and she was more sure as she watched Miss Suvorov, who gaily urged Creighton to call her Tatiana, flirt with him. Even more astounding was Miss Wilton's smile, which became more strained as the dance progressed through its intricate pattern. Shock riveted Natalya, nearly tripping her up, as she realized Maeve Wilton was furious at Tatiana. That made no sense unless . . . Could it be possible Miss Wilton regretted her hasty decision in putting an end to her betrothal to Creighton?

She could not ask, although the question burned on her tongue. When Creighton caught her eyes during the dance, his lazy wink added to her confusion. Was he oblivious to the tension between the two women or simply enjoying the silent battle for his attention?

Natalya was no closer to an answer when the dance came to an end. Hiding her amazement that Creighton followed her and Miss Wilton back to the general, she understood when he bowed over the general's niece's hand and said, "Thank you for the dance, Tatiana. If you will excuse me, my friends, I promised Count Dmitrieff I would show him my colonel's collection of art."

"I would love to see it," Tatiana answered, her soft purr remarkably like Miss Wilton's.

"I would be delighted to guide you about the house later," he answered so smoothly Natalya could not keep from regarding him with astonishment. This rakish side of him was one she had never seen before . . . and it was irritating. She hoped he was not so hypocritical with her.

"Must you go, Count Dmitrieff?" asked Miss Wilton, but her eyes were riveted on Creighton.

"We shall not be long," Creighton said, again seeming unaware of the undercurrent of strain surrounding him.

Miss Wilton raised her chin and snapped, "I was asking the count."

"We shan't be long," Natalya answered. Tilting her head, she flashed Creighton a smile before adding, "And, Miss Suvorov, mayhap when we return, you can give Creighton the opportunity he needs to satisfy something about vodka, which piqued his curiosity today during the hunt."

"What is that?" asked Tatiana, her eyes aglow as she put her hand on Creighton's arm. "Are you curious about its taste?"

"Its aftertaste," Natalya said, trying not to laugh.

In a clipped tone, Creighton asked, "Shall we go, Demi?" He gestured toward the door.

When she heard his stifled laugh as they walked away, Natalya was again amazed. "Please share what is so amusing."

"You."

"Me?"

"Your expression reminded me of my tutor's when I did something he did not approve of." He led the way out into the corridor beyond the ballroom. "If you expect to keep Miss Wilton from turning her attentions to your general, you need to lather her with compliments."

"And half-truths."

"We prefer to call them court-promises, words that mean nothing once the wooing is over." He smiled at her. "Mayhap you need not worry. Maeve has been very attentive to you. I should warn you she can be persistent when she wants something."

"Or wishes to rid herself of something?" The question popped out before she could silence it.

He opened a door at the end of the hallway. "How insightful of you! I should have guessed your keen ears would hear all the scandal about me and Miss Wilton."

"One needs only to spend a few moments with Barclay."

"He does hold on to a secret as well as a sieve holds water."

"Or as well as Miss Suvorov hides her desire for your company."

"Jealous?"

"You asked me that before."

"And you didn't answer me."

She laughed. "I answered you. How can anyone be jealous of nothing?"

Instead of answering, Creighton lit a lamp on a low table by the door. The room flashed to life. It was empty save for a pair of tables set before the hearth. Along the walls, which arched high above them, weapons were displayed.

Natalya walked to the closest wall and put her fingers out to touch the broadsword that hung at eye level. The hilt was so wide she doubted she could close her fingers around it. "How magnificent!"

"I thought you would enjoy this display."

"More than Tatiana will," she said with a laugh as she went to look at a crossbow.

"I had planned to show her another collection."

She turned and copied his sardonic arch of a single brow. "A more private exhibition?"

"Now you sound jealous again."

"No," she hurried to say before either he or her own thoughts could label her words not wholly true, "I simply worry about a friend who has been hurt before."

"A friend?"

"You."

"Are we friends?"

"That is what you called me before."

He closed the distance between them. "True." Suddenly, he grinned. "And, my friend, it is time you learned all you need to know to win a lady's heart."

"I have no interest in winning a lady's heart."

Clasping her hands, he pulled her toward him. "You need to learn to waltz."

"Creighton, we should not—"

"Which makes it all the more delightful." He laughed when her boot heel caught the carpet. "Relax, Natalya."

"If someone were to see you here dancing with a man—"

"But you aren't a man." He drew her against his hard chest. "Just match my steps. Think of it as a new kind of march."

"Creighton—"

"I—"

"No!" She refused to let him interrupt her again. "I have had enough of this silliness." As she turned toward the door, she heard the scrape of steel.

"Natalya!"

She whirled. Her hand came up instinctively to catch the saber Creighton tossed to her.

"If you do not like one sort of dance," he said, jabbing at her with the one he held, "mayhap you would enjoy another."

With a laugh, she raised her sword. "I warn you I am more expert at this than at the waltz."

His smile was almost feline. "So am I."

As she matched his motions, she realized he was not bragging. She could fend off each of his jabs, but she gained no ground against him. Slowly, his smile broadening on every step, he backed her toward the wall. She gasped when she bumped into stone. She tried to slip to her right. He halted her easily. To the left. Again he parried aside her sword. She gritted her teeth and tried to surge forward.

With a laugh, he slipped his saber beneath hers. The tip was a bare breath from her throat, the flat against the underside of her chin.

"Throw down your sword!" he called.

She tossed it to the floor, ignoring its clatter as she watched him closely. Flexing her fingers, she held her breath. He stepped nearer, triumph glittering in his eyes. She shifted. He shouted as her fist came down on his wrist. His sword skittered across the floor. She whirled. He caught her arm, and her breath exploded from her as he shoved her back against the wall.

"You play rough," he whispered.

"I play to win."

"Always?"

"Always." She raised her other hand. He caught it and pressed it to the stones. She tried to pull away. He pinned her to the wall, the firm length of his legs against her.

She raised her gaze to discover his smile had vanished. The fierce fires were burning in his eyes again. She could not read the expression in his shadowed eyes as his mouth lowered to hers in the lightest of caresses. Knowing she should order him to halt, every thought became the delight blossoming outward from his touch. He released her hand, and his fingers slipped along her side in a gentle stroke.

"I always play to win, too," he whispered, his lips brushing hers.

All gentleness vanished as he kissed her again. The caress of his fingers along her back urged her to touch him, even as her breath grew fast behind her thudding heartbeat. She cautiously lifted trembling fingers to his shoulders. As she touched their breadth, it was as if summer lightning seared her. When he cradled her against his strong arm, she let the sweet storm swallow her. The thunder of her pulse careened through her, sweeping aside every sensation but pleasure.

As his lips moved along her neck, his breath grazed her skin, inciting the embers within her into a firestorm. Pushing aside her short curls, he teased her ear with the tip of his tongue. She gasped and pressed closer to him, her reaction immediate and compelling. She wanted to be within his arms, enfolded to his firm chest, exulting in this incredible danger. She would risk anything for—

"No!" she cried, pushing herself out of his arms.

Creighton reached out, but she edged away. "Natalya, sweet Natalya."

"No. Don't ask more of me than I can give," she choked.

"I only ask—"

"Too much!" Striding to the door, she slammed it behind her. She rushed along the hall, knowing she might escape his embrace but not the truth. For one moment, when his arms enveloped her, she had been willing to risk everything she had fought for, everything her family had died for, for just one more kiss.

Fifteen

Petr nodded, but did not slow currying the horse Natalya used. "It shall be as you wish, *barin.*"

"Master?" Natalya asked, surprised. "You have not called me that since we arrived here."

"I feared you would decide you did not want to be the master any longer."

She flinched, for his words warned she had been unable to hide her feelings for Creighton— No, she must think of him only as Lord Ashcroft or Captain Marshall. There must be no more than camaraderie between them. She would never again allow her feminine yearnings to betray her. To too many she owed too much, and she could not forget that in exchange for Creighton's kisses. She would not be just another of his *à suivie* flirtations. He gambled nothing to satisfy his desires. She risked everything.

"I am sorry, Petr, if you thought that." She pulled on her riding gloves. "It is not true."

"Not any longer?"

She could not keep from smiling. What would she have done in the wake of horror if this strong man had not been by her side? Reaching for the saddle waiting by the stall, she said, "I think it would be wise if you accompanied me whenever I must go out with Lord Ashcroft."

"And within the house?"

"You know I always enjoy your company, Petr."

The brush slowed as he looked at her across the horse. Sorrow filled his dark eyes. He nodded. "I will stay close to your side, Kapitán, to serve you as best I can."

"Good." She did not add more, for it would be unseemly. And, she had to own, she wanted Petr's respect too much to reveal how close she had come to losing herself in love. With his help, she would not be so foolish again.

The large room with its comfortable chairs was quiet. A fire crackled on the hearth, although there was no need for heat. The rain coursing along the uneven panes in the window was warm enough to raise a mist along St. James's Street.

Creighton looked over the top of his newspaper as Barclay stormed into the reading room of their club. Smiling, he wondered what was irritating his easily irritated friend now. "Good afternoon, Barclay."

"I might agree if I had a single reason to consider it anything but dreary." He went to the window. "It is raining again. By Jove, I believe I have not seen the sun in a fortnight."

"The weather is much sunnier in Spain or Italy."

"Ha! As if I would give up the pleasures of the Season and go to one of those places." Whirling to face Creighton, he growled, "Are you trying to get rid of me?"

"For what reason?"

"To prevent the duel!"

"Nonsense. That is going just as it should." He smiled as he closed the newspaper, which he clearly was not going to have a chance to finish now. "I always find your company amusing, Barclay. Sit and calm yourself. The day is not so horrid."

His friend's eyes narrowed. "What are you acting so blasted moony about?"

"Moony? I thought I was being pleasant."

"You haven't been pleasant since your colonel told you to—" His mouth became round. "Oh, no! It's that Russian!" With a hiss, he snapped, "You are falling for Tatiana Suvorov, aren't you?"

Creighton smiled. Barclay would be furious to discover how close he was to the truth—and how mistaken. Yes, a Russian filled his thoughts, but not Tatiana. The sampling of Natalya's lips had whetted his hunger for more.

"You have to own Miss Suvorov is unique," he said when he realized Barclay was waiting for an answer.

"Is she?"

Creighton frowned. "What do you mean?"

"She isn't the only woman who traveled with the Russian army." He snorted in derision. "Or our own army. I have heard the tales of the women who follow the troops. They are no better than cyprians."

"Tatiana is no harlot."

"No?"

"I think I can recognize a lady."

Barclay laughed. "You give yourself much credit."

"Do I?" He watched rain splash on the carriages inching along the street.

"You failed to recognize Maeve Wilton for what she is."

He turned to see his friend's grin. "How so?"

Barclay chuckled again. "How can you have come so close to leg-shackling yourself to Maeve and still know nothing about women? Can't you see how your pretty Russian watches any other women who are vying for your attention?"

"I was not of the mind there were any."

"You are a damned hero! Of course there are women interested in the brave Lord Ashcroft."

"Mayhap she is simply curious."

"Or envious." Barclay came to stand beside him. Clapping Creighton on the shoulder, he said, "She will not be long in this country. You must woo the young woman off her feet with something more than a moonlight kiss."

Creighton resisted smiling. If he did not know better, he would guess Barclay had been privy to his thoughts of Natalya. His advice was right on target, albeit for the wrong woman. "No, that is not the way. There is another way."

"What other way?" He grabbed Creighton's arm and choked, "You don't mean to try honesty, do you?"

"What is wrong with honesty?"

"By Jove, you are an air-dreamer! Women do not want honesty. They want compliments and sweet lies."

With a laugh, Creighton said, "Now I know why you have never come within ambs ace of the altar. No, Barclay, I shall not use sweet lies. I have another plan in mind."

"I wish you success."

"I have no doubt it will be mine." He turned back to the window. "I *do* always play to win."

Natalya hummed without paying attention to the melody. She smiled when she saw the perfect shine Petr had managed to put on her boots after she had tramped through the mud at Colonel Carruthers' house. Her appearance would not shame the general tonight when she attended the rout at the house of some duke whose name she could not remember.

This soon would be coming to an end, for word was that the czar was set to embark for England. A few more soirées and she could leave this odd country—and Creighton Marshall.

Her song faded into silence as she went to stare out the window. On the square, several couples were walking. The ladies' parasols were like vibrant flowers in the sunshine. A carriage rattled past, and a child ran among the trees, his nurse in tow.

Closing her eyes, she leaned against the wall. The drapes enfolded her in soft velvet. Of all the mistakes she had made, the greatest one had been to yield to the temptation to taste Creighton's kisses. Petr would remain nearby as a reminder of what she must do and, more importantly, what she must not do.

Her fingers gripped the drapes. There must be somewhere else she could stay during the rest of her sojourn in London.

No! She never had run from what was difficult before. She would not now. It was time to prove her father's daughter was as strong as his sons.

Someone rapped on her door.

"Come!" she called.

A footman entered. He glanced about the room uneasily, and she guessed he was looking for Petr. She was not sure what Petr had done to instill this terrified respect in Creighton's household, but she was certain he found it as amusing as she did.

"For you, my lord." The footman held out a narrow wooden box. "This was just delivered, and the boy said it was for you."

She understood why James sounded dubious when she saw the name on the lid of the box. It had been sent by Madame Barbeau, the *modiste*. "This was delivered for me?"

"That is what the lad said. If it is a mistake, my lord, I shall be happy to have it returned to the shop without delay."

"This is most curious." She was about to hand the box back to the footman, then said, "There may be something inside to explain this error. I shall see what is inside, then I will let you know."

"Very well, my lord."

Natalya closed the door behind the footman. Setting the box on the chaise longue, she flipped aside the latch. Slowly, she opened the wooden lid, not sure what she might see.

Pale blue tissue hid what was beneath it. A card sat on top of it. Eagerly she picked the card up, then tossed it aside when she realized it was printed with the same lettering as carved into the top of the box. She looked for another card, but there was nothing to identify who had had this sent to her or why.

She held her breath as she peeled back the tissue. Her eyes grew wide when she saw the pink silk decorated with the most delicate lace she had ever seen. Cautiously, she reached out to lift a silk chemise from the box. It had been years since she had touched anything so soft.

"Oh, *krásiv!*" she whispered.

"Is that good or bad?"

She whirled and stared at Creighton. He closed the door as quietly as he must have opened it. With a smile, he looked at the silk she held in front of her.

Her face was warm when she turned to drop the pink chemise back into the box. Fearing her cheeks were the same color as the silk, she took a deep breath before she answered. *"Krásiv* means beautiful."

"I agree." He crossed the floor to stand behind her. Reaching over her shoulder, he fingered the silk. He lifted the chemise from the box and ran it along her cheek. Her protest evaporated into the heat surging through her as he whispered, *"Krásiv,* indeed. This color right here is absolutely charming, Natalya."

"You should not be here. Petr will—"

"I thought you gave him orders, not the other way about."

She took the undergarment from him and put it back in the box, closing and latching the lid. "You should know that a good officer always depends on the counsel of his men."

"Or *her* men."

"That is an irrelevant comment."

When she edged away, he chuckled. "Then let me speak of much more relevant matters. Do you like my gift?"

"For whom?"

"For you."

"You had these made for me?"

He sat on the chaise longue and chuckled. "Who else would think of buying such a gift for Count Dmitrieff?"

"Someone with an aberrant imagination, such as one of your friends."

"Not even Barclay has an imagination that bizarre." He caught her hand, pulling her down beside him. "Will you wear these smallclothes which are more suitable for a lady than whatever the Russian army issued you?"

"I . . . I don't know."

"You can, you know." He loosened the button on her high collar. "No one, save you and me, will know that, beneath your austere uniform, you are wearing luscious silk."

"Creighton, you shouldn't." She put her hand over his, but he reached for the next button among the braid.

"You are probably right, but I want to, Natalya." His fingers splayed across the collar of her coat. Even through the thick wool, the heat of his fingers scorched her.

With a gasp, she drew back. "I think you should leave." Standing, she motioned toward the box. "And take that with you."

"I do not take back gifts."

"Then I *give* it to you."

"Natalya—"

She folded her arms and clenched hands in front of her. "Why is this so important to you?" Her eyes narrowed. "Did you tell the seamstress that these clothes were a gift for me?"

"Your secret did not pass my lips at the *modiste*'s shop." He reopened the box and spread aside the tissue. "This is for you, Natalya. You may choose to wear it or give it away to anyone you wish or simply throw it away. I do not attach any expectations to any gift I give."

She touched the knife she wore at her side. "You have already given me a gift."

"And I saw the disappointment in your eyes." He put his hands on her shoulders, but did not try to bring her near. "Just as I saw it when I bought that silly fan for Tatiana. When are you going to accept the truth, Natalya?"

"Which truth?"

"That you can pretend to be a man and that you can persuade the world and its brother that you are a man, but the truth is that deep within you beats a woman's heart." Again he ran a finger along her open collar without touching her. "A woman's heart with a woman's desires and needs." Picking up the chemise, he folded it into her hands. "You are what you are, Natalya. 'Tis nothing to be ashamed of, for you have done what many men could not and what few woman would dare to try."

Natalya had no answer as he patted her cheek as he would a child. He bid her a good afternoon. When she heard him repeat those words as he opened the door, she looked over her shoulder to see Petr standing in the doorway.

"I came as soon as I heard he was within the house, Kapitán," he said, glaring back at the door.

"I know."

"What is that?"

Shoving the garment back into the box, she said, "A most mistaken thing from Lord Ashcroft. A gift I have no use for." She shut the lid.

Petr's face darkened in a frown as he touched the piece of silk caught in the top. "A gift such as this will raise your father from his grave to thrash that *angliski* lord."

"It is nothing." She picked up the box and dropped it on the windowseat. "I told him I do not want it. I shall find someone in the household who would like to have the garments."

He shook his head. "I do not like this, Kapitán. For him to give you such things, for him to think of you as a woman, is *opásny.*"

"Yes," she whispered as she sat beside the box and ran

her fingers along the top. She looked again out the window at the pleasant scene, but an icy shiver cut along her shoulders. So easily again she had been tempted to succumb to the rapture of Creighton's touch. "You are right, Petr. It is very dangerous."

Sixteen

"Will I find this less dreary than the last gathering for the Russians that I attended?" Barclay grumbled as he entered the foyer of the well-lit house. He handed his cape to a footman and stepped aside as Natalya offered her fur-edged hat to the same wide-eyed man.

She looked around and smiled. Her appreciation of elegant design had been honed during this short visit to London. Noting the round window at the turn of the stairs and the glistening stained-glass lily set in its center, she added such a window to her mental list of what she wanted in the dacha she would raise on her father's estate.

"I do so despise boring soirées," continued Barclay.

"I have no idea what this will be like." She hoped he did not intend to be so peevish all evening.

"Surely, Demi," Creighton said as he shrugged off his cloak and set it on another footman's arms, "you have attended many such evenings both before you joined the army and after."

She quickly looked away. She did not want to admire the sleek line of his silver waistcoat and how his black coat and white breeches called forth the memory of his arms around her and his chest pressed to her. Walking toward the curving stairs, she said, "I lived in the country most of my youth, and I was very young when I received my commission. Even during the rare moments when we were not concentrating on preparing for battle or recovering from our most recent confrontation with the French, I preferred the company of Petr and the other men."

"I can understand that," Creighton replied, motioning for Barclay to lead the way up the stairs. "Many a night I preferred the campfire where my men sat to the comfort of my colonel's tent."

She started to smile, then forced her lips to straighten. She could not allow Creighton to persuade her to let down her guard against him. There had been no excuse that would have allowed her to have Petr join them here. Although her sergeant waited outside with the carriage, she must depend on herself within the house. No whispers from her heart could be allowed to overrule her good sense.

Creighton glanced at her when she did not reply, but she made sure she was busy admiring the friezes sculpted with cherubs and roses along the edge of the ceiling. As she walked between the two men through the broad expanse of the door into the room where the gathering was being held, she did not have to pretend to be caught by the beauty. Bronze silk covered three walls and shimmered in the light of the pair of chandeliers set in the center of the high ceiling. The fourth wall was a fantasy mural where mythical creatures wandered in a perfect garden.

"Quite the thing, isn't it?" Creighton asked lowly.

"What?"

"The painting." He put his hand on her shoulder and steered her toward the wall. "The present Lord Lynville's mother was a bit dicked in the nob."

"What?" she repeated.

"Insane."

"Oh." She peered more closely at the artwork. "I suppose if one must be deranged, this is a wondrous result."

"So fanciful, Demi? That isn't like you."

Standing straighter, she locked her hands behind her.

"You sound so sure for someone who knows so little of me."

"But who would like to learn more."

She was saved from answering by the call of her name in a deep, familiar voice. Taking a deep breath, she said, "Excuse me. General Miloradovich wishes to speak to me." She chuckled. "And I would guess, by how quickly she is fluttering her fan, Miss Suvorov wishes your company."

Natalya did not give him a chance to retort. Crossing the room, she nodded toward the general's niece, who was dressed in a confection of pale blue. Natalya doubted if Tatiana Suvorov had worn the same dress twice since her arrival in London.

General Miloradovich raised a quizzing glass to his face and smiled. "Ah, young Dmitrieff. It is you. And Captain Marshall, good to see you again. Talk with my niece. She seems oddly anxious to discuss vodka with you." He jabbed Creighton in the side with a beefy elbow. "If you want to know more about it, you need to ask a man. Right, Dmitrieff?"

"Yes, sir," she answered, fighting her grin as Creighton looked uncomfortable. Served him right for trying to seduce her . . . and nearly succeeding.

Hoping her disquiet was not obvious, she was grateful when the general said, "Come and speak with the duke, my boy. He has many questions about our lancers. Who better than you to answer them?"

"I would be pleased to help, sir."

The general's full face lengthened. "Talk, that is all we can do now. How long will anyone want to hear of the glories of our victories?"

"For as long as you wish to speak of them," she hurried to assure him. She wished General Miloradovich would find a new mistress, so he would lose these glum spirits. "Excuse me, Lord Ashcroft, Miss Suvorov."

"Lord Ashcroft?" Creighton repeated when she started to follow the general.

Again Natalya was saved from answering by the general's demand that she hurry. Throughout the eternally long hours of the gathering, she avoided Creighton. It was far easier than she had guessed, for the curiosity about Count Dmitrieff remained strong. She let the dowagers draw her into conversation and traded tales with the gentlemen, but always she was aware of Creighton watching her. Even when he went into dinner with Tatiana on his arm, Natalya was spared from speaking to him. The general's niece kept his ears busy with prattle while Natalya tried not to yawn during their host's long-winded tales of his experiences in North America during the last British war.

"Had a brangle with my friend Creighton?" The question in a bleary voice was one Natalya would have liked to ignore, but Barclay wrapped an arm around her shoulders and leaned heavily on her. His breath was thick with wine and brandy.

"No." She tried to shrug off his arm.

"Then he must have had one with you. Just as well. Don't want my second being *your* tie-mate." Motioning wildly, he almost fell to his knees. "Creighton, old friend, come over here."

Creighton scowled as he saw Barclay leaning on Natalya. She refused to meet his eyes. Blast the woman! If he had had any idea a kiss would spook her like a fox in a field of hounds, he would have given in to the temptation to kiss her that first night. Then his life would be the one he had planned, the one of meaningless flirtations and card games that lasted until dawn and beyond. He had looked forward to this Season, and now . . . He smiled. She might be furious with him, but this could be even more intriguing.

"Barclay," he announced, "you are sewed-up."

"Just a dram or two."

"You should take him home," Natalya said, her nose wrinkling as Barclay wheezed a grin at her.

"An excellent idea." Creighton slipped Barclay's arm from around Natalya and put it over his shoulder.

"Do you need help?" she asked.

"Another excellent idea." He smiled when she frowned. Mayhap she had thought to be rid of both of them, hoping he would graciously decline her assistance.

Creighton was more grateful for her help than he had guessed as Natalya worked with him to guide a wobbly-legged Barclay down the stairs and out to the carriage. More than once, Barclay nearly tumbled on his nose, threatening to take them with him. More than once, Creighton was tempted to let him do just that.

Barclay laughed as he climbed into the carriage. "A grand party. The Russians are not so boring as I remembered."

"Does he remember anything when he gets this drunk?" Natalya asked.

"Quite the roué you were, Creighton," Barclay continued. "Tonight you were so attentive to Tatiana Suvorov, but I saw how Maeve watched you last time we were together. You shall break both women's hearts in short order if you continue on this course."

"What would you have me do?" Creighton waited for Natalya to enter the carriage before him. He was not sure if it was because he could not disabuse himself of the habit of allowing the lady to go first or simply because he enjoyed the sight of her slender legs climbing the step in front of him.

"Choose," Barclay crowed.

Creighton sat next to his friend, although he would have preferred to share Natalya's seat. As cold as she had been this evening, he would not put it past her to leap out of the carriage and walk back to Berkeley Square if he sat beside her. Folding his arms over his coat, he caught Natalya's eyes as he asked, "And, Barclay, whom would you have me choose?"

"It makes no difference to me." He chortled a wine-drenched laugh. "It may to you." Leaning forward, he slapped Natalya on the knee as the carriage lurched into motion. He nearly fell in her lap. As Creighton caught him, he asked, "What do you think, Demi?" Another roar of laughter filled the carriage.

"I think you chose the right time to leave the party," she answered primly.

"Listen to that!" Barclay's words were slurred with drink. "Chiding me just like an old tough!" He began to sing a bawdy song.

Natalya drew up one foot and rested it across her other knee. "Does he drink like this all the time?"

"It seems he has since I returned from the Continent," answered Creighton beneath the rumble of his friend's voice.

"Then why are you two friends?"

Barclay hiccuped and threw his arms around Creighton's shoulders. "My bosom-bow. Good old Creighton. He—"

Creighton disentangled himself. "Just sit and be quiet, Barclay. We'll have you to bed soon."

He leaned one hand on Natalya's knee and chirped, "Bed? Sounds grand, doesn't it? How about it, Demi, old friend? Put out our weapons in the moonlight tonight? What a skimble-skamble way to have a duel!"

"You *are* drunk," Creighton said, hauling his friend back against the seat. He looked at Natalya, but only dismay dimmed her eyes. Damn Barclay! "Be silent."

"All right." He began singing again.

Creighton shook his head and smiled. Lowly, he said, "I think this is the best we can expect tonight."

"You still haven't answered my question," she murmured.

"Which one?"

"Why he is your friend. Do you feel sorry for him?"

He did not answer quickly. Looking from her shadowed face to Barclay, who was fading into a drunken sleep, he said, "Partly I do, but partly our friendship is based on years of knowing each other." He patted Barclay's arm. "We spent our first Seasons in Town enjoying a bachelor's fare together."

"You were like *him?*"

"I guess I must have been." He watched the streetlamps flicker past. "Although mayhap not, for I cannot imagine Barclay ever being jobbernowl enough to think of marriage." He reached across the carriage and gripped her elbow. Bringing her closer, although she stiffened at his touch, he said, "I answered your question. Now, how about a long overdue answer to mine?"

"Your question?"

"Why am I Lord Ashcroft to you now?"

She peeled his fingers off his sleeve. "You know very well why."

"That answer again. I assure you. If I had any idea, I would not ask."

Glancing at Barclay, she whispered, "We should recall we are nothing more than comrades."

"A dreary thought."

"Creighton—I mean, Lord Ashcroft—" Her lips twitched. "Oh, very well. Creighton it shall be, but that does not change my resolve. Nothing must stand in the way of my plans for reconstructing my father's dacha."

"But—"

A sharp crack shattered the night. Before Creighton could react, Natalya's hand was on his head.

"Down!" she shouted.

More shots were fired. The carriage sped along the road. The horses neighed a warning as they careened around a corner. The carriage skidded. A wheel struck a curb and the horses shrieked. The carriage rocked to a stop.

"What in the blazes—" mumbled Barclay.

"Stay here," Creighton threw open the door. It crashed against a tree. No wonder they had stopped!

Natalya followed. Creighton flinched as something dropped toward her. Then he saw Sergeant Zass on the top of the carriage. She shoved the gun Zass had tossed down to her into Creighton's hands.

"Another!" she called. "For me!"

"Get back in the carriage!" Creighton shouted.

"Don't be absurd."

"Natalya—"

She ignored him. Guns fired over the carriage again. Zass ducked, then, stretching down a long arm, handed her another gun.

A ball struck the carriage. Creighton shoved Natalya back behind the open door and shouted, "Keep down, Barclay!"

"Behind those trees!" she said, pointing to their left.

"How do you know?"

She put her hand on his head again and pushed him down as another gun fired. Crouching in the shadow of the carriage, she whispered, "The direction of the shots, and I saw a flash of gunpowder from there. If we do not fire back, they may believe we are wounded or so frightened we are unable to fight. That might lure them from the trees."

"True, for they cannot rob us from there." Even in the dim light, his teeth glittered as his lips drew back in a snarl. "Damn conveyancers."

Natalya wanted to agree, but there was no time. Any thieves who attacked a carriage like this must be bold. She held her breath as she glanced at the top of the carriage. A furtive motion told her that Petr was waiting for her command. From within, she heard Barclay's soused song start again. That told her he was uninjured.

She tapped Creighton's arm and pointed toward the shadows edging out from the trees. Four men! She had expected more, but she could not be overconfident with these easy odds. A man who made his living by preying on others must have skills as finely honed as a soldier's.

She held her breath. Beside her, Creighton tensed. If he

panicked . . . No, General Miloradovich had told her Creighton was a well-respected officer. *But so is General Miloradovich, and he hides from battle!* She silenced the frightening thought. She could not think of anything but the thieves.

"Dead? Be they all dead?" The rough voice came from behind the carriage.

"Can't be. Ye ain't that good a shot." There was a pause. "Jemmy, did ye settle these folks' hash?"

"Didn't kill no one," answered a third voice. "Told me to let the pop fly over the leathern conveniency, ye did. Know what I'm doin'. I be the best running rumbler in London Town."

The carriage rocked as one of the men kicked it.

"Tepér'!" shouted Natalya.

"What?"

The blast from Petr's gun answered Creighton at the same time she repeated, "Now!"

She fired her gun. The thieves scattered. She gave chase to the closest one. Behind her, she heard Petr and Creighton shouting. She knelt to reload. Something flashed in the dim light.

"Osteregáytes!"

At Petr's warning, she dropped underneath the knife.

With a roar, she jumped to her feet and pulled her sword. Petr's answering growl from her left set her blood to rushing through her like floodwaters along the Dneiper. The battle was on! She met the thief's knife with her sword. Hearing a crash of steel, she did not look to her right.

Petr howled victory just as she put her sword's tip to the center of the thief's chest. His knife fell.

"Please, guv'nor, have mercy," the thief whispered.

"As much as you had for us?"

Even in the dark, she could see his face lose all color. She gave him no time to answer as she herded him back to where Petr had one thief beneath his foot and another pressed up against the carriage. Both wore identical expressions of terror. When she saw Creighton bringing the last one back toward the carriage, she smiled.

She clapped Petr on the arm, then turned to Creighton to congratulate him. Her victorious smile faded as she saw the tight lines of his face. What was bothering him now? The English were so erratic. She could not guess, even once, how they would react.

While the watch was found and the thieves taken away, Natalya waited for Creighton to say something. He stood in stony silence. Not even Barclay's suddenly sober questions were answered. During the rest of the ride back to Berkeley Square, it was as if Creighton had no more life than the statue in the middle of the square.

Even when they entered the house, Creighton mumbled, "Barclay, you know where the guest room is," and started for the stairs.

Natalya stepped in front of him. As he moved to walk around her, she pulled her sword and held it across the stairs. Beside her, Petr did the same, but she motioned for him to put it away.

"Kapitán, you must see—"

"Not now, Petr." Turning to Creighton, she demanded, "What in perdition is wrong with you?"

"Your sword to begin with."

She followed his gaze toward it and saw the stain of fresh blood on its tip. If she had pricked the thief, she had no regrets. Mayhap the fool would think twice before shooting at another carriage.

"Why are you so distressed?" she asked. "We defeated them!"

"It would have been better if we had not had to fight them in the first place." He tugged the sword from her hand and threw it to the floor.

Petr took a step forward, but halted when she raised her

hand. What he growled under his breath sent heat climbing to her cheeks, but Creighton's eyes remained icy.

"Kapitán, before you say more, you should—"

"Damn!" Creighton snapped. "I don't know what he's threatening, but call off your watch-dog. I have never struck a— Damn!"

"Petr, do nothing," she murmured.

"Kapitán, if you will look at what I found—"

"Later," she ordered before switching back to English. "What is wrong?"

"I thought I was done with fighting." He moved closer to her, but she did not back away. "What was amusing when we were jousting with sabers at the colonel's country house was not when we were confronted by knights of the pad. I have had my fill of battle. I want no more."

She fisted her hands at her waist. "So you would not act to protect Tatiana if she were attacked? Or Miss Wilton?"

"That is not the issue."

"Then what is?"

"You like to fight! I do not."

She stared at him in disbelief. "You think I like to fight? You think I wish for a return to the battlefield?"

"Yes."

"You are so very wrong." She swallowed tears that she must never let fall. "I told you how I hated the war. I hated the mud and the blood and the death."

"But you exult in winning."

"Yes." When Petr picked up her sword and handed it to her, she slid it back in the scabbard at her side. "And I have won all I fought so hard to gain. Mayhap, Creighton, you cannot understand because you lost your brother after you decided to join the battle. I became part of the war because I lost all of those dear to me, save for Petr. You could only lose while I could only win." She put her foot on the first riser. "I vow to you that I shall. No one will halt me from getting what I deserve."

He laughed coldly. "Exactly." He pushed past her and climbed the stairs.

She stared after him, then looked at Petr who was frowning. Again she suspected Creighton's answer had a meaning she could not comprehend. She knew she must discover it before all was lost.

Seventeen

"Kapitán?"

At the rap on the door and the call in Russian, Natalya put down the sword she was polishing. She had not thought she would need to use it here in London, but most things about England were proving to be different from what she had expected.

"Petr, *mózhno.*" As she waited for him to enter, she smiled. She would have known it was Petr even if he spoke English. The servants had stayed in the shadows all day. Even Mrs. Winchell had not prattled this morning as she usually did. After the argument in the foyer in the wake of the attack on them, Natalya was sure every servant in the house questioned how to act.

Her smile disappeared when Petr locked the door behind him. Above his beard, his face was etched with lines of strain.

"What is wrong, Petr?"

"I found this in the bag one of the thieves carried." He held out a small slip of paper. His fingers, unbelievably, were shaking. She had never seem him nervous, not even in the midst of the battles around Paris.

"What bag?"

His smile was icy through his beard. "The one I stole from them before the English authorities took them away."

"Petr!"

"What need will they have for it if they hang as they should?"

"English justice is different from ours. That might not be the punishment for such a crime here."

"It should be," he grumbled, then handed her the slip of paper. "The thief fought me for this. I thought it might be important."

"To him, perchance, but to us?"

"Read it, Kapitán." His hands shook again. "Please."

Natalya tilted it so she could read the scratchy writing. Her eyes widened. "Oh, dear God!"

"What is it? Is it bad?"

"Very. 'Tis a death threat."

He put his hand on the blade at his side. "What does it say?"

" 'Kill the Russian and his host on June 13.' " She stared over the page at Petr's abruptly pale face. "They meant to do more than rob us last night." She frowned as she tapped her chin. "But yesterday wasn't June 13. Odd, isn't it? I would have guessed English highwaymen could not read."

"So what do we do?" Raising his chin so his beard jutted toward her, he said, "Give me what command you will, Kapitán, and I will find their confederates and make certain they pose no threat to you again."

"I am not sure what order to give." She stood. "Do you have the bag?"

He hesitated, then murmured, "It will not please you."

"Why?" She held out her hand. "Let me see it." When he placed the small leather pouch on her hand, she gasped. She recognized the beadwork on it as Petr must have. "This is Russian design."

He nodded.

"Is this why you took it from the thief?"

A hint of a smile twisted through his beard. "I saw the design after I relieved him of it."

Untying the strings at the top of the bag, she peered in

it. Her nose wrinkled. The tanner had done a poor job of curing the leather, and it stank. She ran her finger inside the bag and pulled out a single coin. "An English shilling," she whispered.

"Not much to pay for so many deaths."

She chuckled. "Petr, you are constantly practical. I believe you are correct. This orphaned coin may once have had many brothers living with it in this bag."

"So what do you wish me to do?"

"If this were Moscow or St. Petersburg, I would know the law well. Here?" She shrugged. "The customs of the English in so many ways are not like ours."

"We must do something."

"Yes." She tapped her chin. "I wonder why this date is given."

"Will we be leaving by then?"

Hearing the hope in his voice, she shook her head. "Once the czar arrives, he shall wish to confer with the Prince Regent for at least a week." She shivered. "That date is a week from yesterday. They may have been a week off."

"Or they may have been overly eager, and others will be hired to do what they failed to accomplish."

She tapped her chin and nodded. "True."

"So what shall we do?"

"We shall do what we must to save Lord Ashcroft's life."

"And yours."

She smiled coldly. "And to make these fools sorry they ever conceived of this idea."

"Lord Dmitrieff?" came a hesitant voice from the other side of the door.

Petr growled under his breath, but Natalya shook her head. She recognized James's voice. The footman sounded scared, yet it could not be because of the message she held. Unless . . . Creighton was going to his club this afternoon. If he had been attacked . . .

She pushed past Petr, threw aside the bolt, and flung the

door open. The startled footman backpedaled a pair of steps.
"What is it?" she cried.

James swallowed hard, then murmured, "A caller for you,
my lord." He faltered, and his voice creaked, "Is there a
problem, my lord?"

"No— I mean—" She took a steadying breath. "Of
course not. A caller for me?"

"He's waiting in the foyer, my lord."

"Who is it?"

"He refused to give his name." He rubbed his hands on
his breeches. "He is Russian, my lord."

"Thank you. Please let him know I am coming down."
Natalya motioned to Petr to follow her. Switching to Russian, she said, "Let me think about this. I shall ask Lord
Ashcroft some questions about the proper procedures here
in England."

"He will wish to know why you want such information."

"I can foist some tale off on him." She slid her sword
into its sheath and buckled it around her. "I would prefer
not to lie, but I would prefer even more to leave this country
alive."

"So we are still leaving?"

"Petr, what sort of question is that?" She pulled open
the door. "Of course. We are leaving as soon as we can."

Natalya muttered a curse as she saw the disagreement on
her sergeant's face. Her resolve must not lessen. She had
come too far and suffered too much to let Creighton's enticing eyes and even more beguiling touch change her.

Petr's uncommon expression vanished from her mind
when she came down the stairs and saw a familiar man
standing in the foyer. She had not had to suffer Kapitán
Radishchev's company since Paris, and she had begun to
hope the general had left this pompous fool behind. She
should have known better as soon as she saw General
Miloradovich's new mistress the day she had tried to persuade the general to let her move out of Creighton's house.

Radishchev had tried to usurp her place as the general's aide-de-camp but had succeeded in obtaining the position only of finding the general company when he was lonely.

A twinge cut through her. No, she must not let her disquiet betray her into making the situation worse. Radishchev could see no further than his own ambitions, so he would have no idea of the secret she hid.

"Welcome," she said.

The captain cleared his throat as he looked around the foyer, dismissing it with a quick glance. "Where have you been, Dmitrieff?"

"Been? Here, of course, as General Miloradovich ordered."

Radishchev's smile revealed missing teeth beneath his dark mustache. She knew they had been knocked out by an irate husband, not in the midst of battle. "So you choose to obey some orders rather than obeying all the general's orders?"

"I have obeyed every order the general has ever given me."

"Save for the most recent." He laughed coldly, then scowled as he looked past her.

Knowing Petr stood behind her, Natalya wanted to urge her sergeant not to react to this buffoon. Quietly, she said, "If you think to cause me trouble by—"

"I need cause you no trouble when you stand here when the rest of General Miloradovich's officers are gathered on St. James's to celebrate the czar's arrival in England."

"The czar is here?"

He laughed. "What has so occupied your mind, Dmitrieff, that you have not heard the tidings of the grand welcome our czar and the Prussian king received yesterday?" He ran his finger beneath his mustache. "Or should I say 'who'? The general has been much intrigued with your recent companion—the Englishwoman."

Natalya squared her shoulders. She was not going to let

this conversation plunge into meaningless gossip. "I received no orders to come there."

"But you did receive this!" Radishchev picked up an ivory card from the silver plate by the door. Slapping it into her hand, he laughed again.

She resisted snarling back that he must not have delivered the message until now. That would gain her nothing, save more ridicule by this brainless dolt. Quickly she read it. Kapitán Dmitri Dmitrieff was requested—was ordered, she corrected automatically—by General Miloradovich to join his fellow Russians for cards and drinks at 37 St. James's Street before four this afternoon.

With a sniff, Radishchev glanced around the foyer again. "I'm not surprised you did not receive it. What can we expect from the peasants who live in disgusting hovels like this?"

Natalya clenched her hands at her sides. He was determined to infuriate her, as he was each time they had met. He had not succeeded yet. He would not today, although, from the first, she had thought Creighton's house was lovely. Many of her plans for the new dacha had been altered to include facets of this house. Instead, she said, "I shall leave immediately to meet the general."

"Of course you will." He threw open the door, wiping all color from the footman's face. "I trust you will refrain from embarrassing him so again."

Natalya put up her hand as she heard Petr growl under his breath. When the door had closed behind Radishchev, she smiled. "Do not let his worthless words disturb you, Petr."

"He is jealous because no English lady has given him more than a glance." Wistfulness filled his voice as he added, "Maybe we can have the English thieves attack him."

She laughed tightly and patted Petr's arm. As soon as she apologized to the general for being late for this gathering, she would find Creighton. He must be told about the threat, even though she was certain he would not take the news well. No matter how much he wished to avoid battle, it was on once more, and his life would be forfeit if he did not give credence to her warning.

And another she cared about would die in violence. She would not allow that to happen. Not again.

Natalya heard the men's voices resonating from the choke-full room at the top of the stairs. As she entered the room, a glass of wine was shoved into her hand. She was not sure who had given it to her. So many men filled the room, she could not take more than a step past the door.

Her arm was grasped.

"What are you doing *here?*"

She turned to see Barclay Lawson, already elevated by the wine in his glass. He had a bottle beneath his arm. "I could ask the same of you," she said tautly.

"This is our club."

"Your club?" Her eyes widened. "Is Creighton here? I must talk with him without delay."

Barclay shook his head and wobbled. He must be more altogether than she had guessed. "Not a good idea. Not at all."

"Barclay, this is important."

"Not a good idea." He leaned toward her, the fumes of wine on his breath washing over her. "He wants to be alone. Wouldn't even play a few hands with his best tie-mate." He took another drink.

"What is amiss?" Mayhap Creighton had noticed something during the attack on the carriage that warned him of the danger they faced. Dismay filled her at the thought his eyes might have been keener in battle than hers, but she ignored it. He had to be more familiar with the methods of British thieves than she was, so he could have determined from the beginning that they were not ordinary highwaymen. *That* could explain his short temper in the aftermath.

Her hopes were dashed when Barclay laughed loudly

enough to draw attention from those around them. Taking him by the arm, she steered him out of the room and to a corner by a window.

" 'Tis no great secret," Barclay crowed, slipping his arm around her shoulders. He shrugged and drained his glass. "He gets moody like this sometimes. Pay him no mind."

"Do you know what is bothering him?"

He opened the bottle and refilled his glass. Taking another deep drink, he mumbled, "Not that you can blame the man. Not when you, of all people, sweep into London and monopolize the attention of the only woman he ever asked to leg-shackle herself to him."

"Leg-shackle?"

"Marry!" Looking her up and down, he laughed humorlessly. "What do you think that does to Creighton when he sees someone like *you* catching Maeve's eye? Should have let me shoot you right in the beginning and put him out of his misery."

She drew back from him. Leaning her hands on the railing at the top of the stairs, she said, "Creighton made it quite clear all feelings between them were dead."

"As dead as Napoleon's dreams of an empire." He hiccuped and swallowed another drink. "Lord above. Creighton won't even open the room where he proposed to Maeve. It's been left like a shrine—no, more like a mausoleum—" He scratched his nose. "Mayhap more like a—"

She gripped his arm, and he turned his drunken eyes toward her. "Are you speaking of the front parlor?"

"Yes. The one where the door is always closed."

"I know which room you mean." She thought of the morning she had taken breakfast with Creighton on the balcony overlooking the garden and how he had avoided answering her questions about why the room was shut up. Now she understood. "It is shrouded as if someone died within it."

He squinted at her. "Do you mean that *you* have actually been in there?"

"Once."

"Really?" When he tried to focus on her, he tipped toward the wall. She pushed him back upright. He muttered, "Thanks."

"Ne za chto." Leaving him to give his bottle a black eye, Natalya went back to the room where the gathering was growing even noisier. Or maybe it was just that her head ached with too many thoughts.

She scanned the room. It did no good to curse her height when many of the men were more than a head taller than she was. She did manage to greet General Miloradovich, but did not pause to listen to him expound again on how the Russians had defeated the French. The general was telling stories in Russian to his hosts, who could not understand a single word. Just as well, she decided, when she heard his opinions of the English command led by the man who had recently been raised to be Duke of Wellington.

Finding Creighton in the midst of this press might be impossible. Then, recalling what Barclay had said, she edged out of the room. Looking across the hall, she saw a door that was partly ajar. She opened it.

The room was deserted save for a single form hunched in a chair overlooking the street. Sorrow riveted her as she watched Creighton pick up his glass, then put it down untasted. His hand fisted on the arm of the chair, and she heard the low curse he muttered.

He looked up as she crossed the room. Irritation fled from his face to be replaced by amazement, then, just as quickly, the irritation returned. "What are you doing here?"

"Barclay just asked the same thing." She pointed to the chair next to his. "May I sit?"

"No."

She locked her fingers behind her back. "No?"

"Not until you explain what you are doing here."

"General Miloradovich was invited here and wanted his fellow officers to attend."

"Fellow officers, yes, but *you* shouldn't be here."

"I am one of his fellow officers."

His mouth twisted. "This is a gentlemen's club. No women are allowed within its walls."

"I will make all efforts to duck if the roof comes crashing down." Sitting, she said, "We must talk."

"Not here."

"Don't be as stubborn as a mule." She clutched his navy sleeve. "This is important. Someone wants us dead. They want us dead by Monday next."

He regarded her in silence, then stood. "Sorry, Kapitán. I have no interest in your next battle. I am done fighting."

"Even when your own life is in danger?"

"I am still breathing."

She came slowly to her feet. "Even if my life is in danger, too?"

His laugh struck her like a blow. "Who is better at self-defense than you, my dear Captain? You need no one to defend your virtue and your life. I leave you to plot your strategy against whatever enemy you have gained. Or enemies. I suspect you have managed to madden more than you have gladdened since your arrival."

"Creighton!" She stepped in front of him. "You have to listen to me."

"No, I don't. I have finished arrangements for my commission to be sold, and I never will have to suffer the orders of anyone else again." He gripped her arms.

Her breath caught at the potent warmth of his touch. As his fingers splayed across her arms, she moved nearer to him. Her eyes closed as his mouth descended toward hers. She wanted his kiss; she wanted it with every fiber of her being.

With a strangled curse, he released her. He did not turn as she called to him. The door slammed in his wake.

Eighteen

Natalya glared at the ceiling, but her fury was not aimed at the intricate pattern around the brass lamp over her dressing table. How could Creighton be so blasted unreasonable? How could he fault her for being obligated to follow orders when he had known the same frustration at Colonel Carruthers' insistence that Creighton host her? Refusing the general's command to come to the gathering to celebrate the czar's arrival in England would have caused all kinds of trouble she did not need.

A rap sounded at the door.

"Go away!" she snapped.

"Kapitán?"

Swinging her feet off the side of the bed, she called, "Petr, *mózho!*"

He entered and closed the door quickly. His scowl was nearly as dark as his beard.

"What is wrong?" she asked, although she wanted no more problems heaped on her.

"Lord Ashcroft asked you to leave the gathering for the general this afternoon, Kapitán. Such insults must not go unanswered."

"It was not an insult." She slid off the bed and wrapped her arms around herself. She did not bother to ask how he had found this out when he understood so little English. No doubt she had betrayed the truth with her own anger as she left the club this afternoon. Petr had his own methods to discern the truth, and she had been grateful for his insight more times than she could count. "I had no place at that club, which is for men only."

"You are a soldier of Russia, a *bogatyr* who led us to great deeds. You—"

"I am a woman, Petr, even if you do not always think of me that way."

"Kapitán, I . . ." For the only time she could recall, a flush rose above his full beard.

With a mocking laugh aimed at herself, she said, "Forgive me, old friend. It was not my intention to embarrass you by reminding you of the truth."

"I never forget it, but—"

She sat on the chaise longue and looked up at him. "There is no need for apologies. For me, too, it has been easy to forget who I really am. I have spent so long as Dmitri Dmitrieff, I nearly lost myself in the role of my brother."

"And now?"

She motioned toward a chair. "Sit, so I do not strain my neck staring up at you." When he obeyed, obviously uncomfortable with the blue satin surrounding him, she continued, "Now that Czar Alexander is here, we do what we must to make our nation proud. Then we go on with the czar and the general to Vienna. Once our duties there are complete, we return home to rebuild what was destroyed. Nothing has changed, Petr."

"You have."

"Many times in the past." She smiled sadly.

"No, I mean now." He clasped his long hands between his knees as he slanted toward her. He lowered his voice, even though no one could comprehend his words except her. "Do you love this *angliski* lord?"

"Why do you ask?" she asked, struggling to hide her astonishment at his unexpected question.

He stood as she did. "You have not had me slit his throat."

"The war is over, Petr."

"Is it?"

"Even if we still fought the French, the English have been our allies against Napoleon."

"But isn't this *angliski* lord your enemy?"

"Of course not!"

"But he could undo all you have done."

"But he hasn't! He has kept his vow to me. If he had not, everything would have been ruined. I trust him, Petr. At first, I had no choice but to trust him with the truth. Now I trust him with my life after the attack on us."

"And you trust him with your heart," he said grimly.

She shook her head. "He will not heed my warning of the menace stalking us, but I shall not see him die simply for his own pigheadedness."

"If we were to leave—"

"I thought of that, but the order for our deaths has been given and paid for, at least in part. You can be sure the assassins will wish to obtain the rest of their fee."

"So how will you convince Lord Ashcroft to heed your warning?"

"That," she said with a sigh, "is the one thing I have not been able to find an answer to. I only know I must and soon."

Creighton found no welcome beneath his own roof. It was as if he were the outsider and Natalya his host. He avoided his book-room, not wanting to meet her within its seclusion. To be alone with her, to sift his fingers through her honey-gold hair and to enjoy the scent of her sweet skin would add to the torment haunting him.

Damn women!

No matter how often he said that—to himself or out

loud—it did not help. He had expected his life to be simple upon his return to the Season. He had expected flirtations and cards and mayhap a rendez-vous with a woman who was more interested in pleasure than her reputation. Instead, he was saddled with three illogical women. Maeve was determined to show how easily she had set aside her feelings for him while Tatiana was eager to prove how much she wanted to be with him. And Natalya . . .

What had rattled her good sense? If he had not known better, he would have guessed she was frightened this afternoon at the club. Impossible! Not the brave and dauntless Kapitán Dmitrieff. Even before he had touched her, she had been trembling.

"Bah," he grumbled to himself as he shooed the servants out of his bedchamber and readied himself for bed. He had no use for her feminine fears brought on by her imagination and her unwillingness to relinquish the reins of war and live a life of peace. Let her look for trouble where there was none. He wanted only a good night's sleep and the chance to wake on the morrow to the life he should be living.

A scream rang through the house.

Creighton was on his feet, his hand reaching for his sword before he realized he was standing in his own bedchamber. He frowned as he wondered what had awakened him so suddenly his heart hammered against his chest. Sweat clung in an icy sheen to his back, a single drop trickling along his spine.

A scream slashed the night . . . again.

He tore open his door and raced along the corridor. Forms moved in the shadows. He recognized them all. James, the footman, and Mrs. Winchell were lurching down the stairs. From the other direction, Zass lumbered like some beast out of half-forgotten mythology.

Mrs. Winchell cried, "Who is that? It sounds like the scream of a—"

"I know what it sounds like." He did not need Mrs. Winchell speaking the word "woman" even in disbelief.

He hammered his fist on Natalya's door. She screamed again. He tried to open the door. It was locked.

"Damnation!" he snarled. Raising his foot, he struck the door. Pain reverberated up his leg as the door crashed open.

With an ear-splitting shout, Zass pushed past him but froze as he stared at the bed where Natalya was on her knees, her hands pressed to her breast. She was wearing the silk smallclothes beneath her unadorned nightshirt, and Creighton cursed. If anyone else saw her like this . . .

He pulled the door shut behind him. He could not afford time for an explanation when Natalya was mumbling something wildly in her sleep. Beside him, Zass moaned as if he had been sliced through by the sword leaning against the bed.

"What is it?" Creighton asked.

Zass shook his head and moaned again.

Edging around the man who seemed to be rooted to the floor, Creighton inched toward the bed. He did not want to wake Natalya too quickly. He had seen her reflexes and did not doubt she slept with a knife beneath her pillow. It would cut through him before he could breathe again.

"Natalya?" he whispered.

"Mërtvy! Vse mërtvy! Nyet! Nevozmózhay!"

He could not understand what she cried, but Zass did. He collapsed to the floor, a fallen behemoth, his fingers clawing into the carpet.

Creighton reached out to touch her, then drew back as she hid her face in her hands and crumpled into a ball on the bed. Her sobs ripped into his heart, threatening to halt it in midbeat.

"Natalya," he murmured, "wake up. It is only a nightmare."

She threw her arms around him, pressing her face to his chest. Her sobs struck his skin as her tears seared him through his nightshirt. She repeated the words he could not understand.

"Natalya, what is it?" he asked. "In English. What are you saying? Tell me in English."

She pulled back and stared at him, but he feared she was still a captive of her dream when she moaned and pressed her face against him again. "Dead! They are all dead!" she groaned. "It cannot be true."

He clasped her face in his hands and tilted it back. Shocked to see the trails of tears on her cheeks, he whispered, "You are safe here, Natalya. Wake up and see that you are in London."

"London?" She blinked several times, then stared at him in disbelief. She pulled the wrinkled nightshirt up to cover the silk which accented her every curve. "Creighton?"

Before he could answer, a sob came from the floor.

"Petr?" Natalya peered over the edge of the bed, then stretched out her hand to touch Petr's bird's nest of hair. "Petr, forgive me for hurting you anew."

He raised himself to one knee and took her hand. Pressing it to his forehead, he whispered, "I wish I could shred from your mind all memories of that day."

"As I do for you." She squeezed his fingers gently. "Go and find your own bed, my friend. I am sorry to disturb your sleep."

"Let me stay with you. I shall protect you from these demons."

"You can't, for they are within my mind." She motioned for him to stand. "Please sleep, Petr, for you know we have not escaped all that hunts us."

Petr aimed a furious scowl at Creighton, but nodded. "I shall wait on the other side of the door."

Again she shook her head. "Go to bed." Sitting back against the headboard, she whispered, "Maybe our host will heed me now when I speak of the danger that must have evoked this nightmare."

He glared again at Creighton. Stamping to the door, he pulled it open so hard it crashed against the wall. Creighton rushed to close it in his wake. When the doorknob fell onto the floor, Natalya recoiled.

"Don't be frightened," Creighton said as he stuck the broken knob back into the hole. "I shall have it repaired tomorrow."

"How was the door broken?"

Sheepishly, he said, "I wasn't sure what was happening in here." He sat on the edge of the bed. "You screamed very loudly, Natalya."

"I am sorry. Creighton, if you would just listen to me, maybe this shall not happen again."

"I will listen while you tell me what you dreamed."

"That is unimportant."

"Tell me."

She shook her head. "It is best forgotten."

His finger beneath her chin was as gentle as a zephyr, but the power of his touch whirled about her as he said, "Mayhap, but it is not forgotten. It has burst forth tonight."

"It may never again."

"Mayhap."

Leaning back against the pillows, she pulled a blanket around her shoulders. She drew her knees up so she could wrap her arms around her legs. "Thank you for your concern, Creighton, but—"

"Don't lie to me." He gripped her shoulders, pressing her more deeply into the soft mound. "I thought I could always believe what you tell me."

"You did not believe me this afternoon."

"Forget this afternoon." Leaning toward her, he whispered, "Tell me of tonight, Natalya. What haunts you? What unseen battle scars do you carry?"

"None." She shivered, and he moved to sit beside her.

He put his arm around her, drawing her into the crook of his shoulder. "There was no battle, only slaughter."

The words once spoken would not be halted. They spilled from her lips as memory piled on memory, each scene more heinous than the previous one. She clung to him, pressing her cheek to his nightshirt as she whispered of how the French had attacked the dacha without warning in the middle of the night. With Petr's help, she barely had escaped from her bedchamber as every building on the estate was being set afire. She had not been able to return to help any of her sisters or her mother or younger brothers or any of the old retainers.

The sound of screams had followed them as Petr took her to a hiding place he had devised for this very reason. At dawn as the flames were dying in the brighter glow of the sunshine, they had crept back to discover they alone survived the holocaust.

"There was no one left," she whispered, staring at the night sky through the open drapes. "The bodies were unidentifiable, so we knew they had been tortured before they were slain. As I stood there on that morn, I vowed to see the French pay for their crimes against my family." Tears rolled along her cheek, but she did not wipe them away. "And I have."

"You have avenged the family that the French took from you, but," he murmured as he tilted her face toward him, "what a cost it has exacted on you." His fingers splayed across her cheek in a questing caress. "You have given up the days when you should have had no thought more serious than which gown to don for the next party. You have sacrificed the nights you should have spent playing the coquette with a dashing suitor. You have set aside the life that should have been yours." His fingers ran along her lips gently as his voice softened to a whisper. "Natalya?"

"Yes?"

"When does the masquerade end?"

"What do you mean?" She sat straighter so she could see his face more clearly, although tears still blurred her eyes.

Again his fingers coursed along her cheek, his fingertips brushing her brows. "You will be given your father's lands as Count Dmitrieff. What then?"

"I will oversee the rebuilding of the dacha and bring the fallow fields back to a rich harvest. Those who wish to work with me shall be given land and the protection they deserve. I shall—"

"Be Count Dmitrieff." He pressed his mouth over hers with fleeting fire. As she gasped, he whispered, "Natalya, for whom are you rebuilding? For those who died? Or for those who should come after you?"

"I . . ." She swallowed roughly. "I am not sure."

"I am sure there will be no heir to your estates if you continue to live your brother's life. When will you set the lie aside?"

She kneaded her fingers on her knees. When he put his broad hand over them, she laced her fingers through his. "Creighton, if it is known how I have bamblusterated everyone, all may be lost."

"So what do you do?"

"I shall do what I must." She drew her fingers from beneath his and wiped her face. *"Óchen'zhal',"* she whispered.

"What?"

She struggled to smile weakly. "I mean I'm sorry. I should not be weeping like a child."

"Why not?"

She looked up at him. "I am not a child."

"No," he murmured, his fingers uncurling along her cheek, "you are not. You are a woman who has seen atrocities that haunt your sleep."

"I thought I had forgotten."

"How could you?"

"You have."

He laughed tersely. "You seldom misread someone else,

Natalya, but, when you do, you miss by a country mile. I have not forgotten a moment of the mud or the blood or the stench of gunpowder."

She did not resist when he leaned her head against his shoulder. "I did not know. You have said so little."

"What could I say?"

"I don't know." Her smile was weak. "I do not like saying that."

"You say it very seldom."

She faced him, being careful the blanket remained around her. "Creighton, there is one thing I do know, and you must listen to me. You are in danger."

"No more of that." He stood, his scowl as fierce as Petr's. "I have no idea what has put such ideas in your head, but the war is past, Natalya. It is time all of us let it go." He turned toward the door.

"Don't go," she whispered.

"Natalya . . ."

"Don't go." She caught his hands in hers. "Don't leave me alone, Creighton. I have never been alone before I came here, for I always slept with my sisters. Then I shared a tent with Petr. I cannot face those dreams alone tonight."

He hesitated. "If I send for Zass, he would be back here in a heartbeat."

Rising to her knees, she put her fingers over the center of his chest that was bared by his open shirt. "I want your heartbeat beside me tonight."

"You are asking me to—"

"Hold me. Just hold me and protect me from what I can no longer fight by myself."

Creighton took a step toward the door, then stopped. Did she know what she was asking? Only if she had truly been a man could she understand his longing to forget all his pain in the pleasure of her touch. How much restraint did she think he had? With the pink lace peeking past the blanket to bring to life his fantasies of her soft against him, he wanted no more talking, no more arguing. He wanted her.

"Please," she whispered. "I don't want to face this alone tonight."

With a moan, he swept her to him. He captured her lips beneath his. Against his mouth, her breath grew ragged with a desire he longed to gratify. He did not loosen his embrace as he looked down into her softened face. Her lips offered an invitation he could see repeated in her eyes. As she reached trembling fingers up to his face, he turned to kiss them.

He was pleased when her fingertips tipped his mouth toward hers. Never before had she initiated such intimacy. His arm encircled her waist, and her pliant curves pressed temptingly to him. Sitting on the bed, he leaned her back over one arm. As his mouth tasted the silken skin of her neck, his hands slipped to the curve of her waist in its luscious silk.

The magic of her mouth beneath his lit a fire deep within him. As he reclined her back into the pillows, he lost himself in the rapture where nothing existed beyond the delightful sensations found in her arms.

"I'm not sorry I promised to keep the truth of your sex a secret," he whispered against her ear. "You look so delicious in this silk. I want no one to know that tonight except me."

Quivering, she combed her fingers up into his hair. "I will hold you to that promise."

"And I shall hold you to me." He smiled as her lips tilted when he bent to claim them anew. "All night long."

Nineteen

A bejeweled world of raindrops decorated the trees beyond the open drapes. Its brightness woke Creighton. Cramped muscles protested. Opening his eyes, he stared at the top of a bed. This was not his room. He scowled and struggled to recall where he was. Why wasn't he in his own comfortable bed? Why—?

A gentle motion beside him sent a smile spreading slowly across his lips like the morning sun flowing across the rug. In the curve of his arm, her soft blonde curls caressing his chest, Natalya slept as innocently as a baby. Stains from her tears ruined the perfection of her rose-dusted cheeks.

He smiled as his gaze roved along her body which was supple against him. Beneath her nightshirt, the silk chemise clung to her curves, as enticing on his skin as the caress of her hand resting between her cheek and his chest. A soul-deep craving nearly choked him as he admired the gentle rise and fall of her breasts. His fingers tingled with the longing to stroke her lovely legs that had slipped from beneath the coverlet. Even though he had seen them often encased in wool pantaloons and shining boots, he ached to tangle his legs with them as he pressed her back into the pillows.

The battle last night had been within him while he held her. He longed to teach her of the ecstasy they could share, but he had not. Natalya was unlike the other women cluttering his life. She dared him to be what he truly was. She saw past the roué he had tried to be when he persuaded Maeve to be his bride and the dashing blade he had pretended would become a hero on the battlefields of France. In her honesty, she had touched his heart in ways he had not guessed a woman could do.

She offered him respect. He could offer her no less.

He touched the delicate lace on the chemise he had ordered for her. What had seemed the perfect jest to play on her after seeing her delight with the fabrics in the *modiste*'s shop now seemed as cruel as a taunt. If she had had the choice, she never would have donned a smaller version of her late brother's uniform and assumed his identity to repay the French for devastating her home and family. She had done what she must to survive . . . as she still did.

She had clung to honor and obligation, even when she was forced to accept a challenge to duel Barclay. Then she had agreed to do all she could to halt it. Now it was time for him and Barclay to recall what honor was.

Brushing her hair aside, Creighton tenderly kissed her cheek. He fought to keep from chuckling as she batted the air with her hand as if to shoo away an annoying insect. That, as much as her request for him to hold her all night, told him how thoroughly innocent she was about the passions they could savor in this bed.

His eyes narrowed, and he swept her into his arms. As he kissed her with every bit of his aching desire for her, her hands slid along his arms to wrap around his neck as she answered with her own ardor.

She breathed something he could not understand. He guessed her words were in Russian. A pulse of jealousy struck him as he wondered if she spoke to a lover who would comprehend those words. He pushed that thought aside. Natalya was not like Maeve, who delighted in surrounding herself with admirers whom she could not bear to marry on the chance she might lose a single one of them.

When Natalya gave her heart, it would not be in exchange for anything but her lover's heart in return.

Regretfully, he raised his lips from her soft ones. The time was wrong for what seemed so perfect. How he longed to convince her to continue with this later . . . when every inch of her was awake and suffering this exquisite torment he fought.

It might yet be possible. There was so much to be said between them, but not now. First, he must speak with Barclay.

Creighton tiptoed to the door. The knob rattled as he slipped his fingers around the door to open it. When the hinges creaked a warning, he almost laughed. Who would have guessed he would play the hero beneath his roof?

He stretched and rubbed sleep from his eyes. By Jove, he had not slept so well in weeks. He sighed under his breath as he went into his own rooms to bathe and dress.

It was time for things to change . . . whether he wished it or not.

Creighton swung off the horse and took the steps from the street two at a time. Rapping on the door, he looked along the walkway. No one was about, save for the peddlers who brought fresh produce and milk to the houses on this square.

He knocked a second time before the door was opened by a bleary-eyed footman. "Good morning, Allen," he said, as he entered.

"My lord—good morning. Is Mr. Lawson—er, are you expected at this hour?"

"Not likely." He pointed to the stairs. " 'Twould be better if my look-in doesn't disrupt the rest of the household. Take yourself off to the kitchen and get some coffee. I can announce myself."

"My lord, Mr. Lawson is still abed."

Creighton chuckled and climbed the stairs. He resisted the temptation to squeeze in his shoulders as he went up the twisting stairwell. This house was as spacious as his, but the dark colors made it seem as cramped as a cave. No doubt Barclay would be as ferocious as a bear being woken from its hibernation.

He rapped on the bedchamber door and called, "Barclay, are you in there? Alone?"

Hearing grumbling, he stepped back as the door opened. Barclay stood in his nightshirt and a single stocking. His shoes and the rest of his clothes were scattered between the door and the bed, which was too neat to have been slept in. When Creighton saw the imprint of the pattern of the rug on one side of his friend's face, he resisted laughing. He would have to urge Barclay to be more insistent that his man help him to bed on nights when he was as drunk as an emperor.

Barclay squinted toward him. "Who— What is happening? Did someone die? Oh, dear lord, I'm not supposed to be at the park, am I?"

"Not unless you have challenged someone other than the count to a duel."

He cradled his head. "I don't think so. Creighton, where did you go? I had planned on you to keep an eye on me at White's. I depend on you, you know."

Creighton took his arm and steered Barclay around the clothes on the floor to a chair by the window. When his friend moaned, Creighton pulled the drapes closed. He drew up another chair. Its feet struck the floor, and Barclay groaned more loudly.

"Egad, Creighton! Think of my head."

"You should think of it yourself before you drink another bottle of wine into oblivion."

Barclay frowned. "If I wanted a lecture, I could go home to my father. What's wrong with you, Creighton? You used to match me drink for drink, and we had such good times."

"I guess the war changed me more than I thought."

"Or maybe it's that blasted Russian captain you have living with you. Does he nag at you like a wife?"

Creighton leaned the chair back on two legs and chuckled. "To own the truth, I enjoy the count's company. More than you can imagine." He laughed again. "That is why I came to tell you it's over."

"What's over?" He rubbed his eyes. "What is so blasted important you have to wake me at this ungodly hour?"

"It is nearly seven."

He shuddered. "An ungodly hour when I sought my bed less than two hours ago."

Creighton went to the door and called for coffee to be brought, then sat again by the window. "Do you think you can wipe the cobwebs from your brain long enough for you to heed what I have to say?"

"I shall try."

"Good, then listen to me. I want to put an end to your plan to duel Count Dmitrieff."

"Fine."

"Just fine?"

"What else do you wish me to say?" When a footman came to the door with a tray, Barclay took a cup and leaned into the steam. Sipping, he sighed. "I was finding it all quite boring anyhow."

"Be clear on one thing, Barclay."

He peered over the top of his cup. "Anything, if you will take your leave and let me get back to sleep."

"Make no other challenge to the count."

"Fine. I vow to you I'll never challenge anyone ever again if you will just get the hell out of here."

Creighton stood and patted Barclay on the shoulder. When his friend moaned, he swallowed his laugh. "Get some sleep. We have the reception for the czar tonight."

"Tonight?"

"You won't want to miss it. I understand they are serving vodka."

Barclay groaned again, and Creighton took sympathy on his friend. Bidding him to get a good rest, he went down the stairs and out onto the walkway to his waiting horse. He glanced toward Berkeley Square, then, with a sigh, swung into the saddle. Dealing with Barclay had been the easy part. Now *he* must do what he could to help Natalya grasp her dream.

She had risked her life and her reputation for a single reason. That waited for her in Russia. From the first, she had told him nothing must keep her from returning there. Including him.

He groaned as deeply as Barclay had. Blast it! He had done the honorable thing in buying that commission. Now he wanted to enjoy himself with a fair lady who fit so perfectly in his arms.

Impossible! He owed her the duty of assisting her. To do that, he must not give in to his yearning to hold her again. It would not be easy, but it would be the right thing.

The right thing had never seemed so wrong.

Natalya opened her eyes as she heard footsteps pass in the hallway. She squeezed open one eye and was astonished to see the sunshine had already climbed onto the foot of the bed. Sitting, she stared at the indentation in the mound of pillows next to where she had been sleeping.

She touched the pillows, but Creighton's warmth had vanished. Pulling one of the pillows to her, she pressed it against her face. His scent remained, reviving the wondrous dream of lying in his arms. With him beside her, the past had been banished, and she had delighted in each moment of being with him.

Knuckles struck the door, and she looked up, startled. Hadn't the door been open before? She had thought it had come ajar in the middle of the night. It must have been no more than her imagination. If Petr saw her acting this want-witted . . . She pulled on the dark-red dressing gown and reached for her pantaloons.

The door swung open. Mrs. Winchell's face flared with embarrassment, and the housekeeper hastily turned her back as she said, "My lord, forgive me. I didn't think the door would open so easily."

Natalya buttoned her pantaloons in place. " 'Tis not your fault, Mrs. Winchell."

"This arrived for you." She did not look at Natalya as she held out a slip of paper.

"Thank you."

As the housekeeper rushed away, Natalya read the short message. She should have expected as much. General Miloradovich wanted all his officers to gather at his house immediately. They must plan their greeting for the czar.

She looked wistfully at the bed. She had hoped she might enjoy breakfast with Creighton on the balcony again this morning. Even more, she had hoped they might savor a few more of the stolen kisses in that private spot.

Reaching for her uniform, she sighed. Creighton might be able to set aside his commission and his duty to follow orders, but she could not. Not yet, not when she was so close to getting what she wanted.

And what you need? The question came, unbidden, into her mind. It was one she could not answer, one she dared not answer, for she had fought too hard to give up now. She could not give up, even when she was no longer certain if the prize she sought was what she really wanted.

"Here you are, stranger."

Natalya smiled as Creighton came up to stand beside her in the crowded ballroom. She admired the lines of his strong body, which had cushioned her so sweetly last night. His black coat and white breeches were the perfect foil for his red hair. At her side, her fingers tingled with the yearning to run them up his arms and draw those arms around her in a heated embrace.

"I left a message that I would be with my fellow officers all day," she said.

"Miloradovich must be nervous about putting on a good show for the czar."

"I believe he is. He met with various officers throughout the day." She laughed as she looked at the ballroom with its grand gilt walls. Music lilted on the air that was heavy with cigar smoke from the room across the hallway. "Mayhap he fears that the czar will realize the truth about him."

A light voice twittered, "Good evening, my dear Count Dmitrieff."

Tensing as Maeve Wilton ran a fan along her coat sleeve, Natalya could not keep from admiring the painted fan. It was decorated with ribbons that matched the ones at the high bodice of her gown, which was as unblemished as Creighton's breeches. With pearls laced through her hair and about her neck, she looked as beautiful as one of the angels painted onto the high ceiling.

Natalya swallowed roughly. She could not keep from admiring Miss Wilton's ensemble nor could she keep from noting how Miss Wilton complemented Creighton as they stood side by side. They were an undeniably handsome couple.

Swallowing again, but unable to shift the sudden clog in her throat, she said, "Good evening, Miss Wilton."

"Oh, I must insist that you call me Maeve." She fluttered her eyelashes. "It is not so difficult for you to say, is it?"

"No, Maeve."

"How charming my name sounds in your endearing accent!"

Natalya glanced at Creighton. It seemed unbelievable that Maeve would make believe that he was not standing here, but clearly that was what she intended. "I am glad it pleases you, Maeve. Would you care to join Creighton and me while we discuss the czar's arrival in London?"

"Creighton, how are you this evening?" she asked with a pout.

"Simply noting how charming my name sounds in the count's endearing accent," he said, chuckling.

Maeve snapped her fan closed. "Do not be impossible, Creighton!"

"I was being honest. Something I have discovered it is wise to be all the time." He turned to Natalya. "Wouldn't you agree, Demi?"

She struggled not to laugh. Poor Maeve did not need to be humiliated more by what she could not understand! "Honesty is always the wisest course."

Maeve slipped her arm through Natalya's. "Do let us go to where the dancing will be. I enjoyed our last dance so much."

"That must wait until later, I am afraid," Natalya answered, disentangling her arm from the other woman's. "I have my duties to perform this evening, which may prevent me from enjoying your company as I would wish."

"Duties? What duties?" She rounded on Creighton. "Is this of your doing? I have seen how you watch the count and me. Jealousy is not an attractive thing, my lord!"

He held up his hands. "The count's duties are his own and his country's. I am here merely as his host."

She started to snarl back a response, then turned to Natalya. "Forgive me, Count. I look forward to seeing you when you have completed your duties." She held out her hand.

Again Natalya had to fight to keep from laughing as she bowed over Maeve's fingers. Her eyes were caught by Creighton's, but she looked hastily away. As furious as Maeve was, her anger would be nothing in comparison to how she would feel if Natalya chuckled.

"Very nice," Creighton said quietly as Maeve hurried off

to the admiring crowd of ladies she seemed to gather at every occasion.

"Maeve?"

"No, your handling of her. I own never to being as capable."

Natalya stepped closer to him and lowered her voice. "Creighton, if I had had any idea she would develop a true affection for Count Dmitrieff, I would have put an end to this long ago. I never meant this to hurt you in any way."

"Hurt me? What do you mean?"

"I know of what happened between you and why you left London to join the army and——"

He drew her back into an alcove. "Who has been filling your head with drunken stories?"

"Barclay."

He rolled his eyes. "Who else?"

"He is worried about you."

Creighton laughed shortly. "Mayhap, but I suspect he is more worried about himself. He chided me first thing this morning because I didn't stay with him at White's yesterday to be certain he got home and to bed safely."

"This morning?"

"I asked him to withdraw his challenge for the duel, and he agreed with less reluctance than I had anticipated."

"Did you go— I mean . . ." She was not sure what she intended to say. Anything she could imagine saying would reveal her feelings too clearly when he had said nothing of his own.

A flurry of emotions swept through his eyes, too fast for her to comprehend a single one. "Natal— Demi, we need to talk."

"Yes."

"I assume you have to stay here until the guests of honor appear."

"Yes." She put her hand up to his face and tilted it so ⌐ gaze met hers. "Creighton, you must listen to me about the danger you are in. The murderous threat in the note Petr found is now a day closer to its deadline."

"Not that again! You have this annoying habit of getting something in your mind and not letting it go, whether it is logical or not." He laughed softly. "Just like a woman, Demi."

"Please. This is no time for jesting. You must heed me." She ran her thumb across his lips and sighed when his breath warmed her skin. "You heeded my needs last night. Let me heed yours tonight."

His voice became husky as he gripped her elbows, drawing her nearer. "I know you don't mean what you are saying. I could easily think only of how much I need you against me without even a hint of silk separating us."

"Then listen when I tell you what Petr found in those thieves' possession. It—"

"Lord Ashcroft!"

Creighton released her as Tatiana Suvorov came toward them. "My turn, I fear."

"Yes." Natalya was shocked to hear relief in his voice. Was he so happy to use Tatiana as an excuse to put space between them? She had thought he wished . . . No, she was unsure of anything. She longed to speak to him of last night, but she had no chance to add more as Tatiana greeted Creighton with a bold kiss on the cheek.

General Miloradovich's niece was dressed as elegantly as Maeve, and she flipped open her fan to reveal it was the one Creighton had purchased for her. "I hope you do not think me brazen when I wish to show off what good taste you have, Lord Ashcroft," Tatiana said in her breathy voice. In the same sour tone that Maeve had used when she greeted Creighton, she added, "Good evening, Count Dmitrieff."

Not taking Tatiana's outstretched hand, Natalya dipped her head. *"Dóbry vécher, grazhdánka."*

"Good evening, miss," Creighton said, chuckling.

Tatiana gasped. "I did not know you spoke Russian, my lord!"

"Only what I have learned from Demi."

"Demi?"

"My friend Count Dmitrieff." He patted Natalya on the shoulder, then offered his arm to Tatiana. "Allow me to get you something to drink, Miss Suvorov."

"Da." She dimpled. "That means—"

"Yes," Creighton said with a warm chuckle that sent a chill through Natalya. As he led Tatiana into the ballroom, he went on, "As you can see, Demi has proven to be an excellent teacher."

At a laugh behind her, Natalya turned to see Colonel Carruthers. "I doubt if Miss Suvorov would need to teach any man much more than that one word." He cleared his throat as guilt settled on his face. "Forgive me, my lord. That was not something meant for anyone's ears but my own."

"There is nothing to forgive when we are much of a mind." She smiled.

"If she plans to do something that could wound Captain Marshall—" He chuckled. "Allow me to beg your forgiveness again. I sound like an old tough guarding her young charge."

"Creighton is important to you. That is nothing to be ashamed of, sir, for I am well aware of how an officer comes to depend on his men."

When her name was bellowed, Natalya sighed. Not a single conversation this evening was going to go uninterrupted, but she could not dawdle when General Miloradovich shouted for her to join him along the corridor beyond the ballroom.

Instead of a greeting, the general demanded, "You did not answer the questions I posed to the rest of my staff this 'noon, did you?"

"No, sir," she answered, not adding that he had not asked her.

"What do you think of London, Dmitrieff?"

"It is very full of people," she said evasively, not sure what answer he sought.

"As any city is." He laughed. "I forget you prefer dirt beneath your feet. What do you think of the English?"

"They seem to enjoy their endless entertainments."

The general rammed his fist into a table beside him. The vase on it wobbled. She steadied it as she stared at him. What had she said to distress him? Her words had been innocuous.

"Endless!" He grumbled something she could not understand under his breath. "They act as if the war never happened."

"The people I have met are curious about it."

"As they would be curious about some new creature out of Africa." He fisted his hand on his beefy hip. "That is what we are, Dmitrieff. Some exotic monkey to entertain them until they are bored and go onto something else."

"In Russia—"

"It will be no different. We are an anachronism, Dmitrieff, in this time of peace."

She forced a smile. "I am sure the czar has many plans to use a man with your skills, General. Peace just brings us a different type of battle to fight."

"Battle?" He scowled so fiercely, she almost drew back. "So that is how you see it? Growing potatoes and raising pigs is as worthwhile as slaying our enemies?" He waved his hand. "Begone, Dmitrieff. I should have known you would not be able to see past that farm of yours."

"General—"

"Begone."

"Yes, sir," she said, backing away.

Natalya turned as horns heralded the arrival of the evening's guests of honor. Not able to see over the heads front of her, she sighed. First Creighton refused to listen to her, and now the general.

Her sigh became a silent moan of resignation when Maeve rushed to her side and hooked her arm through Natalya's so she could lead her into the ballroom and "introduce my dear, dear friend, Count Dmitrieff, to my closest family." Natalya was not sure how anything could become much worse, but she feared it would before the czar's visit was over.

Twenty

Natalya yawned as she picked up the newspaper and scanned the headlines on the first page. Every article was focused on the visit of the Regent's allies. She must read it to Petr later, although she doubted if he would do more than laugh at the English people's preoccupation with how the czar looked and what his sister the Grand Duchess Catherine of Oldenburg wore and why the Czar of All the Russias had again turned down the Prince Regent's invitation to stay at St. James's.

"No doubt he wishes some time to be with the Grand Duchess," she said, as she turned the page. Gossip never had appealed to her, and, since her arrival in England, she had come to wonder how the British had won a single battle. Too much talk and little too action seemed the hallmark of the *ton*.

"Looking for your name in the society columns?" Creighton asked as he came into the breakfast-parlor. His coat was slung over his arm, and he tossed it on an empty chair. With his hair still damp from his morning ablutions and his cravat only loosely tied, he seemed more at ease than she had ever seen him.

She resisted reaching out to take his hand as he passed her. When he went to the sideboard, she stared at the table. Not once had he said a word about coming to rescue her from her nightmare and staying to hold her through the night. Mayhap she was the air-dreamer to imagine there might have been more to his feverish kisses than the light-hearted flirtation he shared with Tatiana. She put her fingers to her lips and choked back a gasp. Had he kissed Tatiana, too? How many times had he told her he was little different from his best friend? Barclay seldom was sincere, and he certainly would never give his heart to one woman.

"What do you say, Demi?" Creighton asked, his voice still teasing. "Have you become like *tout le ton* and seek your name in the morning paper so you might remember what your befuddled brain cannot recall in the morning?"

"I had not considered it might be newsworthy enough to be there."

"Mayhap others have." He served himself from the side-board and sat facing her at the round table. "The carefree gentleman can often find his cares much less free after his name appears connected to a lady he barely knows but had the misfortune to speak too many words to within earshot of a matchmaking mama."

"I doubt if that is the case for either of us."

"Really?" He snatched the paper out of her hands and paged through it. "Aha! Heed this, my dear Demi." He struck a pose and read in a pompous tone, " 'Last night during the gala presentation of the Prince Regent and his guests before the dinner hosted by George, Prince of Wales, it was noted that one of our country's honored guests was much in the company of Miss Maeve Wilton. Count Dmitrieff of—"

"You are hoaxing me!"

"Am I?"

She seized the paper. It tore in two. With a laugh, he pointed to the page he still held.

"I would like to see it, Creighton."

"I doubt that." Tossing it in front of her, he stabbed at the middle column. "However, if you insist, there it is."

In disbelief, Natalya read the tiny print. She began to

chuckle. When he asked what she found so amusing, she said, "You did not read far enough. Otherwise, you would have been as delighted as I to learn that Lord Ashcroft's name is here, too."

"Blast!" He stood and peered over her shoulder. "My name and hers! Does Tatiana read English?"

"I'm not certain she reads Russian, but you can be sure someone will read it to her."

"Blast!"

"You said that already."

Grinning, he took his seat and jabbed his fork into his scrambled eggs. "The woman needs no persuasion to continue her pursuit of me. Do give me advice, my dear count, on how to deal with your countrywoman, who has such firm convictions."

"I would gladly give you advice." Natalya folded the tattered newspaper and set it aside. "The advice I have wished to offer you now for two days."

"To get myself a chaperone if I expect to be with Miss Suvorov?"

"No."

His smile vanished, and she knew her intense tone had reached him. "If this is in reference to what you've been prattling about since the general's party at White's, I have no wish to hear it."

" 'Tis no jest, Creighton. Chance smiled on us when Petr found the note."

"Mayhap he arranged for it to get you out of here. You know he hates it here."

She scowled. "Don't be absurd! He cannot read nor write Russian. He can't even speak English!"

"Fine education you give your servants."

"You are changing the subject."

"I was bored with the other one."

Grasping his wrist, she clamped his hand to the table. Eggs flew across the table, but she ignored them as she gasped, "Are you trying to prove you are as want-witted as Barclay? Is it so important for you to become like him again that you cannot see the danger in front of your nose?"

"I see only splattered eggs." He pulled away and scooped the eggs back onto his plate.

"As splattered as you may be."

"By Jove, you have a lurid imagination."

She shook her head. "I have seen what happens to a body on the wrong side of a gun. You have to face that you are in deadly danger."

"You think someone wishes to kill me?" Creighton laughed again and reached for a muffin. "Why would anyone wish to kill me now? The war and its barbaric sport is past."

Natalya clenched her hands. She could think of one reason someone would wish to see him dead: his dashed stubbornness. Instead of answering, she unbuttoned her coat and reached under it. She pulled out the slip of paper Petr had found and tossed it on top of his plate of eggs. "I think the reason why is less important than the simple facts in front of you."

He picked it carefully and shook a piece of egg from it. His brow furrowed as he read it. With a derisive snort, he dropped it back in front of her. "You aren't the only Russian in London, and I am not the only host."

"We are the only ones to be attacked."

"And they failed. The attack was not even on the day in that blasted note." He stood and shoved his plate aside. "I shall not live my life cowering in my house. That's how this whole nation was acting when Napoleon threatened to cross the Channel. Hiding like rabbits in a hedgerow. Too many died stopping him for us to remain so timid."

"So you will be foolishly fearless instead?" Setting herself on her feet, she said, "If you will not watch out for your own welfare, then I am obligated to."

He groaned and shook his head. "Do me no favors, Count

Dmitrieff. I have no wish to be included in your unending war."

"It has nothing to do with war."

"Then with what?"

She faltered. If she spoke of how she yearned to safeguard him as he had her, he might laugh again. She could not endure to hear him belittle the night that had been so precious.

Picking up the torn newspaper, she folded it. "Mayhap you are right, Creighton. Mayhap the threat is not for us. That means we must be doubly alert to the danger surrounding our friends and compatriots. It is our duty to—"

"Duty! I want nothing more to do with duty."

"So you can be just like Barclay Lawson?"

"If I wish to. That is the whole point of being a free man. To be able to choose how I wish to spend my life."

"Even squander it?"

"If I wish to." He seized her shoulders.

Before she could do more than gasp at the bolt of pleasure ripping through her at his touch, he pulled back his hands. She raised her arms to his shoulders. He moved aside, his face naked of expression.

"I do not want you guarding me like a sentry, Natalya." His voice was whetted with an anger that shocked her. "Keep yourself and your huge bear of a watch-dog away from me. Do your duty for Russia here and wherever else you go. I want no more of this."

Natalya stared after him as he grabbed his coat and charged out of the room. Moments ago, he had been joking with her. She stared down at her hands. Just the promise of her touch had sent him fleeing.

Tears filled her throat. She should be grateful for his cold words. He was right. Her duty was not here. It was to her family, as it always had been. Letting herself become bedazzled by the caresses of an Englishman would betray her vow to get her vengeance on those who had slain her family and to see the latest Count Dmitrieff in the restored dacha amid burgeoning orchards and fields.

"My lord?"

She forced a smile for James. "Good morning."

"Here are the messages that have been delivered for you this morning, my lord."

Thanking him, Natalya read through the dozen notes as she walked toward her room. Count Dmitrieff would become quite the one to dine about amid the Polite World if she accepted even half of these invitations. She winced as she opened one with florid handwriting. It was to remind Count Dmitrieff to be certain to call during Maeve's next at-home.

The last one was addressed to both her and Creighton. She broke the sealing wax and unfolded it. With a smile, she read it. Colonel Carruthers was hosting a masquerade ball on Monday night next. Monday night next! The date of the threat in the note. Creighton would insist on attending, even though he could be the target of murderers.

She must protect him from his own folly. But how? A slow smile spread across her face as she stared at the sunshine sweeping all the shadows from the stairs.

A masquerade ball was perfect for what she needed. The assassins would be looking for Lord Ashcroft *and* Count Dmitrieff. If she went in disguise, no one would guess the truth of her identity, for her face could be concealed behind a full mask. A domino would be too dangerous.

Yes, a mask would work. She could watch over Creighton without him knowing she was there. It would be perfect. All she needed was the right costume.

Her smile broadened. She knew just the perfect one.

Natalya spread the skirt across the bedcovers and smiled. Borrowing this gown from the laundry behind the kitchen had been easier than she had guessed. The heavier material of a servant's dress would conceal her lack of proper small-clothes to wear with it. She frowned. What did a fine lady wear beneath those slender, sheer gowns?

A deep gasp burst from behind her. She gathered up the gown and rolled it into a ball as she turned to see the astonishment on Petr's face.

"Don't sneak up on me like that!" she cried.

"Forgive me." He fingered his beard as his eyes narrowed. "What is that?"

"Nothing of import."

"A dress?"

"Yes, but—"

"For you?" He frowned. *"Grazhdánka* Natalya, you must be careful of which path you choose now."

Natalya stared at him, astounded. He had not called her *"Miss* Natalya" since the day they crawled from their hiding place to see the horror left by the French. That day, as they took a pledge to see their enemies pay for their crimes with their lives, she had become his captain.

"Petr, you are worrying needlessly. It is nothing but a serving woman's dress."

"For you?"

"There is to be a masquerade ball."

"And you will go as a woman?" He shuddered. "I feared this would happen."

"What would happen? I do not understand."

His scowl etched lines deep into his tanned forehead. "The *anglíski* lord. He wants more than friendship from you."

"You are wrong. He let me know at breakfast that he wishes me out of his life with all speed."

"You believed him?"

"Of course. He made his feelings quite clear. He does not believe the threatening note you found presents a peril to him, and he wishes to live his life as he alone sees fit."

His beard jutted toward her. "He lies."

"How do you know that?"

"I am a man. I know how a man thinks."

"Good." She dropped the wrinkled dress on the bed. "Then enlighten me, for I cannot understand why he resists my offer of our help to protect his life and ours. It makes no sense."

"It is not my place to say anything."

She fisted her hands on her waist. "Be honest with me, Petr. Give me some insight into why Creighton is acting as he is."

"I know only what I have seen, and, if you wish me to be honest, I shall say I am not sure if your father would be pleased to see his daughter share the bed of an *angliski* lord."

Her eyes widened. She had not been mistaken. The door *had* opened to her bedchamber the night Creighton offered her comfort from her memories. Petr must have come to check on her. He would have seen . . . She must not think of that now, for even the memory of Creighton's arms around her urged her to rush to him so he might enclose her in those strong arms again. She had as lief to think how stubborn he was, and how she must save his life, whether he wished her to or not.

Rubbing her hands together, she said, "You need not worry about my father's dismay, for Creighton has no interest in marrying anyone. He wishes to be as free of hindrances in his life as his inimitable friend Barclay Lawson."

Rage lowered his brows. "He would dishonor you and——"

"Lord Ashcroft has done nothing to dishonor me." She looked away so she did not have to hide her pain as she spoke the truth, "He sees me as a comrade-in-arms, as you and the other men do."

"In his arms?"

"Petr!"

He picked up the dress and snapped wrinkles from the fabric as he held it in front of her. Handing it to her, he said, "I am glad, for I have no wish to stay in this pale country. I long for the fresh air and beauty of our homeland. Will we return there soon?"

"I pray so." She smiled grimly. "Once I am certain we all have survived Monday next."

The *modiste*'s shop was empty when Natalya opened the door. The heavy aroma of roses nearly drove her back to the street. She took a deep breath of the pungent air off the walkway, then plunged inside.

The *modiste* peeked out from the back of the shop. She was not wearing the generous smile she had when Creighton had entered the shop.

Natalya brushed her hands against the simple material of her gown. It announced her place in society as surely as if she wore a sign. Mayhap she should have gone to another shop, mayhap serving lasses did not come here, but she was unsure where she might find another *couturière*.

"Are you Madame Barbeau?" she asked, thickening her accent to mock Tatiana's.

"Yes." She edged out of the back. "Are you one of the Russians?"

"Yes, I am *Grazhdánka* Butovshyj. Miss Butovshyj." Smiling, she turned slowly to look at the bolts of fabric displayed on the wall. "I have heard you are one who can work miracles. I need a gown for a masquerade."

"What do you seek?"

"Silk." The word popped out before she could halt it.

"Excellent choice, mademoiselle."

Natalya smothered her wince at the French phrase. The *modiste* had also lost much because of that Corsican beast, so it would behoove Natalya to ignore how being addressed in French sickened her.

"Do you have an idea of a color?" continued Madame Barbeau. "With your golden hair, you would look very classic in white, but you can wear nearly any shade to a masquerade."

She touched a mother-of-pearl silk set on the lowest rack. "How about this?"

"That is *très cher.*" She eyed Natalya, clearly trying to appraise the number of coins in her purse by the quality of her clothes. "Very expensive."

"The occasion is special. All of the lady's household should look their best." She lowered her voice. "The Regent himself may be in attendance."

"If you wish." She jotted some numbers on a sheet of paper and offered it to Natalya. "The matching mask would be a few guineas more, depending on how much lace or gems you wish on it."

Natalya hoped her gulp did not reach the seamstress's ears. She had been with her father when he negotiated for a pair of fine horses. Their price had been less than what this dress would cost. "I will agree if you can have the dress ready for me to wear Monday next."

"Monday next? Impossible."

"But, Madame Barbeau—"

"Impossible!" She muttered something else in French under her breath.

"I shall pay half in advance."

The *modiste's* eyes narrowed as a sly smile tipped her lips. "All in advance."

"But if the dress is not finished—"

"It shall be finished." She held out her hand. "However, I must delay not a second more."

Natalya reached into the bodice of her gown to draw out her leather purse. As she counted out the coins, Madame Barbeau sniffed and added that she would include a proper reticule for Natalya.

"Thank you," Natalya said, trying not to think how few coins remained in the bag. "When will I need to come in for fittings and—"

The street door opened. Natalya turned and stifled a groan. How much more could go wrong today?

"Bonjour, madame," Maeve Wilton called out in a cheery voice. As she untied the ribbons on her wide-brimmed straw bonnet, she said, "I see you have another customer."

"One of the Russians visiting our country," the *modiste* answered with so much pride that Natalya would have guessed the Frenchwoman had sought out Natalya for her business.

"Russian?" Maeve raised a quizzing glass to her eye and asked, "Do I know you?"

"I think not, *grazhdánka,"* she said, edging toward the door.

"Odd, for I am almost certain we have met before." Maeve slipped off her paisley shawl and smiled at the *modiste.* "Mayhap it was here."

"Mademoiselle Butovshyj is visiting my shop for the first time," the seamstress said.

"Do not hurry away," Maeve urged. "Come and talk with me while Madame gets us some tea."

Natalya glanced at the *modiste,* whose lips were pursed at the idea of running errands for her patrons. "I believe she is busy."

"Nonsense. She always brings me tea." Maeve smiled with arrogant self-assurance. "Don't you, Madame?"

"Certainly, Mademoiselle Wilton." The seamstress went toward the back of the shop. "Once you have enjoyed your tea, I can take your measurements, Mademoiselle Butovshyj."

Maeve swept the pattern books from the table and sat in the closest chair. Motioning for Natalya to take the other, she said, "I know we may never have met, but I have had the good fortune to be introduced to several of your countrymen. Do you know Count Dmitrieff?"

"The name is known to me, although I have not met the count in London." As she sat, her feet pressed against the floor, eager to speed her out of the shop. "He is not within our household."

"He is staying with Lord Ashcroft. Do you know anything of the man?"

"I have heard he is a war hero."

Maeve waved that aside as Madame Barbeau set a tea tray in front of them. Not even bothering to thank the *modiste,* she replied, "That matters nothing to me. Does the count have a wife?"

"No." She bit her lip to keep from laughing. This was all so absurd. Never had she imagined such a *contretemps* when she first had chosen to fulfill her brother's obligation to the czar.

"A fiancée?"

"None that I have heard of."

Raising her quizzing glass, Maeve peered through it. "Are you sure we have not met before this?"

"I am only recently arrived in London. We came with the czar's party." She pointed to the *modiste,* who was hastily gathering all she needed to make the dress for the masquerade. "I have had time only to come here in order to have a gown ready for the assembly in honor of the Russian delegation."

"Monday next," muttered Madame Barbeau. "She gives me only until Monday next to make a gown fit for such an evening."

Natalya opened her mouth to reply, but Maeve interjected, "Pay her no mind. Madame mumbles like that every time I come in."

"Grazhdánka—"

"Maeve. You must call me Maeve." Her forehead furrowed. "What is your given name?"

"Natalya." She was unsure how many other names she could reply to without revealing the truth, so her own name might be best.

"So you know nothing else of the count, Natalya?"

Deciding to take the offense, she poured herself a cup of tea and said, "You seem obsessed with the count. Do you have affection for him?"

"Not exactly, but I wish to know more of the man." Maeve smiled secretively as she stirred more sugar into her tea. "I do not know how things are done in Russia, but here the way to a man's heart is often through another man's."

"So you wish to convince someone else that you have affection for him by pretending to be bemused by the count?" She smiled. She did not have to ask who was the target of Maeve's campaign, which seemed as carefully thought out as an attack on the French. Creighton must still hold a place in Maeve's heart, or, she corrected herself as she noted Maeve's possessive smile, Maeve Wilton intended to ensnare his affections anew. "Your English ways are most confusing."

"Men are confusing."

On that, Natalya was ready to agree wholeheartedly. Somehow she had to determine why Creighton was acting the way he was before both of them ended up dead. She hoped this was the way, or Maeve Wilton might soon be weeping at the funerals of both Count Dmitrieff and Lord Ashcroft.

Twenty-one

When boot heels pounded into the room, Natalya did not look up from cleaning her own boots. She recognized the sound of Creighton's furious steps with an ease that threatened to break her heart anew. During the past few days, he had said barely a score of words to her.

Without the courtesy of a greeting, he demanded, "What do you mean by leaving me a note that you aren't attending Colonel Carruthers' masquerade tonight?"

"I do not wish to go."

"Are you afraid?"

"Afraid?" She looked up at him, then quickly away before she found herself admiring the excellent cut of his coat and how his breeches accented the strong line of his legs. "Do not be absurd! I am not afraid of your *angliski* thieves." She bent to rub harder against the spot on her boot.

He snatched it away.

"Creighton!"

Tossing it into the corner, he said, "I would appreciate your undivided attention, Natalya."

"Creighton, watch what you say!"

His snort was as outraged as any she had heard from Barclay. "Why do you expect everyone else to heed me when you pay me less attention than the mud on your boots?"

"When you act like this, you should not be surprised that your petulance is ignored."

He reached toward her, then clamped his arms across his chest. "Dammit, Natalya!" He cursed. "Don't glare at me! I shall call you what I wish."

With a sigh, she drew off her other boot. She set it by the chair and stood. "I am tired of this endless round of parties where everyone talks and no one says anything. Please extend my apologies to Colonel Carruthers, but I doubt if anyone will miss me amidst the gaiety."

"So you are just going to hide here like a coward?"

She clenched her hands in front of her. "I am no coward."

"I think you are." He leaned on the back of the chair and smiled icily. "Are you going to strike me with your fists?"

"No." She forced her fingers to uncurl. She did not want to hit him; she wanted to draw his arms around her as she melted to him. If he would lower his guard for even a moment, she might— No, she could not. She must not.

"No? Afraid?"

"I would not be silly enough to bruise my knuckles on your hard head when 'tis clear even such a blow would not be enough to knock sense into you. Today is June 13. Today is the day the Russian and his host may die."

Turning slowly with his arms outstretched, he said, "No holes in me yet."

"Only in your skull!" She tapped his forehead.

He caught her wrist in a grip as strangling as a vise. Something flickered in his eyes when his fingers softened to stroke the inside of her wrist. Then he pushed her hand away, saying, "Enjoy your evening alone, Natalya. I hear General Miloradovich plans to leave for Vienna soon. Good riddance to both of you."

"Where did you hear that?"

"From the good general himself." His smile remained

cold. "Mayhap you would hear the same if you didn't cling to this house like a child afraid of its shadow."

Natalya gathered up her boots and left him to stew in his own misconceptions. Dash it! She was going to save his neck, if for no other reason than to prove that she was right. Then . . . She did not want to think of then or why General Miloradovich was planning to leave London so soon without telling her.

Natalya turned slowly in front of the looking glass. The sensation of silk against her legs and curling around her shins was almost decadent. For more than two years, she had worn ponderous boots and the bulky wool uniform of a cavalryman. She turned again to look into the glass and gasped.

Reflected back to her was her memory of Mama. Touching the white ribbon in her hair, which possessed the same gold aura as her mother's, she swept her hands along the sides of her gown. Slowly, her fingers touched the bodice. As a child, she had rested her head against Mama's breasts and been comforted in the wake of a nightmare.

Just as Creighton had comforted her. Yet his embrace had been so unlike Mama's, for Mama had offered solace and Creighton's arms promised passion beyond even her most daring fantasies.

That was over!

She would make sure he survived the night, and then she would leave. She had to go back to Russia and do as she promised, even if it broke her heart utterly. Let him stay and become just like Barclay Lawson while he flirted with Maeve Wilton. If he wanted that life . . . She swallowed roughly. She could not believe he did.

Pulling her thickest cloak from the back of the chair, she flung it over her shoulders. More carefully, she pulled the hood up to conceal her hair. She took her reticule and opened it. Seeing the glitter of brass on the pocket pistol inside it, she closed the top and hid the bag beneath the cloak. It would give her only a single shot, but that might be all she needed.

She was ready to face whatever might be thrown in her way. Hearing the rattle of the carriage in front of the house, she peeked through the curtains. She watched Creighton get into the closed carriage.

Dropping the drapes back into place, she skulked out into the hall. She must follow closely, or all might be lost even before the masked ball began. Even spending her last coin on a hired carriage would not be too much if she could thwart the assassins.

Natalya's heart thudded against her chest as she crossed the brightly lit foyer of Colonel Carruthers' house. With her mask in place, she was unrecognizable, but so were many of the other guests. This was going to be more difficult than she had imagined.

A footman stepped forward to take her cape. She handed it to him along with the engraved invitation.

"Whom shall I announce?" he asked, as correct as a new recruit on parade.

"Natalya Butovskyj."

"Butov—"

"Butovskyj," she repeated slowly.

He nodded and, giving her cloak to a maid, he motioned for her to follow him up the broad marble stairs. The ballroom was awash in music and conversation beneath the brightly lit chandeliers. Inside the doorway, she saw General Miloradovich with Kapitán Radishchev hanging on every word. Radishchev would be pleased Count Dmitrieff was not here tonight. It would give the fawning fool a chance to gain more of the general's favor. She wondered if Radishchev knew of the plans to leave London.

With his back straight, the footman bowed toward her

and then to Colonel Carruthers, who was wearing a full dress uniform that must have been uncomfortable because he was shifting from one foot to the other.

The footman stumbled over her name again, so Natalya offered her hand to the colonel and said, "I am Natalya Butovskyj. Thank you for inviting the members of the Grand Duchess's household to your gathering this evening."

"You are welcome." He kissed her hand lightly. "I thought the Grand Duchess had sent her regrets that no one would be able to attend because the household was going to the theater with the Prince Regent and his party."

She hoped her laugh sounded genuine. "She did not want to offend you, Colonel, by ignoring your generous invitation. She knows how I love masquerades."

"That is no surprise," answered a deeper voice.

Natalya whirled to see Creighton standing behind her. Even with a black domino hiding half his face, nothing could diminish the strength of his gaze. Beneath his ebony coat, his silver waistcoat glittered in the light from the chandeliers like a vest of jewels.

"Creighton, do you know Miss Butov—?" Colonel Carruthers smiled as he said, "A most impossible name for our English tongues, I fear."

"Then she must grant us all the favor of allowing us to call her by her given name." He offered his arm. "Do allow me to escort you in, Natalya."

She did not hesitate. To do so might cause a scene she could ill afford. As he wove a path through the guests, without pausing to speak to any of them, she whispered, "How did you recognize me so swiftly?"

He ran his finger along her bare shoulder. "I knew as soon as I saw this skin, which was so soft against my chest for one wondrous night." He led her out onto a balcony that was draped in the thickening shadows of twilight. Lifting aside his domino, he said beneath the blithe music of a country dance, "I thought you were not coming tonight."

"I had hoped to save you from your own folly," she said, pulling off her mask. She stuffed it in her reticule along with the small pistol.

"By dressing like a princess?" He laughed. His fingers brushed her cheek, then he clasped them behind his back as he looked past her, frowning. "Did you hope to confuse your so-called executioners by having Count Dmitrieff vanish? Or are you just trying to avoid Maeve, who has been searching every corner of the ballroom for the good count?"

"Do you harbor such animosity toward her that you would have me hurt her when I must leave?" Her eyes widened as she gasped, "Or do you see the count as a safe rival for her affections? If she is enamored with me, she will not betray you by seeking another man's company." She laughed coldly. "What a perfect dolt I have been! Did you use her as heartlessly, too? Is that why she gave you your *congé?*"

"If you were a man, I would demand you meet me on the field of honor for such words."

"Creighton, don't."

"Don't?" Bafflement threaded his forehead, and she knew he had not guessed she would reply as she had.

"Don't be as pompous as Barclay." She ached to run her hand along his jaw, which was smooth from his recent shave. She longed to rest her cheek against it while she enjoyed the sharp scent of his cologne. "You never challenged any of Maeve's other admirers to a duel. Why me?"

"Because I do not want you spending so much time with her. She may give you wrong ideas."

"About you?"

"About how a lady should act."

"How is that?"

"With honesty."

"Honesty? *Ya ne ponimáyu.*"

"Do you understand this?" Grasping her cheeks, he pressed his mouth over hers.

She slid her hand up his arm, encircling his shoulder as her breath grew unsteady against him. His arms enfolded her to his chest. His heartbeat matched hers in a swift race to delight. As his hands glided along her, waking every inch of her to the pleasure of his caresses, she pressed closer. Never had she wanted to be within a man's arms as she did now. Even when she was not with him, he haunted her every thought.

She moaned softly as he bent to place a line of searing kisses along the skin above the low neckline of her gown. Slipping her fingers beneath his coat, she splayed them across his back as the moist probe of his tongue explored the dusky secrets within her mouth. Soft, wordless sounds emerged on her ragged breath. Warmth emanated from deep within her, for each place he touched her flamed hotter.

He chuckled with satisfaction as he buried his face in her hair. As his cheek brushed hers, she turned his mouth against hers. Unable to control her own craving, she feasted on the sweet flavors of his lips. She sighed as he raised his mouth from hers.

"Creighton . . ."

He put his finger over her lips. "This sweetness is what you must never lose. Your honesty and your ineffable innocence are such a splendid part of you, Natalya. Maeve is as calculating as a horse thief trying to peddle his stolen wares at a fair."

"Even Maeve is not so horrible," she said, not quite sure why she was defending the Englishwoman.

"No? See for yourself how different you are from other women."

He drew her to another door along the balcony and pointed to a group of women who were talking intently an arm's length in front of them. Her eyes widened when she saw Tatiana Suvorov stroll over to them, although she should not have been surprised. Tatiana seemed determined to attend every function during her stay in London.

Tatiana looked down her nose at the Englishwomen and asked, "Do you know if Lord Ashcroft has arrived?"

Even from where Natalya stood, she could see the superior smile Maeve wore as she answered, "Yes, my dear Creighton is here. I saw him earlier." She turned to another of the ladies. "Is he alone?"

Creighton chuckled as he walked back to the thick stone railing. Leaning on it, he crossed his arms over his chest. "So you see, Natalya, you were right. You and I are in peril, even though the only danger to me is Miss Suvorov's intention not to leave London until she leg-shackles herself to me, and the only danger to you is an amorous Maeve."

"You are wrong."

Laughing, he said, "This night will be unbearable while Maeve makes sure I regret not bringing the good count here." He caught her hands and drew her toward him. Whispering against her ear, he asked, "Do you think she suspects how I am trying to keep my rival far from her eager charms?"

Natalya stared at him. "How can you be so witless? She cares nothing for the count, save as a tool to make you so jealous you will vow your undying love to her as you once did."

"You are mad!"

"No, for she has told me nearly as much herself." She walked back toward the ballroom, being careful to avoid the door where the women stood. Putting her hand on another door frame, she turned to face him. "She let you escape from her web once, but is now determined to wrap you up again as tightly as a spider does a fly."

He put his hand over hers. As he edged around her, so he stood between her and the ballroom, he said, "And she thinks to hold me there until she decides if there is another feast more enticing." He chuckled. "Dear Natalya, if for no other reason, I would have to be delighted you have come to London to provide Maeve with a bit of her own bitter medicine. How wildly she has fought to entice Count Dmitrieff into her net! It has been a joy to watch."

"You are no gentleman, Creighton Marshall!"

"And neither are you, Natalya Dmitrieff." He pressed her hand to his lips. When she gasped softly as the heat of his mouth flowed through her, he whispered, "You are, as you always have been, a most beautiful woman."

With a smile, he drew her away from the door. He turned her lightly beneath his fingertips so he could view her from every angle.

"Do you approve?" she asked when she faced him again.

"You shall think me mad."

"Because you approve?"

"Because I miss the sight of your limbs which are obscured by this silk."

She laughed. "You are mad! The wool of my uniform hides more than it reveals."

"I did not mean that." He bent to whisper against her ear again. "Do you recall the morning after I held you in my arms all night?"

She put her hands on his chest and pushed him away. "You left without saying a word to me." Sudden tears blurred the starlight.

His arm slipped around her waist and pulled her back to him. Her breath burst from her as he held her tightly against the wall of his chest. As his fingers drifted up her back with the rhythm of the waltz spilling from the ballroom, he asked, "How could I speak to you when the only words on my lips were of how luscious you looked when I woke to find you curled against me as guileless as a puppy and as sensuous as a siren? 'Twas then I could admire your bare limbs, for they were draped over my own legs."

When heat climbed her cheeks, she whispered, "I did not know."

"Did you know I kissed you when I could not resist tasting your luscious lips one more time?"

"I dreamed— I mean, I thought it was a dream. I—"

"Let me remind you."

Her smile vanished beneath his mouth as she savored the kiss she wanted to relish for the rest of her days . . . and all her nights. It was all the sweeter because she knew it was impossible.

"You may be correct," Creighton said as he led Natalya from the dance floor back out onto the balcony. With a pained expression on his face, he limped past the other couples who had come to escape the crowd in the ballroom. "You may never learn to waltz."

"I believe you stepped on my toes more than I did on yours, my lord."

"Impossible."

"But my soft slippers cannot hurt your toes as your shoes have mine."

He let a roguish smile tilt his lips. "Shall I kiss each injured toe to speed it on its way to recovery?"

"My toes?"

His arm around her waist pulled her tightly to him. She was perfect in his arms. "They must be as scrumptious as the rest of you, my dear Natalya."

"I think you are mad."

"I think I would like to prove you wrong." He tilted her mask up, but paused as he looked past her. "Blast!"

"What is wrong?"

"That," he said, as Barclay called Creighton's name again as he bumped into the door, then stumbled through it onto the balcony.

He was surprised when she laughed. "Don't fret," she said softly. "If he is as foxed as usual, he won't guess who hides behind my mask."

"Natalya—"

"Don't fret."

Barclay lurched toward them. Wine splashed from his glass, gaining him a scowl from a dowager checking on her young charge, but he simply bowed toward her without pausing. Raising the glass, he drank deeply. "Your colonel knows his wine, Creighton."

"I am sure he would appreciate you telling him so." He tugged on Natalya's arm. Dammit! He should have seen that this might happen. He had to get Natalya away from here.

"Where is he?"

"About somewhere." Again he tugged on her arm. "Check the card room."

"I shall." Barclay turned, then looked back over his shoulder. " 'Tis nice to see you much more yourself. Do I call you 'Natalya' or 'Count Whatever-Your-Name-Is' tonight?" He laughed. "Quite the masquerade!" He suddenly frowned and reeled back to them. He put out a finger toward Natalya's bodice.

With a gasp, she pulled back.

"You *are* a woman!" Barclay choked. He squinted at Creighton. "She is a woman!"

"I know."

"You know?" He swayed, then grasped onto the railing. "How long?"

Creighton put his hand on his friend's arm. "Barclay, this must be kept a secret."

"How long have you known?"

Natalya whispered, "From the beginning."

Barclay's face bleached. "You mean you would have let me duel a woman?"

"We tried everything possible to keep the duel from taking place," Creighton said quietly.

"I could have killed a woman!"

"Unlikely." Natalya wished she had remained silent when the bald man scowled.

Creighton hurried to say, "Forget the duel and forget you saw Natalya like this." He aimed a scowl at Barclay, who regarded him with a drunken smile. "Forget it. Do you understand?"

He shrugged and nearly fell to his knees. He waved aside Creighton's hands. "Sure. Why not?" With a loud burp, he turned toward the ballroom.

Natalya took a step to follow. She halted when Creighton ran his finger along her shoulder. She quivered. With fear or fury . . . or delight?

"It appears," he whispered, "despite your assertion to the contrary, one of us is a gentleman."

She frowned as Barclay tottered back into the ballroom and began to speak to a lady with hair as white as untrampled snow. "But if he tells someone else—"

"Who would believe him when he is as drunk as an emperor?"

"And when he is not in his cups?"

"He is asleep."

She relaxed and nodded. "As long as he does not talk in his sleep." Putting her hand on his arm, she whispered, "I have come so far and worked so hard to protect my father's legacy. My struggles must not come to naught because he cannot keep his counsel." She sighed. "I am leaving soon. Then it shan't matter."

He drew off her mask and tossed it onto the balcony's rail. He wanted to see her shimmering smile when he spoke of what throbbed within his heart. "Natalya, stay a while longer."

"Here?" She smiled. "I intend to keep an eye on you until midnight and—"

"Forget that damned threat. Don't leave with Miloradovich. I have tried to put some distance between us because I know your heart is focused on rebuilding your family's estate. But the truth is, I do not want you to go. Stay in London." He swept her to him. "Stay with me."

He pressed his mouth over hers, not wanting to hear her say she must leave. He held her tightly, for he wanted to

give himself the chance to memorize her. Bending her back
over one arm, he deepened the kiss until she softened
against him, a captive as he was of their escalating passion.

Raising his head, he delighted in her soft smile. Her hand
against the back of his head brought his lips back to hers.
He forgot all the reasons why he was stupid to let another
woman lure him into her enchanting spell. Everything vanished from his mind but the craving rippling through him
with each touch of her slender hand.

"Stay with me," he murmured against her lips.

"I must go back to Russia. I must . . ." Her sigh sent
shivers through him as he teased her ear with his tongue.

"Stay with me." He framed her face with his hands and
looked down into her glazed eyes that glittered with the
promise of the ecstasy he could unleash. "Do not tell me
no, Natalya. Think of what I ask."

"I am uncertain what you are asking. Do you ask me to
be your wife?"

Natalya bit her lip to silence her anguish as his hands
fell back.

He started to answer, then sighed. "No."

"Then what do you ask?"

"I'm asking you to stay with me."

"As your comrade or as your mistress?"

He cupped her chin in his hand. "I think it is impossible
for us to turn back from what we have shared. I want to
spend my nights with you in my arms. For the past week,
we have tried to deny the truth, Natalya, and we have been
miserable. You belong with me."

She pulled away. "I am not a possession."

"No." His fingertips brought her face back toward him.
"But can you deny the truth of what we feel when you are
in my arms?"

"No, not the truth."

"Then stay with me."

Natalya lowered her eyes as she walked to the deepest

shadows along the railing. "You ask the impossible. I must go back to Russia."

"Would you have stayed if I asked you to marry me?" He put his hand on her arm and turned her to face him.

"No, for I have vowed Count Dmitrieff will rebuild my father's dacha. I cannot break a blood vow."

He brushed her cheek with his lips. "Will you stay with me tonight, Natalya? If we cannot have more than this one night, will you deny us this?"

"I . . . I don't know." She yearned to throw herself into his arms and tell him the truth within her heart.

"Will you think on this and give me an answer while I get you a glass of something to put the color back into your face?"

She raised her hands to her icy cheeks. "Yes."

He put his hand over hers. "I hope your answer when I return is the same."

Natalya leaned on the railing as Creighton walked into the ballroom. Was she mad? Even to consider sleeping by his side and then leaving, never to see him again, was insane. Yet this might be her last chance to know the real love she could share with a man. She touched her abdomen. This might be her only chance to give her father's name an heir and herself a part of Creighton to take with her. How could she hold his child in her arms and not weep for the love she had relinquished in order to do as she vowed? She hid her face in her hands and fought not to cry.

Deep voices jarred on her ears, yanking her from her misery. Two men strode along the balcony. She tried to ignore them. What did she care what problems they had when— She stiffened. The men were speaking Russian!

Clinging to the shadows, she strained to hear what they were saying in such desperate whispers. She clenched her reticule as she heard, ". . . and, with Alexander dead, everything shall fall into place."

"They are at the Theatre Royal in Covent Garden at this

very moment." A rumbled laugh reached her ears, teasing her with its familiarity. She did not take time to try to identify it as she heard, "The czar shall not live to see the end of the merriment on the stage. Dead, just as we planned."

Natalya pressed her hands over her mouth. Dear God! Creighton had been right. The threat had not been for them. It was for the czar and the Prince Regent. She had to get to the Theatre Royal and warn them.

Creighton!

No, she could not waste a moment. Not even to find him.

The two men continued along the balcony. She followed the railing in the other direction, then hurried toward a door into the ballroom.

She heard a shout. She spun. The two men were running toward her. Gathering up her dress, she raced into the ballroom.

"Ostanovítes!" came the bellow from behind her.

She had no intention of stopping. She ran back through the ballroom. Looking back, she saw the men gaining on her. Dash these silk slippers! She kicked them off and pulled open her reticule.

A hand grabbed her arm. She shook it off and raised the pistol. The sound was deafening as she fired. The ball struck a chandelier, sending crystal flying. Women screamed. Men shrieked.

She ran down the stairs and out onto the walkway. Pulling the reins from the hand of a startled groom, she mounted and raced down the street.

She had been a fool. The war was not over. She must warn the czar and keep the battle from flaring to life again. For if Alexander were slain on English soil, the fragile truce might fall apart . . . and she might have to face Creighton across a battlefield.

Twenty-two

Closing the fur collar of her uniform around her throat, Natalya strode toward the front stairs. Her sword slapped her leg comfortingly, and, at her waist, her pistol drew down the sash. She hoped she would need neither of them. The theater would be filled with those eager to see the Regent and his guests. Hints that the Regent's wife might appear would add to the number crowding the floor and filling the boxes.

Even if she succeeded in stopping the assassination attempt, the ensuing uproar would reverberate through the rest of the czar's stay in England. Alexander might order all his delegation immediately to Vienna. She would have to leave Creighton. She did not want this too-short, sweet interlude ending so soon.

But if she failed, this diplomatic visit between England and Russia could end in war. Both she and Creighton would be called to fight. How could she ride into the blinding smoke of cannon fire and slice into the enemy when he might be at the other end of her sword?

She could not fail. War had claimed too many of those she loved. She would not let its horror steal Creighton's life as well. If she could save his life, she would do anything, even sacrifice her own.

"Petr!" she called up the back stairs. Where was he? She

had thought he would be pacing the hall, ready to demand how she had skulked out of the house without him knowing.

No answer.

She started up the stairs, then paused as the front door crashed open. Natalya halted as she heard, "Is she— Where is— What the blazes is her name? Where is Natalya?"

She gripped the railing. The garbled words were unquestionably in Barclay Lawson's voice. Frowning, she vowed to repay him for his drunken idiocy in delaying her. She had no time to make up some lie to keep him from rushing back to Creighton with the truth.

The footman answered, "Natalya, Mr. Lawson? There is no one of that name here."

"Dmitri— By Jove, why can't those blasted Russians have decent names that a man can pronounce?"

"Count Dmitrieff?" James supplied. "I do not know where the count is, Mr. Lawson. I can have a knock placed on his door. He might still be within because he did not go with Lord Ashcroft to—"

"Not *he!* Her! Natalya Dmitrieff!"

"Mr. Lawson, mayhap you should sit down. I fear you are befuddled."

Natalya smiled and bit her lower lip to keep her laugh from swirling down the stairs.

"Where is she?"

"Mr. Lawson, please." She heard amusement in James's voice, although he remained gracious. "Please sit, and I shall do what I can."

"Find her! Blast these Russians! They have manners better suited to a pigsty."

Natalya shook her head, smiling. Barclay was always the same when he was in his cups. The whole world was beneath him, and it tried to draw him down to its ignoble level. Her urge to smile vanished when Barclay shouted after James, who was walking toward the back of the house.

"Find her! Creighton sent me to find her posthaste. 'Tis

time to introduce her—really introduce her this time—to
Maeve Wilton. Thinks it's about time the two came face-
to-face. Time to make Maeve sorry she spurned him.
Bother, man! Go and find the chit!"

"No," she whispered as she edged away from the steps.
Creighton could not plan to break his pledge of silence.
Even if he thought she would deny him his request to stay
with him tonight, he should not be turning immediately to
Maeve! He could not, not if he were the man she believed
him to be.

Squaring her shoulders, she ran to the back stairs. Nothing must stop her from warning the czar. Not even her own
broken heart.

Creighton stepped out of his carriage. A hand seized his
in a death grip. Gently, he peeled away the fingers to free
himself. "You will be fine, Maeve."

"Oh, Creighton, please let me stay here with you." She
pressed her hand to her bodice, offering him a good view
of the cleavage above it. "I am so deeply unsettled. To have
someone firing a gun at a ball—I fear I will swoon."

"I believe if you were going to, you would have done so
by now." He closed the door. When she peered out the window, he said, loudly enough so the coachee could hear, "I
shall have the carriage take the smoothest streets to your
house."

"Dear Creighton, don't leave me like this."

"You shall be fine."

Her plea became a pout. "It is that Russian woman, isn't
it?"

"Yes," he said, slapping the side of the carriage. He did
not have time to disabuse Maeve of her misapprehensions,
even if he had wished to. Let her think he wished to hurry
to Tatiana's side when, in truth, the only woman on his
mind was Natalya.

She must have fired the gun in the ballroom. No other woman would be there with a pistol. The few witnesses, who were not so hysterical they could not be believed, had agreed a woman had shot the gun. It had to have been Natalya, but whom had she been shooting at and why? Where was she now?

He rushed up the steps as the carriage went around the square. Pushing past James as the door opened, he shouted, "Where is the count?"

"Just what I wanted to know," grumbled Barclay. "Where is she?"

Creighton seized his friend by the lapels and demanded, "What in perdition are you doing here?"

"Came to find Natalya."

Looking over his shoulder, Creighton snapped, "Close the door and your mouth, James. Not a word to anyone, do you understand?"

"Yes, my lord," he replied, although his baffled expression contradicted his assertion. He scurried away.

Barclay eased out of Creighton's grip and hiccuped loudly. "Where is she? She should be here. I saw her riding neck-or-nothing from Carruthers' house."

"So you followed her?" Creighton wondered if any jury would convict him if he strangled Barclay right here and now. It would be, in his estimation, justifiable homicide.

"Wanted to bring her back and let Maeve see her real competition." He dropped to sit on the first step.

"Who knows you plan to do that?"

"Just told that witless footman of yours. Argued with me like a child, he did."

James edged around the corner and whispered, "My lord?"

"Yes?"

The footman cringed at his sharp answer. "Thought you might want to know that Count Dmitrieff was seen just a few minutes ago in the kitchen. He—" He swallowed roughly. "The count took his horse and rode off."

"What was he wearing?"

"Wearing?"

"Yes, man, answer me! What was he wearing?"

"His uniform, I suppose. One of the girls in the kitchen mentioned it was a hot night for all that wool and fur up under his chin."

Creighton swore. "Was that after Barclay spouted off the truth?"

"The truth?" James's eyes grew wide. "Then the count is a woman? He is a she?" He gulped as Creighton glowered at him. "Yes, my lord, it was after Mr. Lawson's arrival and demand to see him—er, her."

Creighton pounded his fist on the newel post. "She had to have heard you, Barclay. You must have been fed with a fire shovel as a lad! That dashed big mouth of yours!"

"I wanted to talk to her. I assumed she would come here. I was right. Where else would she go?"

Creighton did not think the question was worthy of an answer. Where else, indeed! Natalya had proven she could defeat any knight of the pad, and, by now, she might be anywhere in London or beyond. Something had sent her fleeing from the ball as if she were Cinderella. Something had changed her from this evening's faerie princess back into a Russian cavalry captain.

But what?

Dismissing James again, Creighton said, "If you had kept your mouth shut, Barclay, and let me do what I know better than you how to do—"

"I know you are the brave and dashing war hero, Creighton, but the point of the matter was that you had your hands full with two women at the moment that shot went off." He staggered to his feet. "I saw you encircled by them. That Russian woman was fawning over you, and Maeve was acting like the queen of the May. I couldn't do

anything about Tatiana, but I thought it would do Maeve
good to see exactly whom she intended to use to make your
nose swell with jealousy."

"You moonling! Do you think I care what Maeve
wants?"

"You always have. Far too much." Barclay tried to square
his shoulders but clutched the banister to keep himself on
his feet. "Egad, Creighton! You have never appreciated a
single thing I have done for you."

"And what have you done for me other than endangering
Natalya by spouting off the truth?"

He grinned broadly. "I persuaded Maeve you weren't
ready to settle down, so she took up with that chucklehead— What was his name?"

"You did what?" He gripped his friend's lapels again. He
was about to shake him when Barclay's face turned a threatening shade of greenish gray. Shoving Barclay aside, he
demanded, "How could you interfere with my plans to
marry Maeve?"

"You really didn't want to marry her." He collapsed back
onto the riser and looked up at Creighton like a faithful
pup. "Besides, we were having too much fun for you to
buckle yourself to any woman."

"So you decided that my not marrying her would make
me happy?"

"I decided that you not marrying her would make *me*
happy." He belched, and the gray tint deepened. "And you,
too, Creighton. We were enjoying our bachelor's life too
much to put an end to it so soon. Bleat all you want, but
the truth is that you are glad you didn't marry her."

Creighton fought back his anger. "Yes, but not for the
reason you interfered with our plans."

"It's because of *her*, isn't it? You are befuddled by a
woman who wants everyone to think she's a man!" He
laughed and slapped his thigh. The motion knocked him
against the banister.

"Natalya! I have to find her!"

Squinting, Barclay peered at him. Creighton cursed and pushed past him. He took the stairs three at a time, shouting for Zass. If the man were still here, then Natalya could not have gone far.

Mrs. Winchell hurried toward him. "Thank God you are here, my lord. I believe we have had thieves in the house."

"Thieves?" His stomach lurched. Could Natalya have been right about the stupid threat? If the assassins had come while she was here alone, it might not have been her the kitchen girls had seen but a man paid to kill her.

"This way."

He followed the housekeeper into the front parlor. Ignoring the shrouded furniture, he ran to the back of the room. He stared at the empty gun case. Glass was littered on the floor and crunched beneath his boots as he walked closer. In the dim light from the hall, he saw a bloody cloth on the carpet. Someone must have wrapped it around a fist and driven it through the glass. The pistols and gunpowder were gone.

Bending, he picked up the cloth. Natalya? He could not believe that. She would be wiser than to risk herself like this. With a curse, he tossed it back onto the floor. Mayhap not Natalya, but Zass would shed this much blood and more to help her.

"Was anyone seen?" he asked as he pulled his sword from the ruined case.

Mrs. Winchell wrung her apron in her hands. "No one, my lord. You know none of us are supposed to be in this room."

"Blast!" His own stupid order, which had done nothing but make him look like a gawney, had allowed Zass or someone else free access to the guns. Even as he had chided Natalya for not letting go of what had happened, he had kept this room as a memorial to his own stupidity. "Get someone in here to clean this up."

"In here?"

"Yes, clean up the whole room. 'Tis time all of us put the past behind us."

Her next question was halted by shouts from the lower hall.

Creighton rushed out of the room. He ignored Mrs. Winchell's shriek when he passed her. He tightened his grip on the hilt of his sword as he ran down the stairs. Too many times tonight he had not been prepared. He would not be caught so again.

A man stood in the middle of the foyer. He wore a navy coat over dusty white pantaloons. Tawny hair twisted across his forehead and matched the thick mustache over his taut lips. As he shoved past James, his assertive steps slowed, and his gaze locked with Creighton's.

"Are you Lord Ashcroft?" he asked, not waiting for the harried footman to announce him.

"Yes. Who are you?" He had no time to waste on pleasantries, not even with this man whose single question had been enough to label him as Russian.

"I wish to see Kapitán Dmitrieff."

Creighton shook his head. "He is not here."

The man's stern face softened only slightly. "I wish to see Kapitán Natalya Dmitrieff."

Hearing Barclay's soft curse from the bottom step, Creighton lowered his sword so the tip rested on the carpet on the stairs. It would be a reminder for the Russian not to do something he soon would regret. "Who are you?"

The man climbed partway up the stairs and reached beneath his coat.

"Take care, Creighton!" cried Barclay.

The Russian ignored Barclay as Creighton did. He drew out a card, and, bowing, handed it to Creighton as he said, "Lord Ashcroft, I need to speak with Kapitán Dmitrieff immediately. Would you please inform her of my arrival?"

"The captain is not here." He risked a glance at the card

and laughed shortly. "How do you expect me to read this? It is in Russian. Who in blazes are you?"

The man peered around the foyer. "Is there someplace where we can speak in private?"

"Don't let him come any closer!" Barclay called, jumping to his feet. "You can't trust him."

"Ignore Barclay," Creighton said with a sigh. "We can speak in my book-room."

"We can speak there without anyone overhearing?"

"Yes, of course." Looking past the Russian, he ordered, "Mrs. Winchell, let no one interrupt until I ring."

"Yes, my lord," she answered uneasily.

Creighton had hoped Barclay would have the good sense to go home, but his friend stumbled up the stairs after them and into the book-room. Praying Barclay would not be ill on the good rug, Creighton closed the door and turned to the man who still had not told them his name.

"No one shall overhear us now," Creighton said, fingering the hilt of his sword. "I would appreciate the courtesy of your name, sir."

"Dmitri Dmitrieff."

"But you are dead!" choked Barclay.

Creighton was glad Barclay had uttered the jobbernowl words before they had burst from his own lips. He appraised the Russian anew. Although the man's eyes were brown, they had the same tilt as Natalya's. Even more revealing was the stubborn angle of his chin, which was a twin of Natalya's when she was exasperated and determined to have her way.

Frowning, he asked, "If you are truly Count Dmitrieff, where have you been while your sister has been fighting the French in your stead?"

"Fighting those among our own countrymen who would be traitors to Russia." He sighed through taut lips. "I had no idea she had assumed my name and life until a few days ago. My lord, I must speak with Natalya immediately."

"As I told you, she is not here."

"Where is she?"

He hated to own to the truth, but there was no other way. "I haven't seen her since she raced out of the masquerade ball this evening."

"Alone?"

Barclay stepped forward. "No one was brave enough to go after her when she shot at the chandelier in the ballroom, save for me."

"And you are?"

"Barclay Lawson." He grinned and fell back onto the settee.

Dmitrieff turned back to Creighton. "That man is completely intoxicated."

"A normal state for him, I fear."

"Can he be believed? Did Natalya fire off a gun in the middle of a ballroom?"

Creighton leaned his sword against the mantel. "A gun was fired, reportedly by a woman. I assume it was her."

"Who else?" Dmitrieff rubbed a scar along his left cheek. "Do you have any idea why?"

"She was being chased," crowed Barclay.

"Chased?" asked Creighton at the same time as Natalya's brother. "By whom? Why didn't you say something about this before?"

"You never asked." He closed his eyes and folded his hands over his forehead. "I don't feel so good."

Creighton pulled him up to sit. "Who was chasing her?"

"Two men."

"What did they look like?"

"Couldn't see too well."

Dmitrieff muttered, "That is understandable."

"Barclay," snarled Creighton, "what *did* you see?"

"Not much."

Creighton sighed and released him. Looking at Dmitrieff,

he said, "We can ride for my colonel's house and check the list of guests."

"That could take hours to chase down every man."

"Won't take long," murmured Barclay.

"Why?" Creighton put his hand on the back of the settee. Had he been this lost in drink before he left for the war? Never caring about anything but his own pleasure and a way to escape his aching head the next day, so he could join in another game of cards?

"Weren't that many there."

"The room was full."

"Not of Russians."

Dmitrieff gasped, then asked, "Russians? Are you certain?"

"One wore a uniform just like Natalya prances around Town in." He laughed and slapped his leg. "She looks much better in it, though."

Dmitrieff snarled something. Creighton could not understand the words, but Dmitrieff's tone instantly identified them as curses.

"What is wrong?" Creighton asked.

"Natalya is in great danger."

"How—?"

"I have no time to explain. I must stop her."

Creighton chased him down the stairs, catching Dmitrieff's arm before the man could rush out the door. "Explain while my horse is brought."

"My lord, this is not your battle."

"It is if Natalya's life is in danger."

Dmitrieff's face creased in a swift smile that vanished as quickly as it had appeared. "I am pleased Natalya has found a friend in you, my lord. She has been alone too long."

"Save for Zass."

"Petr is here?"

Creighton nodded. "In London. He has shadowed her nearly every moment of her stay." He shoved aside the memory of the few times when he had delighted in her company without Zass lurking nearby.

"If he is with her now, she may have a chance of surviving."

"Surviving what?"

"The assassination of the czar and his host, the Prince Regent." He opened the door. "I will explain on our way. We must not delay, or the alliance and all of us may die, too."

Twenty-three

The street in front of the theater was clogged with carriages and those who wanted to see the leaders in the Alliance against Napoleon. Creighton threaded his way ruthlessly through, using the butt of his hand whip to herd spectators out of the way. Curses were fired at him, but he paid them no mind. He had to get into the theater to warn the Prince Regent and the czar.

Tossing his reins to a footman by an ornate carriage, he leapt from his horse. "This way!" he shouted to Dmitrieff as he paid for two admissions.

They rushed into the foyer. They could hear laughter from the audience. The show was going on, uninterrupted.

"Where is she?" Dmitrieff asked.

"I don't know. She should have been here by now. She had a head start on us even if we had not stopped at—"

He cursed. "Unless she was halted."

Creighton turned back toward the door. "We need to find her."

"We need to stop what may happen here at any moment. We can't wait." Dmitrieff glanced around the foyer. "Where do we go?"

"One of the boxes, I'm sure, but which side? We may not have time to search them all."

"Do you know which box the Prince Regent is using tonight?"

"The wrong one" came an answer from their left.

Creighton whirled, flinching as he recognized the Russian accent. "Who in perdition are you?"

A short man laughed as he pulled a pistol from beneath his coat. "We knew you would come. We have been waiting for you, my lord—Ashcroft, isn't it?"

"Dmitrieff, run!" He reached for his sword.

Another gun was pressed against his back. The man in front of him laughed again. "Dmitrieff? Can't you recognize your own guest?"

Creighton risked a glance over his shoulder. As he had feared, Dmitrieff was surrounded as well. He looked back at the short man. "Who are you?"

The man in front of him shoved him down a narrow corridor. He opened a door hidden in the shadows. "Someone who is going to give you a last, futile chance to be a hero, Ashcroft. They said you were with the woman who eavesdropped on us."

"And who eluded you to sound the alarm." He laughed tersely. Natalya must still be free if this man had not discovered the truth. "No doubt, by this time, she has gone to warn Count Dmitrieff."

"You should have been sensible like the count and stayed away from here."

Creighton did not answer as he was shoved into the darkness. He gripped a banister when his foot dropped onto what must be a step. Behind him, he heard Dmitrieff curse. The pistol prodded against his back, and he went compliantly down the steps. A dull glow appeared in front of him. As the floor smoothed in front of him, he tried to determine where they were. They were heading toward the stage, but near the outside wall. Boxes and painted boards were stacked haphazardly along the walls. This must be a corridor the stagehands used to store scenery. The boxes had to be right above their heads.

A familiar odor assaulted him. Gunpowder! Horror

choked him. Were these blocks attempting to copy Guy Fawkes who had tried centuries before to blow up Parliament? An explosion from here would rock the whole theater. If there was a fire, it would rush up the stairs, cutting off the escape for everyone in the boxes on this side.

He heard a shout. In Russian! These men were planning to kill their own czar. Why? He did not understand.

Rounding a corner, Creighton cursed. A dozen men were slumped together in the cellar. One form was unmistakable among the barrels he knew must contain gunpowder. "Miloradovich!"

The general straightened. He snapped an order.

"Ashcroft!" shouted Dmitrieff. "Be—" A gurgle was followed by a thump.

Creighton whirled. He caught the raised hand with the pistol aimed at his skull. Knocking the gun to the floor, he struck the Russian in the gut. He raced to scoop up the pistol. A brawny arm snaked around his neck. He was shoved up against a wall. Pain crashed through his head as it struck the stone.

Miloradovich snarled again.

Creighton repeated the last word, "Zass?" He stared at the bearded man in the moment before agony exploded through his skull and all thought, even that Natalya might walk into the same trap at any moment, vanished.

Natalya jumped from her horse. Lost! She had gotten lost twice in the curving streets of London. Even getting directions had failed to help her. She could see none of the landmarks in the dark.

She ran to the door of the theater. She did not get far before two hands grabbed her. She was whirled to look at a burly man. He stuck his hand under her nose.

"I've no time for this," she said. "I have to get inside."

"Pay first."

"Pay?" She patted her waist. Dash it! She had left her English coins in her reticule. "I don't have any money right now. If you will let me go inside—"

"Pay first," he grumbled.

"Will this be enough to pay for it?" She pulled her sword.

He shrieked and released her, calling for the watch. She tossed the sword at him. He let it clatter to the stones at his feet, then stared at her in silence.

"Enough?" she asked again.

He nodded.

She did not wait to see if he said anything else. She ran into the theater. Hearing laughter, she did not know which way to go.

Her eyes narrowed as she saw someone in a military uniform slink around a corner. She could not discern what nation it belonged to. She followed and discovered a small door ajar. It broke the pattern of the wall. She peered into it. When she heard footsteps coming from within, she edged behind the door. She held her breath as fingers came around it. A low laugh rang in her ears. She knew that laugh! She heard it when the two men were talking in Russian on Colonel Carruthers' balcony and during the hunt and . . .

"Radishchev!" she whispered as he began to close the door. One of her fellow officers was planning to murder the czar?

She struck his head with her pistol. He fell to the floor with a crash. She held her breath, but no one came running. Pushing the door open with her hip, she checked what was beyond. Stairs! This was not going to be easy.

Sweat was dripping down her back by the time Natalya got the unconscious man propped on the top step so he would not tumble down and alert whoever was below. She had nothing to bind him with, save for her belt. It was clumsy, but she hoped it would hold him long enough for her to discover what was happening.

Drawing the door nearly closed, for she was unsure if

she could open it from this side once it was shut, she tiptoed down the stairs. Voices struck her. Russian voices! How could that be?

When Natalya reached the bottom of the stairs and saw the glow of lanterns, she was certain she must be in the midst of a nightmare even more horrible than the one that had routed Creighton. Barrels were stacked next to a wooden column. A man was opening one of the lanterns and reaching under his coat for a piece of tinder. A coat just like hers!

"Hurry, you fool!"

She moaned as she recognized the voice, now that it was no longer distorted by the stairwell.

General Miloradovich!

She inched closer. Her foot struck something soft. Stretching down with her left hand, she touched a damp stickiness. Blood! Was the man dead?

A lantern shifted, splashing light across the prone man's face. Creighton! What was he doing here? She knew she had no time to get an answer, even if he could give her one. Something glittered on the ground beside him. Another pistol! She grabbed it and rose.

"Light it," ordered the general. "Hurry, so we can get out of here."

The man held the burning tinder to the fuse. It caught and flared.

"No!" Natalya shouted. She jumped from the shadows, firing her pistol.

One man reeled back, clutching his chest. Shouts filled the cellar. She raised the other gun. She screamed as flame pierced her arm. The gun fell to the floor. Blood flowed down her arm.

Miloradovich kicked her pistol away and laughed. He pulled out his own gun, then lowered it, laughing. "Stay here and die, Dmitrieff. I knew I could not trust you, the great hero of Mother Russia. You fool. You naïve fool! You could have joined us and gotten the rewards we can get only from battle."

"Battle? What do you know of battle?" She fought to keep her voice strong. "You know we will stop you."

He frowned. "How? Who?"

She took a steadying breath. He must believe she had alerted someone who could halt him. She must be careful what she said. "As we stopped your other assassination attempt on us."

He sneered. " 'Tis a shame that failed, for your death would have caused enough commotion to give us cover for our work." He gave a deep belly laugh. "Not that it matters. We shall succeed, and you shall die."

"You shall not succeed. I—"

He struck her wounded arm with the gun. With an agonized scream, she collapsed to the floor, fighting for her senses while pain raced up her arm. As if from a deep hole, she heard his laughter as someone called for everyone to flee while there was time.

Their footsteps vanished up the stairs. She heard the sizzle of the fire in the silence broken only by her struggle to breathe. Wet coursed along her arm. Pushing herself to her feet, she fell back to her knees. The fuse! She had to cut the fuse.

She crawled to where it was burning rapidly. She tried to pull her knife. Her fingers refused to close on it. Something crashed overhead. Gunshots? Impossible. It must be applause. Those fools! They had no idea they were sitting on death.

Her knife. She had to get her knife.

Broad fingers closed over hers. She moaned and tried to pull away, crying out when she bumped her wounded arm against a barrel.

"Let me help, Natalya."

"Creighton!"

She watched, struggling to hold on to her wits, as he

pulled her knife and tried to slice through the tar-soaked rope. With a curse, he moved to a length closer to the barrels. He shouted in triumph when he cut it. Kicking away the burning rope, he stamped it beneath his boot.

Another crash came from above. It was a gunshot!

She forced herself to her feet.

"Natalya, wait!"

"No time to talk now!"

"I had no plans for talking," Creighton said roughly as he whirled Natalya into his arms. "You calf-headed, want-witted . . ." His words became a low moan as he captured her lips.

Wanting to stay in his embrace, she pulled away. "Wake your friend. We have to keep them from getting away."

"My friend? Natalya, don't you—"

"We have to stop them!" She was trying to reload her gun even as she ran to the stairs. Her fingers fumbled as pain swelled through her arm.

"Natalya, wait!"

Creighton's voice echoed up the stairs, but she did not pause. If she stopped, she was not sure she could get her feet moving again. She burst out of the door and heard shouts from the street. Holding her gun at ready, she ran outside.

Dozens of men were milling about. They wore uniforms, but ones she did not recognize. She blinked. Yes, she did. They matched the one Colonel Carruthers had worn at the masquerade ball.

A hand on her arm slowly lowered her gun. She looked back to see Creighton's face that was etched with blood from a wound on his temple.

"It is over." He pointed to where a score of soldiers surrounded Miloradovich and his men. The Russians were being herded into a cart.

"How—?"

"On our way here, we stopped to alert the colonel of

trouble." He brushed her hair back from her face and whispered, "I'm sorry I pooh-poohed your threat. You were right."

"Not completely."

"Close enough. If—" He shoved her behind him and pulled his knife as a huge man lurched toward the cart, then turned to them.

"Petr?" she gasped. "No!"

An English soldier stepped in front of him. Petr swept him aside with a growl. He lumbered toward Natalya. Shouts filled the night.

Natalya saw guns being raised. She pushed past Creighton and rushed to Petr. They could not shoot him! As she grasped his arm, she heard the order to hold fire.

Looking up at him, she whispered, "Tell me it isn't true. You can't be with them!"

Creighton caught her uninjured arm and pulled her back from Petr. As if he understood Russian, he said, "He was with your friend Miloradovich below."

"Petr, how can that be?"

Again he did not give the bearded man a chance to answer. "Touch her, Zass, and you will be missing a hand."

"*Nyet,*" he said.

"*Da,*" Creighton snarled back with a tight smile.

Natalya stretched out her fingers to Petr. "Why were you with them?" she whispered.

"To protect you, *Grazhdánka* Natalya."

"Protect me?"

He nodded. "I heard rumblings of what they had planned, and I knew you would not be a part of it, for you have too much honor. But I feared they would turn on you like the rabid beasts they are. So I joined them to try to halt them, and—" When he teetered and collapsed to one knee, she rushed to put her hands under his arm. The weight nearly drove her onto the ground, but she eased his way to sit back against one of the columns at the front of the theater. More dampness ran along her sleeve.

"He is hurt!" she gasped, then repeated the words in English. "Creighton, help us."

"What is wrong with him?" he asked, clearly not willing to waste sympathy on Petr.

"U menyá bolít golová," the big man mumbled.

"What did he say?"

"He has a headache," answered a deep voice before she could.

Looking over her shoulder, Natalya stared up at a face out of her memories. Slowly she rose and put out a tentative hand. Would the phantom vanish if she touched it? Her forehead furrowed as she whispered, not believing her own eyes, "Demi?"

"Kóshka!" He held out his arms.

She threw her arms around him, then winced as pain erupted up her arm. "They told me—"

"I know what you were told." He brushed her hair back from her face. "I am sorry, *Kóshka.*"

"Kóshka?" Creighton asked.

"Cat," Demi said with a chuckle. "A nickname she gained the first time she followed me up a tree too tall for her and then could not find her way back down. I see, little sister, you have, like a cat, continued to land on your feet."

"Where have you been?" She touched his face, wanting to be sure *this* was no dream.

"Fighting to halt insurrection from within our army." He glanced at Miloradovich and his men. "This was not the first attempt to put an end to Alexander's life. There are many who do not like the czar's vision for Russia's future."

Shouts from the theater silenced every voice in the street. Natalya stared at the people emerging from the theater. She could not mistake a single one. The first, a man who seemed nearly as round as he was tall, was beyond doubt the Prince

Regent. He was followed by a handsome man who offered his arm to a woman almost his height.

"The czar!" she breathed. She feared she would not be able to take another breath as Alexander turned to look at her, asking a question she could not hear the answer to. Her feet seemed melded to the stones as he and the Grand Duchess came toward her.

Czar Alexander looked to her right. "Kapitán Dmitrieff?" he asked, staring at Demi.

"No, I was—I am Lieutenant Dmitrieff." He bowed and took a step back. Taking Natalya's unwounded arm, he pushed her forward. "This is Kapitán Dmitrieff. Natalya Dmitrieff."

She tensed as she stood before the Czar of All The Russias. Never had she imagined this moment. Even in her grandest dreams, she had dared to hope for no more than a missive from the czar's ministers returning her father's lands to her. Now those lands would be Demi's, as they should be.

The czar's blue eyes widened. When his sister said something too soft for Natalya to hear past the rush of trepidation in her ears, he chuckled before saying, "You are an odd cavalry officer."

She tried to speak, but it was impossible. Even when she swallowed deeply, she could manage little more than a whisper. "I wished to revenge my family's deaths by fighting the French. There was no one else once I believed the French had killed the rest of my family."

"Come forward." When she hesitated, he added, "Be brave as you always have been, Kapitán Dmitrieff."

She obeyed and started to bow. Then, although she feared she looked absurd, she curtsied. Before the czar, she could not pretend to be what she was not. She must be honest as she had longed to be for so long.

Fingers under her chin tipped her face up. Looking into Alexander's round face, she saw compassion in his eyes. "I understand I may owe you my life as well as my sister's," he said quietly.

" 'Twas Lord Ashcroft who cut the fuse," she replied.

"With his knife?"

"With mine." She took a deep breath to try to steady her trembling voice. She had not been this frightened when she went into battle. "I am glad to be able to serve in whatever way I can."

"That much is clear." He glanced to where the wagon with Miloradovich was disappearing around a corner. "I have heard much of you and your exploits from a man I thought I could trust with my life. It appears his words about your bravery may have been more honest than his pledge to defend Russia. Is your pledge as failing as Miloradovich's, Kapitán?"

"It has never changed from the moment I took it. I hold it dear."

"Yet you served the very man who would have brought the flames of war back to consume us all."

Natalya scraped her tongue along her arid lips. She winced when she tasted her own blood, but kept her voice even. "General Miloradovich was afraid of peace. I wish it with all my heart." Glancing to her left, she delighted in the warmth surging through her as Creighton smiled.

"So it would seem." The czar motioned for her to rise. "You have saved me and my sister and our allies this night. Speak the reward you would wish, Kapitán."

"I wish only to see my brother assume my father's lands and titles."

"That is no reward, for both your father and your brother have served me loyally. I have no cause to deny Dmitri Dmitrieff what he rightly possesses." He chuckled. "I offer you a reward. What do *you* wish?"

Taking a deep breath, she did not hesitate. "I wish to return to being myself. I would ask to be released from my service to the army."

"You want nothing else?"

Again she looked at Creighton. His smile hinted at the delight of his arms enfolding her. Yes, she wanted so much more, but fulfilling her dreams was something Czar Alexander could not do. Only one man could make those dreams come true, only the man who had conquered her heart in spite of her efforts to keep him from claiming it.

When the czar chuckled and motioned for Creighton to step forward to stand beside her, Natalya did not dare move.

"You are?" Alexander asked.

"Captain Creighton Marshall, 10th Hussars." He bowed his head to the czar.

Colonel Carruthers emerged from the crowd that had gathered. He cleared his throat. "As of next week, your grace, he will be known only as Creighton Marshall, 6th Viscount Ashcroft."

"Does this man deserve such a title?"

"His father—"

"Not of viscount, for that is no more than an accident of birth. Does he deserve the title of captain?"

Colonel Carruthers smiled. "Tonight was not the first time he has proven himself to be a hero. A dozen men live this night because he rescued them from an enemy ambush, although he was shot himself."

"You were shot?" Natalya gasped. She clamped her lips closed when Alexander chuckled.

"It would seem," the czar said, "you have hidden your record of bravery from my kapitán."

Creighton rubbed his left arm. "The wound was less severe than the one Natalya received tonight."

"Both of you are worthy of the title of hero, although it seems to be one neither of you wish." The czar glanced at his sister and smiled. "I grant you your request, Kapitán. Your service as a cavalry officer to me is complete, save for one thing. As your final command from your czar,

Kapitán Dmitrieff, I order you to say yes when Lord Ashcroft asks you to be his wife."

"But—" She gulped, realizing she had been about to gainsay the czar.

Creighton put his hand on her arm and turned her slowly to face him. His eyes twinkled in the lights from the theater as he brushed his lips against hers. When her arms rose to his shoulders, he said, "I'm waiting, Natalya."

"For what?"

"For you to say yes." His thumb beneath her chin tipped her face up toward him. "You have told me so often how you always obey orders. Will you disobey this one?"

"I thought you didn't want a wife."

"I didn't realize how much I needed you until I thought you might be lost forever." He kissed her cheek. "I guess I tried to be a hero one time too many, for I did not want to keep you from obtaining your dreams, even if it cost me my heart to let you go."

"I did not want to go." She brushed her fingers against his cheek, then leaned her head on his shoulder. "I want to stay here with you."

His thumb tilted her chin back so she could see his smile. "Now you need not go. There is another Count Dmitrieff to reconstruct your father's dacha. Nothing prevents you from obeying this order."

"Save that you have not asked me to be your wife."

"And when I do, what then?"

She laughed as she brought his mouth toward hers. "Then I suspect I shall never obey another order save to love you with all my heart."

Author's Note

The character of Natalya Dmitrieff was inspired by a real woman named Nadezhda Durova who served in the czar's army during the Napoleonic Wars. Miss Durova served the czar as a decorated cavalry officer for a decade, fighting in many pivotal battles. In her case, many of those around her, as well as the czar, knew she was a woman during her service.

I would be delighted to hear from any readers. Please write mr c/o Zebra Books, and a self-addressed stamped envelope is appreciated.